DESIRE WITH A DIFFERENCE

Izzat Yar Khan

MINERVA PRESS
NEW DELHI
MIAMI LONDON SYDNEY

DESIRE WITH A DIFFERENCE

ISBN 81 7662 054 8

First Published 2001 by
MINERVA PRESS
13 Palam Marg
Vasant Vihar
New Delhi – 110 057

Printed & bound in India
for Minerva Press (India) Pvt. Ltd.

DESIRE WITH A DIFFERENCE

Contents

Pleasure and Politics

I

It was a fine dawn in the Rajputana desert. Anarkali got up quietly from beside Prince Salim, who was sound asleep. She looked out of the window. Dawn was breaking, ushering in a new day. 'Days come and go,' she said to herself. 'But no day is similar to the one it replaces. There is good news and bad news. There are wishes and desires. The small ones get fulfilled, while for the big ones, there is only hope.'

Anarkali came back and stood beside the luxurious royal bed. She looked lovingly at the sleeping Prince. He was thirty-two; but he thought that his thirty-two years had brought him nothing of which he could be proud. He was handsome, very handsome, tall, muscular, broad chested and strong. Young women were attracted towards him and wanted to be loved by him - some because of his magnetic physique and some because they entertained the fond hope of becoming the consort of the future Emperor of India. Anarkali belonged to the former category. She was drawn towards Salim, in spite of herself.

The young girl, hardly twenty, did not want to disturb Salim's sleep. She knew that sleep is good for him and would relax his body and mind. She looked at the goblet of wine and the two cups on the table beside the bed. Besides wealth, Salim liked wine along with his women. The previous night Anarkali had drunk less but Salim more and both had felt themselves transported for some time into a state, where the two bodies had become one, the two souls separate. Anarkali also noticed a portrait of a woman the Prince had sketched the day before. She picked up the portrait. She wished it had been hers. She was a bit disappointed to see that it was that of a woman more beautiful than she. A woman whom, as far as she knew, neither she, nor Salim, had seen before. Or perhaps...

Anarkali turned away quietly towards the door. Just then. Salim opened his eyes and called her softly. She came back to him like a love-bird to her partner, into the warmth of the nest.

'It is too early to get up, Anar,' he said, making room for her in the bed. 'Your pillow is still warm.'

Anarkali lay down beside him and began to run her pretty, long and thin fingers over the hair on his chest.

'Salim', she said, 'I know you are a good painter, but tell me whose portrait is that in the corner.'

'I do not know,' he said, 'but that woman keeps appearing constantly, in my imagination. I don't know why.'

'Have you seen, or met this woman?' she asked.

'I don't know,' he replied. 'I might have seen her as a growing up girl, but where and when, I can't say.'

'She does not look like a common woman,' she said. 'She looks like a lady of high rank. She is a ravishing beauty. The faint smile on her beautiful lips is like a bud that has just begun to blossom. Is she your ideal of a beautiful woman?'

'Yes,' said Salim softly. 'She is my ideal of a beautiful woman.'

'And will you love her and marry her,' she inquired, 'if some day her real self comes before you?'

'I don't know if this ideal woman is married or unmarried,' said Salim. 'If she is married, I cannot marry her. If she is unmarried, I shall be happy to love her, to marry her, to remain devoted to her, but on one condition – she should be sharing and caring. If I love, I want to be loved in return. If I care, I want to be cared for. If she shares her secrets with me, I will share my secrets with her. If, with beauty she has brains, she will learn statecraft, and once I become Emperor of my beloved Hindustan, I shall leave the administration of this great country in her hands. Perhaps her influence will prove beneficial in affairs of the State. It is also possible that if she forms a faction of her own, there will be resentment among other factions; perhaps more powerful factions and then her influence will be baneful, not only for me and my successors, but also for the common people who are the backbone of my country.'

'Is she your dream queen?' Anarkali asked, with no disappointment on her cheerful face.

'It seems so,' Salim said. 'Otherwise why does she come cropping up in my imagination? If I try to draw your portrait, it is her figure and form that I draw; not yours.'

'How do I look to you, in comparison to her? I am real, your dream queen is non-existent,' said Anarkali.

'Yes, you are real,' said Salim, pressing his masculine body closer to hers. 'But something in me tells me she exists somewhere in our land, unconsciously waiting to love me and to be loved by me.'

'Salim, you are a Mughal Prince', said Anarkali. 'You are the Heir Apparent of a vast and mighty Empire. You should be practical, not a dreamer. You should be a realist, not a romantic. You should change your attitude to life and prepare for the great role you are expected to play, when you become Emperor.'

'Anarkali,' said Salim, 'you don't understand. I am a Prince by accident of birth. By the same accident, I could be a beggar, a nonentity, belonging to the riffraff of society. At the same time, I am at heart an artist, painter, a lover of music, song, dance, an aesthete and a lover of beauty. I believe there is beauty everywhere, only if one has the mind and the eyes to find it, to perceive it and to appreciate it.'

'You talk like a philosopher, Salim,' said Anarkali. 'Sometimes I understand you and sometimes I don't. But tell me, am I not young, beautiful and desirable? You send for me more often than any other girl, in your expanding harem.'

Salim smiled at this question. He paused for a while, closed his eyes as if thinking for a proper reply, opened them again and looked into the sparkling eyes of the young woman, reclining beside him.

'Of course, you are an intelligent girl, Anar and you are young. You are not yet twenty. You are beautiful – breathtakingly beautiful, I should say. That you are invited more than any other girl in my seraglio is itself a proof that you are desirable. I don't know what your real name is, or who your parents are. When they first brought you before my mother, she was so enchanted by your beauty and youth that she gave you the title of Anarkali, by which you have come to be known. Anar means pomegranate and kali means bud. You are as beautiful as the pomegranate bud in colour, in touch, in delicacy.'

'You are simply repeating what I have often been told by others, several times,' said Anarkali, opening her lips in a half-smile, which revealed her symmetrical white teeth. 'What I want to know is something different.'

'I am coming to that,' said Salim. 'I can say from my own experience that you have the right figure, the right face, the right contours, the right curves, the right proportion of parts to the whole, the right complexion...'

Anarkali interrupted him. 'Salim,' she said, 'you are talking like a painter, appraising a new model. I want to hear you speak as a lover, to a girl who is drawn towards him, as a needle towards a magnet, wishing every day for his invitation, to enjoy the pleasure of companionship.'

'Partnership, Anar, not companionship,' said Salim. 'Your partnership has a uniqueness of its own. You are an active partner as well as a sleeping partner. You are voluptuous, you are luscious like a peach and you please all my five senses. To look at you is a feast for the eyes, to hear your voice is like listening to soft music, to touch you is to feel the softness of silk, to kiss you is to taste pure honey and to have you by my side, is to inhale a fragrance as intoxicating and delicious as our royal wine.'

'You speak like a poet, Salim,' said Anarkali, gently pressing his hand. 'If I am really such as you describe, why do you need so many girls in your growing harem?'

Salim said, 'A very good question indeed. The harem is not a beauty bazaar, where you can pick and choose and buy. The harem is like one's personal store of fresh fruits. There are grapes, pomegranates, melons, watermelons, mangoes, plums, cucumbers, papayas, oranges and pineapples. You can't have them all at once. So you pick up only one or two, just for a change of taste. Variety, you know, removes sameness, monotony, and ennui.'

'If you feel that a woman is a fruit which is to be reduced to its skin and stone and then disposed of as garbage,' said Anarkali, 'then you have a very shabby opinion of women. I am afraid such an opinion hurts – it hurts me and perhaps it also hurts other sensitive women.'

'Pardon me, Anar,' said Salim apologetically. 'This is more or less the truth. Whatever be its faults – and the faults are numerous – the harem is an age-old institution devised for Princes and Kings, for their pleasure and necessity.'

'By the same logic,' replied Anarkali in her soft voice, 'there must also be a harem of young and handsome men for Princesses and Queens for, as you say, their pleasure and necessity.'

'I agree with you,' said Salim. 'There you have a perfect point. Unfortunately – and I repeat the word unfortunately – the world has been dominated by men and domination implies exploitation and subjugation. As long as this state of affairs continues to exist, gender discrimination will continue unabated.'

'Is there no room for love and marriage, devotion and security in what you call your personal store of fresh fruit? Am I not entitled to the happiness of a stable marriage to one who enjoys – and I use your own words – my voluptuousness, my lusciousness, my sensuousness?'

'Under the prevailing circumstances, Anar,' said Salim suavely, 'there is no such entitlement you speak of and I am sorry that it is so. We Princes and Kings are hardly allowed to marry the woman we love and are happy with. There is more to our marriages than meets the eye. Our matchmakers keep in mind rank and status, family advantages, diplomatic or political gains, so that our marriages, though celebrated so lavishly, are often a matter of compulsion rather than, as they should be, of free choice.'

'This is most unjust,' said Anarkali politely, 'especially when Prince and Kings are supposed to be dispensers of justice.'

'You are right, Anar,' said Salim, patting her cheek as if to suggest that she and other women like her, should go on enduring the mental and emotional agony caused by this glaring injustice, simply because they are women. 'As far I can see, there is no remedy. Perhaps centuries will roll by without tackling your problem. I am not a seer, but I do feel that social change is necessary. This change will come slowly and gradually. The upholders of the existing social order resist change because change will deprive them of their power and their right to shape the lives of others.'

'Salim, I am not complaining. I have nothing against you. I

know how things are and so do the other women in every nobleman's harem.' said Anarkali quietly. 'I was simply raising a point; not pressing it.'

'I understand you very well,' said Salim candidly, 'and my sympathies are with you and other women like you. I have heard that my father, Emperor Akbar, has in his harem, roughly speaking, about five hundred women. The year has only three hundred and sixty-five days. That leaves one hundred and forty-five women surplus. Moreover, there are days of illness, of hunting, of military campaigns, when one is too absorbed or weary to have any desire. Such occasions increase the number of surplus women, and as such, your suggestion of a counter harem, of handsome, young and desirable men is, in principle, quite logical and acceptable.'

Anarkali smiled and her smile removed the coldness that was creeping into the conversation. 'Salim,' she said, 'you know it well that I have never asked you to love me or marry me and I never will. I do not want you to get into trouble on my account. That is proof enough of how much I love you. I believe that love is something which is deeply felt and no instrument can measure its depth. Words are also inadequate for it. The times we have spent together have been some of the happiest hours of my life. But I would not like to live on their memory. When I feel you no longer need me, I will take your permission to seek a suitable man, marry him and have children by him. Of course, the husband I speak of, will not be a Prince like you or a nobleman, but he should have enough to keep me and my children in comfort. I will do so before my beauty and youth begin to fade away and fade away they must, one day or the other.'

The cry of the muezzin calling the faithful to prayer and the bells of the temple calling the votaries to worship, were distinctly heard in the palace. The morning air of the Rajputana desert was clear and fresh. It was time for Salim and Anarkali to get up from their bed.

'Come,' said the Prince, 'let us have a bath. My classmate Muhammad Sharif, is coming to meet me. I have invited him to breakfast. He is the only person who is open-minded like me and gives me his honest counsel.'

II

The breakfast at eight in the morning was sumptuous. All the dishes had been tasted before being served, lest there should be an attempt by some unscrupulous official of the royal kitchen to poison the Heir Apparent, the future Emperor Jahangir. When Prince Salim and Muhammad Sharif had their fill, Sharif jocularly remarked, 'Do you remember, Salim that ten years ago you were suspected of bribing one of the court physicians, Rahmat Khan, to poison your father?'

'Yes, I do,' said Salim, laughing. 'It was an intrigue by my enemies to discredit me in my father's eyes. Who the intriguers were, I have been unable to find out.'

'Perhaps, as was subsequently diagnosed by Bhim Nath, the herbalist, there was no attempt at food poisoning at all,' said Sharif. 'The whole thing could be a canard. But certainly Rahmat Khan lost his job; Bhim Nath was rewarded; the official tasters severely reprimanded and your good name tarnished.'

'Quite true,' said Salim. 'You know me through and through, Sharif. You know I love and respect my father. Everybody knows I was a child born of many a prayer on the part of my father and mother and the blessings of the saint Shaikh Salim Chishti, after whom I am named. The twins, Hasan and Husain, who were born to my parents died five years before I came into this world. I was the apple of the eye of my relatives and the darling of all, especially of my father, the Emperor, who wanted an heir and successor to his mighty throne. As such, I was a pampered child and grew to be an ease-loving man. All tantrums were tolerated instead of being frowned upon. As a consequence of my thoroughly spoiled childhood, I grew up to be, what I am today.'

'You were fun-loving,' replied Sharif, 'but your enemies – whoever they were - started a whispering campaign, that you were impatient to wear the crown of your father, without waiting for his natural death. It is good that the whole thing cooled down in due course. Security within the palace was stepped up. The court physicians were politely asked not to allow anything that could denigrate their profession. However, your name was never mentioned. This did save your face – at least to all appearances.

What still lingers in the hearts of your enemies, nobody can say. At least, their plot of character assassination against you, ended in a fiasco.'

'No, Sharif, no. The plot still continues,' said Salim vehemently. 'Do you know why I have been sent to Ajmer – to this desert? It is to keep me away from my dear mother, the Queen and from the court of my beloved father. The men who dislike me are Abul Fazl and Raja Maan Singh. Abul Fazl is close to my father and he believes in the vastness of Fazl's knowledge as historian and astronomer. He has written the *Akbarnama,* to flatter my father and gain his favour. Raja Maan Singh, I admit, is an honourable man and a fearless warrior. He was inducted to my father's court at the instance of the Queen-mother. But he keeps a zealous watch over me, either by himself or through his paid agents. He prefers my son Khusrau to me. It is this shrewdness of the Raja that irks me.'

'Salim, my dear friend, what you say may be true,' said Sharif. 'But as far as I know, you have been appointed Governor of Ajmer to reduce the growing power of Rana Amar Singh of Mewar. If his power grows disproportionate to his territories, Mewar will pose a threat to the unity and integrity of the Mughal Empire. But you are not doing your duty. You were trained as a soldier, not as a sufi. Why do you shirk from combat? If you don't put an end to this threat now, its dimensions will grow unmanageable, when *you* succeed to the throne.'

'How can I explain my reluctance to fight everyone? Half of my blood, through my mother, is Rajput blood. The Rajputs are a brave and proud people. They are my own kith and kin. Rana Amar Singh's father, Rana Pratap Singh, has now become almost a legendary figure. He felt that the marriage of my mother, a Rajput Princess, with my father, was an insult to Rajput honour. For this reason, he spoke harshly to Raja Maan Singh and he, in turn, replied in equally harsh words. It is a quarrel between two gallant Rajput Princes. I don't come into the picture.'

'Yes, you do, Salim, you do,' said Sharif. 'The marriage of Princess Jodha Bai with the Emperor of Hindustan is an accomplished fact. It cannot be undone, which perhaps is what Rana Pratap may have wished. You, Prince Salim, are the living proof of the process of that inter-religious marriage. You cannot be undone. No one can push you back into your mother's womb. You have to take up arms and cry halt, to Rana Amar Singh's growing power. Otherwise this rivulet, by joining with other tributaries, will turn into a deep and mighty river, which will be difficult to ford.'

Salim heard Sharif patiently, but he was not convinced. He said, 'I am not ashamed of being my Rajput mother's son. In fact, I am as proud of it as my father holds my mother, in the highest esteem. My mother is as chaste as Sita. That is why she is addressed in the palace as Mariam Zamani or Mary of the World.'

'This is beside the point,' said Sharif. 'The point is, why don't you rise to the occasion and curb the increasing power of the young Rana? It is for this express purpose that you were sent here.'

'The truth is I don't want to engage Rana Amar Singh in a big and bloody battle, which may ultimately spell his doom. He is fighting gallantly to preserve his little hereditary principality. He has every right to preserve it as the Emperor has every right to preserve his Empire. I appreciate the young Rana for his valour, his pride which, in other words, is the courage of his conviction. I want to be his friend, not his inveterate foe.'

'There is something in what you say,' said Sharif coolly. 'After all, you are a chip of the old block. With enormous resources of warfare and manpower, your father could not subjugate a few thousand miles of Mewar. He waged an intermittent war against Rana Pratap for nearly a quarter century, but he never set his foot on the soil of Mewar against his implacable foe. He sent some of his best generals to humble the chivalrous Rana. Perhaps your mother and her relatives at court used their influence to keep your father at a safe distance from the already devastated Mewar. You too, like your father, are deliberately distancing yourself from Rana Pratap's son.'

'There are other things in my memory which desist me from action,' said Salim to his old friend. 'My father appointed Abdur Rahim, son of Bairam Khan as the Governor of Ajmer. He was given vast powers to mobilise a strong, attacking force. On night, Amar Singh, affectionately called Ammu by those who loved him and among those with whom he was popular, captured a Mughal camp on the bank of the river Bevas. The inmates were a part of Abdur Rahim's harem. Ammu brought them before his royal father. Rana Pratap received the ladies courteously. He made arrangements forthwith to escort them back to the Mughal commander. He said to Ammu that the honour of women was dear to the Rajputs. He added that the edifice of Rajput society was built on that noble plank. To lay hands on women was, in the Rana's opinion, tantamount to denouncing the traditions of chivalry the Rajputs are justly proud of. He advised his son never to be guilty of such a lapse. This incident has left an indelible impression in my memory. How can I fight such nice people?'

'That incident also impressed the Mughal General as well as your father. The Emperor reciprocated in a fourfold manner. First, he ordered an immediate cease-fire. Secondly, he issued a proclamation to all imperial soldiers to refrain from doing any harm to Rajput women, with the proviso that any infringement of this proclamation would invoke the severest penalty. Thirdly, the chivalry of Rana Pratap struck a responsive chord in your father's heart and increased his respect for the Rana. Lastly, Abdur Rahim was ordered to return to the base camp at Ajmer. Mewar, is still hallowed by the blood of its martyrs, the valiant Rajput men and women. Perhaps, Salim, you do not want to make the Mewar soil redder,' said Sharif.

'The Rana and his family are worthy of respect and admiration. When my father heard of Rana Pratap's sad demise, tears welled forth from his brave eyes. Rai Dursey wrote an impassioned elegy on the Rana's death. He recited it in the court. It had some anti-Mughal bias and all feared that he would be chastised for this effrontery. But, contrary to such an apprehension, my father not only honoured him by inviting him to sit on his right, but also rewarded him with valuable gifts. Such an act is what I admire most, in my father,' said Salim. 'I also wish to emulate him in such display of tolerance, understanding and appreciation.

'Further, Salim, as far as my knowledge goes, the dying Rana took a pledge from his chiefs and faithful companions to stand guarantee that they would support Prince Ammu until he regained his principality,' said Sharif. 'You are helping the young Prince by being absent from any possible scene of battle.'

'Precisely,' said Salim. 'Let us negotiate. Let us talk. Let there be some give-and-take, so that the political conflict may be minimised, if not resolved. Our differences with the young Rana can be narrowed down with each successive meeting. Extremism has no chance of prospering. Ammu knows this; I know this; my father knows this. A policy of peaceful coexistence will suit Ammu, me and the Mughal Empire. The notion of peaceful co-existence is based on the principle of live and let live. What I would like to suggest to my father is, that he should find a tactful and cool man and send him to Prince Ammu, as Chief Negotiator. Meanwhile, let there be a complete cease-fire, to provide the peace process an opportunity to succeed. Violence should be the last resort, to be used when all other measures have failed.'

Sharif had been listening attentively to what Salim was saying. He said, 'The policy you have outlined is a sound one. It certainly keeps bloodshed at a distance. Prince Ammu and his Bhil followers adopt hit-and-run tactics. The Aravalli hills are certainly favourable for guerrilla warfare. The Mughal army is not trained in guerrilla tactics. It is time that a fairly sizeable contingent should be specially trained in guerrilla warfare, under the auspices of the Central Government. In fact, the scope can be widened further. The trained guerrillas of the Centre should teach at the provincial centres which should be set up under the direct control of the Governors of our provinces. The guerrillas are good for mountainous terrain, forest regions and ravines, because these areas are not only easily accessible but also provide relatively safer places for camps and storage of food and weapons. Moreover, these guerrillas should serve on a permanent basis and be paid from the provincial or central treasury, as the case may be. The Mughal army is trained to fight face to face in open fields. It is vulnerable to the guerrillas and is not fully effective.'

'It is a good idea,' said Salim, nodding his head. 'Sometimes, Sharif, I have serious doubts whether guerrilla fighting is chivalrous at all.'

'Whether guerrilla warfare is chivalrous or not, whether it is hitting from the front or the back, whether it is valour or cunning, is beside the point,' said Sharif reflectively. 'What is important is, who wins. It is well known that everything is fair in love and war and you yourself practise it – in love.'

This brought a radiant smile on the pink lips of the young and handsome Prince. After a pause, he said, 'Sharif, if you do not object, I have a mind to recommend you to my father to put all these suggestions before him and persuade him to accord his approval. Of course, the old-timers will oppose you tooth and nail, but I know my father: he welcomes new ideas provided, he is fully convinced. Besides, as my old friend and class-fellow, you have easy access to him. You have also some friends at court. First, meet my mother, convey to her my profound regards and esteem, ask her blessings for me and pat my son Khusrau on both his cherry-like cheeks.'

'You mean I should be the Chief Negotiator between Rana Amar Singh and the Mughal Government?' Sharif inquired. 'Well, I will try my best. Whether I succeed or fail in my endeavours, is altogether a different matter. I will also meet your wife, Princess Maan Bai and certainly pat your son Khusrau. He is a lovely boy.'

'Sharif, state affairs apart, I am fond of Maan Bai. She is the mother of my son. She is the most curvaceous and beautiful among the Rajput Princesses at the court. They affectionately call her Shah Begum. She is devoted to me and my son, but she is highly jealous when she hears that I have relations with other women.'

'Don't you think that if you are privileged to have extra-marital relations, why should she be emotionally starved when you are away from her, for such long periods of time?'

'Sharif, I understand what you are driving at,' said Salim. 'You are right. Either I should be with her at Agra, or she and Khusrau should be with me, wherever I am. She will be delighted to visit Pushkar and the shrine of Khwaja Muin-ud-din Chishti. I will personally take her to both these centres of pilgrimage. Let her pray there, that she and I enjoy the love and mutual strength that comes from togetherness.'

'Amen,' said Sharif, rising up, to take leave of the Prince.

III

It was between nine and ten. The October evening of the Rajputana desert was cool and refreshing, but not chilly. The large room of the Governor's palace was beautifully and tastefully decorated. Chandeliers hung from the ceiling and the light from hundreds of candles illuminated the room, for a festive occasion. In the centre was spread a large Persian carpet with beautiful floral designs. There were white cushions and soft pillows to recline against, on which officers of the province sat, in order of social precedence. The Diwan, or the Finance Officer of Ajmer Province, the Bakhshi or Provincial Chief of the army staff, and the Kotwal, a military officer who looked after civic amenities and law and order, sat on the right side and three noblemen on the left. They were dressed in all their finery and were in a jolly mood, after a day's arduous work.

On the side opposite the entrance there was a raised platform, gracefully carpeted, with embroidered cushion seats and downy, long, round and thick pillows, to serve as a backrest. Three impressive personalities sat there – Prince Salim who was the Subedar or Governor, in the centre, his class-mate Muhammad Sharif on the Prince's right and Anarkali, gorgeously and attractively dressed, to his left. At the bottom of the dais, facing the six guests, sat the musicians – the head musician or vocalist, Ustad Shah Khan, a renowned tabla player, a sarangi player, a flute player, a cymbal player and a matka player. They were six in all. Facing the dais sat an eighteen-year old girl Gulshan, one of the best kathak dancers in the courts of the Rajput princes. She was the cynosure of all eyes. She was dressed in pink. The colour reflected itself on her young and agile body, in the soft light of the chandeliers, adding a sensuous touch to her complexion. Her dress revealed her cleavage and parts of her well-formed back. She was expected to do three or four rounds of dance, each better than the other. She had come at the invitation of the Governor and brought her own Ustad and musicians. Ustad Shah Khan, Gulshan and her instrumentalists had come with a determination to give their best performance, win the hearts and goodwill of the Governor and his topmost officers and noblemen, besides getting a rich reward from Salim. All sat in expectancy, awaiting the signal from Prince Salim, for the dance to commence.

The Prince's dress was of silk and embroidered with gold and silver threads. His eyes met the young kathak dancer's and an unspoken message passed between the two, which Ustad Shah Khan was quick to notice. His eyes expressed approval. Salim whispered to Sharif, 'I had a busy day. I had received a cleverly-worded letter from my father. I told the messenger to wait outside for an hour. After having composed an equally diplomatic answer in my mind, I called the Persian calligraphist, dictated the letter to him, asking him to put it in a more refined language.'

'What did the Emperor write to you about?' Sharif asked.

'The usual pieces of advice which a father gives to a son, far away from him, together with his blessings that I should acquit myself creditably in my efforts to diminish the power of Rana Amar Singh,' said Salim. 'I want some relaxation to remove the day's tension. Shall we begin the performance?'

'Go ahead,' said Sharif. 'Everybody is waiting.' The Prince waved his right hand, and the musicians started playing a well-orchestrated, romantic tune, for a few minutes. The tune was a happy one, conveying the happiness of a lover and the beloved who have met after a long time.

The dancer, Gulshan, rose. She was a tall and slim girl. Ustad Shah Khan began to sing some preliminary notes and Gulshan began her footwork. The bells in her anklet jingled and her bosom heaved and she began to dance graciously. Ustad Shah Khan began to sing a quatrain, singing each line slowly and clearly, modulating his voice according to the feeling expressed in the quatrain. It was a Persian *rubai,* dealing with the carefree attitude of two young people, in love with each other. A rough translation of the rubai would reveal that a lover who has been waiting for his loved tells her on her arrival:

Do sit beside me and be gay,
And fill the cup so that we may
Together drink the wine of youth
And thus postpone the Judgement Day.

To the accompaniment of merry music, the young girl rendered the feeling and the request of the lover through the language of her beautiful and provocative figure, as if she herself was the real beloved, of the imaginary lover. She came dancing towards the dais and sat there for a moment, as if she was responding to the request of her lover. Then she got up, picked a goblet of wine in her right hand and a cup in her left and acted the role of filling the cup with wine and then raised the cup to her fresh, smooth, pink lips. The voice of Ustad Shah Khan, the orchestrated sounds of the musical instruments and the body language of Gulshan, together with her youth, beauty and skill, lent an air of enchantment to the performance, which lasted for about ten minutes. There was a short interval of rest for the performers. The Prince clapped his hands and maids appeared with silver trays, which were placed before each guest. Each tray contained dry fruits from Iran and Afghanistan. The tray placed reverentially before Salim was gold polished. The maids reappeared with other small trays, on each of which was a silver glass, filled with the juice of the famous scarlet pomegranates of Qandhar.

The second round of the dance began. It was called *abhinay* or acting. To the accompaniment of appropriate music, to which her ears were professionally attuned, Gulshan swiftly changed her postures, using with skill the gestures of the head, the eyes, the lips, the hands and the feet. She was trying to convey feelings in a series of interlinked situations – of expectations, of satisfaction, of disappointment, of recognition and finally, of joy. The audience interpreted the movements according to their own understanding.

The abhinay reflected the restlessness of a young village girl, preparing herself for a rendezvous with her lover. She does her simple make-up and looks at the small hand mirror, to ascertain if she looks good and desirable. She then picks up an earthen pitcher and goes out towards the village well. On the way, she stands beneath a peepal tree and looks here and there for her lover. She looks disappointed when she does not find him. She looks up the road and sees a young man coming on horseback. When he approaches nearer, she recognises him and her face lights up with joy.

The rendering of the most exciting moment of a village girl's life was so artistic and exquisitely skilful, that almost all among the selected audience felt enraptured. The Prince now wanted Gulshan to sing a song in her melodious voice. Sensing the amorous mood of the audience, Gulshan signalled to her instrumentalists to play a tune for sometime and create an 'atmosphere.' She sat at the centre of the hall with the audience on her three sides, so that her voice could reach her listeners equally. The musicians seemed to understand which song Gulshan wanted to sing. Ustad Shah Khan looked at the bright young girl encouragingly. Then she sang a Persian song. An approximate translation of which would be:

In me is fire, in you is fire,
In eyes there shines repressed desire,
Two throbbing hearts are our empire,
For something sweet we both aspire.

I shall remember, Laila dear,
What you whisper in my ear,
You tell me to remove all fear,
You vow you ever will be near.

Your youth is like the vernal bloom,
Your beauty drives away all gloom,
For thrills, your heart has ample room,
And all the things enchanting loom.

The tingles of these golden hours,
Your curls of hair are fragrant bowers,
Your glances are delightful showers,
Your smile is laughter of the flowers.

There is the magic of this place,
There is the silver of your face,
There is the glamour of your grace,
There is the warmth of your embrace.

The girl sang each line of the song clearly, in her mellifluous voice, sometimes repeating a line which she thought had won the appreciation of her audience and emphasising the feeling in every line with movements, bringing out candidly that the present opportunity must be made the most of. When she had finished, Prince Salim took off from his neck a valuable string of white pearls and threw it at the dancer-singer, who promptly caught it in both hands as if accustomed to the art of catching such precious gifts. Then she bowed and *salaamed* the Prince and his guests, according to the Mughal etiquette and sat down on the thick, soft Persian carpet.

The first to depart was Anarkali, who went into the inner rooms of the palace. The Prince bade goodbye to the guests. Muhammad Sharif also took leave to go home. The musicians picked up their instruments and left, one by one. Gulshan gave the string of pearls to Ustad Shah Khan who bowed ceremoniously to the Prince and withdrew discreetly.

Salim and Gulshan were left alone. Salim rose from his embroidered velvet cushion seat and Gulshan stood up to reciprocate his sentiments. He laid his hand gently on her shoulder and said, 'In me is fire, in you is fire. It is a good line. I like it. The opening line should lead to the conclusion of your song - the warmth of your embrace.'

The innuendo was not lost upon Gulshan. She had heard of the amorous performances of the Prince. Perhaps, they had been exaggerated by the girls who had related them, to excite and inflame her. Gulshan was no novice. She was well versed in responding to the eroticism of the Rajput princes and noblemen. Now she was curious to know about the future Emperor of Hindustan.

The Child of Many Prayers

I

The dimensions of the seraglio of an Emperor is no evidence of his happiness. A childless Emperor always yearns for a son, an heir, a successor to his Empire. Akbar's beloved Queen, the beautiful Jodha Bai, had borne him not one, but two sons, two years after her marriage. The twins had been named Hasan and Husain. But they died in their infancy and the Emperor was childless again.

One night, Akbar said to his Queen lamentingly, 'What is the use of conquests – of Chittor and Ranthambor and Kalanjar and others? Where is their future ruler? Almost five years have passed since Hasan and Husain left us and I still have no son.'

'Is it my fault, Sire? What about your other bed companions?' said the Queen, without the least anxiety, for she knew that Akbar loved her, with all his heart and soul.

'I never said it is your fault, Jodha,' said Akbar. 'Perhaps the fault, if any, lies in me.'

'No, Sire, the fault does not lie with you, or me, or your other love-mates. You are around twenty-six and I am two years younger than you. Have patience and your wish will be fulfilled one day.'

'The blood of my father Humayun and my grandfather Babar, runs in my veins. They feared early death and so do I,' said Akbar. 'I invited several Hindu and Muslim holy men to the palace and had discussions with them. They did not share my gloomy thoughts. They were sceptical. One of them said, death walks behind us during the day and sleeps with us, during the night.'

'What did he mean by these metaphors?' the Queen inquired.

'What he meant was simply this: we do not know when we will die. Death may come early or late, but it will come one day or the other – when, where, and how, we cannot predict. One of the holy men, who had no faith in astrology, also said that a middle-aged astrologer died, just when he had consulted his horoscope, made complicated calculations and concluded that he would live for another twenty years.'

Jodha Bai came closer to her husband. She put her lovely hand on his shoulder reassuringly and said. 'You have instituted what you call the Yogi-seat, after Chittor was captured. The Yogi-seat is close to your throne in the Diwan-i-Khas. Spiritual teachers of eminence and renown, whom you invite for discussions, occupy this seat. It has come to my knowledge that a Sanyasi of Mathura is here in Agra, these days. People call him Swamiji. Send him an invitation, with all honour, for tomorrow evening. He might accept it. Ask him what the duties of a king are. In his discourse, you may find a solution to the problem that baffles you.'

'You are right, Jodha,' said the Emperor, highly pleased. 'You are always right. I will send the holy Sanyasi of Mathura a cordial invitation tomorrow morning. I may not get a son or successor, but I will at least gather some gems of wisdom.'

II

The Sanyasi of Mathura sat in the Yogi-seat in the Diwan-i-Khas. Akbar's throne was close to him. No invitation had been extended to anybody else to attend the Sanyasi's discourse. It was a purely private affair between the Emperor and the Sanyasi. The holy man had covered his body with a single piece of saffron-coloured cloth. His hair was long and grey with years and he was lean and thin, which indicated self-denial. There was an expression of deep contentment on his face. He sat cross-legged in the Yogi-seat, with his eyes closed.

'Most revered Swamiji, my honoured guest,' Akbar addressed him with the deference due to a holy man. 'I know you have renounced the world and its ways to seek spiritual truth. I do not want to know whether you are a celibate, a brahmachari, or a married man, who has abnegated his wife and children for a higher pursuit. You must have had good reasons to take up sanyas. But my question is not related to this aspect of your personal life. I should be very happy if you are kind enough to enlighten me on the rights, duties, and obligations of a king and how should these rights, duties, and obligations be continued, after his death.'

The Sanyasi heard the Emperor attentively, his eyes still closed. After a few moments, he said in a calm, unperturbed and soft voice, 'Akbar Badshah, you are a tolerant King and you must take all possible measures to preserve yourself and your dynasty, for your own good, for the good of the dynasty and for the good of the millions over whom you rule, without discrimination of any kind. Your destiny as King and the destiny of the people of Hindustan are interlinked. If you prosper, the people prosper; if you go the evil way, so do the people. This ancient country has a fertile soil, ample opportunities for employment, trade and business and the people look towards you, as their friend, philosopher and guide.'

Akbar listened with rapt attention. He said, 'Swamiji, I understand.'

'Akbar Badshah,' resumed the Sanyasi, 'it is your duty to ensure a peaceful succession to your throne. The preservation of dynastic lineage is a must. Your successor must be fully taught the rights, duties, and obligations of a just king. If this is not done, there will be confusion and chaos. The peace in the lives of the people will be shattered. A man is not destined to live forever. His span of life is short, very short. You, as King, cannot accomplish in one lifespan all you envisage, for the people and the country. For their attainment a number of lifespans are necessary. It is therefore one of your obligations to have children and get them instructed in carrying on your good work, in letter and spirit, from the point you leave it. A gap in the dynastic lineage is never a good thing. This is as true of the common man as of the king. Sons serve as bridges that join one age to the other. It is in this way that lands governed by good kings maintain a uniform pace of growth and development.'

The Emperor became sad after he heard the Sanyasi. The holy man had spoken the truth. But Akbar had no son. The Sanyasi raised his right hand to confer blessings on the Emperor. The raising of the right hand also signified that he had no more to say. Akbar got down from his throne, walked to the Yogi-seat and stood before the Sanyasi in silence. 'I thank you, Swamiji,' he said and bowed to the holy man.

Akbar retired to his private chambers. His mind was like an arena of war, where his wish to have a son battled against the unseen forces of nature beyond his control. It took him two days to calm himself. He ordered his attendants to see to it that no one, not even his Queen, should disturb him in his voluntary isolation. During these two days, he had ransacked his brain to find a solution to the problem.

III

Akbar came out of his self-imposed confinement on the third day. His face seemed serene. He had made up his mind. He summoned the Lord High Steward, an important dignitary, to his presence and said, 'Meer-i-Saamaan, we have decided to travel to Sikri on foot. It is a place abounding in rocks, boulders, shrubs and wild beasts. Shaikh Salim Chishti resides there, in a small hut. We intend to see him.'

The Lord High Steward bowed low and said, 'All arrangements will be made, Your Majesty. Covering twenty-three miles of dusty road on foot, Your Majesty, is well worth the rare audience of the saint. Everybody in and outside Agra, venerates the Shaikh. He is a man of God. His piety is well known to all.'

Akbar interrupted his Lord High Steward, 'The Shaikh remains deliberately cut off from the world. He keeps his body and soul together on whatever a few devout people offer him and even of this, he eats very little. He is often absorbed in profound meditation. He is oblivious to all that goes inside and outside the tiny village. He does not want kings, or rich people, to visit him. He considers them a distraction. We want you to convey to him, humbly and respectfully and tactfully that we ourselves are coming to seek his blessings. This *darwesh,* living in voluntary poverty, is spiritually richer than the Emperor of Hindustan.'

'Yes, Your Majesty,' said the Meer-i-Saamaan, bowing. 'A meeting between an Emperor, with riches and luxuries at his beck and call and his subject, the dweller of a poor hut in the wilderness, will be a sight which will astonish the world.'

'We are not going to the saint as Emperor,' said Akbar. 'We are going like a beggar, asking favour from a man rolling in spiritual riches. Saints are like benign intercessors and God listens to their pleadings on behalf of favour-seekers, because of their selfless devotion. We kings and emperors, on the other hand, are largely motivated by diplomacy, which conceals our ulterior motives.'

IV

The Lord High Steward himself, went to Sikri on horseback the next morning. He left his Arab horse tied to a tree, beside the dirt road and set out on foot towards the saint's hut. He sat on a boulder near the hut and waited patiently for the holy man. He was happy that he, too, would have the privilege of being near the Shaikh and having a conversation with him. After a wait of about two hours or more, the Shaikh emerged from the hut and, without noticing the well-dressed dignitary sitting on the boulder, started walking slowly towards a spring, nearby.

The Meer-i-Saamaan followed him, saluted him with due deference and conveyed to him, in a humble and respectful manner, Akbar's wish to have an audience with him, after two days. The saint was bewildered. It was all so unexpected. He nodded assent and the Lord High Steward said words of deep gratitude. He saluted him reverentially, withdrew a few steps backwards facing the Shaikh, according to court etiquette, as if the Shaikh was no less august a person than the Emperor. Finally he departed to tell Akbar of the success of his mission.

The Shaikh found himself in a difficult situation. The contrast between the environment around him, his own way of simple living and high thinking and the refined court environment and lavish lifestyle of the Emperor and his dignitaries, was irreducible. Since he had given his consent to receive Akbar, his first thought was to return to his hut, pick up the broom of twigs and sweep the hut clean. He did it himself, but the bare, mud floor, looked unfit for the Emperor to sit on. There was no cot, not even a broken stool. He himself slept on the bare floor. But he had an old and partly torn piece of cloth, about half a yard long, which someone had given him, to cover his head. He spread it in the centre of the mud floor: this was the best seat the Shaikh could offer the Emperor.

The saint's next problem was, what refreshments he should place before the Emperor. He had no earthen water pitcher, but an old bowl in which he could fetch water from the spring. The Emperor, he thought, was accustomed to grapes and pomegranates, but he had only wild berries, which grew in the bushes. Having decided about how to welcome the Emperor, the Shaikh waited for him.

V

Akbar arrived at Sikri with a small entourage of about fifty men. A few scholars and pious men were a part of the imperial pilgrimage party. Shaikh Muhammad Bukhari and Hakim Ain-ul-Mulk were among them. It took Akbar and his fifty other pilgrims a day and a half, to cover the twenty-three miles of dusty road, from Agra to Sikri. The Emperor and his party reached the hermit's abode at noon. The Emperor had discarded any insignia of royalty, He wore a simple, cotton dress. He walked up the rough-hewn flight of stairs, leading to the Shaikh's humble dwelling. The saint rushed out of his modest hut to welcome his imperial guest. The Emperor bowed low, to touch the saint's feet. The Shaikh drew back and held out both his arms, to embrace Akbar. This was the most formidable meeting. No one had ever seen a powerful emperor humbling himself before a penniless saint.

The Shaikh welcomed the royal visitor with the recitation of a couple of verses from the Quran. Then he led the Emperor to his meek abode, about fifty yards away. He stopped at the threshold and looked towards the *Shahinshah* with an apologetic expression in his eyes. Akbar understood the saint's thoughts about the bareness of his dwelling. He took the initiative and stepped inside. He looked around the single-room hut and said, 'I am thankful to God. This is the abode of peace. God has at last given me access to it. I wish I could live here, for the rest of my life. This place is heaven on earth. One can feel the presence of Allah here. Allow me, revered Shaikh, to share your peaceful lodgings, at least for a, few days.'

The Shaikh did not know what reply to give. He felt that the

Emperor, unaccustomed to hardship and self-abstinence, could not live there. Akbar seemed to grasp the hesitation hidden in the silence of the saint.

'Venerable Shaikh,' Akbar said, 'my soul is finite. It yearns to merge itself with the Infinite Soul. The merger will bestow peace, for which I have longed, in vain. It is only here, where you dwell that I can find the peace of mind I have been searching, for so long.'

The saint felt disconcerted. He had never heard such a request from a ruling king before. He did not know how to respond to this strange entreaty. He was, however, convinced of the Shahinshah's genuine humility. He recalled some of the Quranic verses which extolled the virtues of humility. He recited them in a low voice and then stood speechless. He could not muster courage enough to ask the Emperor to squat on the tattered piece of cloth. Akbar extricated the saint from his embarrassment. He did not wait for formal permission. He sat down cross-legged, on the dusty floor and implored the saint to take his seat on the time-worn piece of cloth, by his right hand. The Shaikh did so, bewildered at what was happening.

Akbar said, 'Revered saint, I have come to pay you my homage, belated though it is. It is an honour to sit at your feet and ask for your blessings, in the performance of my duties. I have been wanting, for many years, to come to this hallowed place. It is pilgrimage for me. You are my spiritual preceptor and I beseech you, to initiate me into the mysteries of what lies behind this world of sight, sound and smell. I may be a Shahinshah to others, but I believe I am the lowliest of all mankind. I have come to learn first-hand, the secrets of life and death. My hopes rest on your munificence and your supplication to God Almighty, on my behalf. I shall not tire you by saying more.'

Akbar had touched the innermost chords of the Shaikh's heart. He was moved with Akbar's total self-surrender.

'Holy Shaikh,' Akbar continued, 'I beg you to allow me the benefit of your company for a few days.'

The Shaikh wanted to say 'no', with a sweep of his hand. But, before he could make this gesture, Akbar quickly forestalled him, saying, 'Do not turn me away. I am a humble seeker of divine knowledge.'

The Shaikh nodded approval. He went out towards the bushes. Akbar also came out and sat on the very boulder on which the Meer-i-Saamaan had sat, three days before. He waited expectantly for the host's return. After a while, he saw the Shaikh coming towards him with a handful of wild berries on a leaf. Akbar stood up as a mark of respect. The Shaikh presented the Emperor the leaf, full of wild berries. Akbar received the gift gratefully. These freshly picked wild berries seemed to the Emperor a priceless treasure, because it came from the saint himself.

Akbar's entourage stood at a distance. Every man there, had been watching with awe, what was transpiring between the Shahinshah and the saint. The Emperor made a sign to all his fifty men to come and pay their respects to the saint.

'Shaikh Bukhari,' Akbar said. 'I want you to perform, in consultation and co-operation with the officers concerned, four important projects – one, the construction of a mosque and a school in the vicinity of the saint's hallowed dwelling; two, preparation of food in our royal kitchen and its distribution to the entire population of Sikri, for as long as the holy saint allows us to stay here; three, the construction of an all-weather cottage, for the Shaikh's residence; and four, adequate provisions for the upkeep of the mosque and the school, as well as for the comfort of the venerable saint.'

The Shaikh hung his head in submission to Allah and then addressed Akbar, 'Your Majesty, my riches are my poverty. I beg of you not to deprive me of these riches. I would request Your Majesty to leave me alone with my poverty and my God. My happiness lies only in these two. The all-weather cottage and my comfort, for which you are solicitous, will interfere in the pursuit of my ultimate goal of self-realisation.

'As for my prayers and blessings, I cannot say what they are worth. But I will invoke the Creator of the Universe for the fulfilment of your heart's desire. God Almighty, in His compassion, may respond with favour. My faith in Him, is total. Let us pray here and now and remind ourselves that what He does and what He does not do, is all for the good of mankind.'

Akbar and the members of the pilgrimage party raised their hands. The words of the Shaikh and the conviction with which he spoke them, overwhelmed Akbar.

VI

Shaikh Salim led Akbar back to the hut. Once inside, the Emperor felt as if peace was descending upon him, layer upon layer, like flakes of snow. He laid himself down on the mud floor for a brief rest, regardless of the whiteness of his cotton apparel. The Shaikh busied himself in his afternoon prayer and meditation. Akbar did not fall asleep. He felt as if he was sharing the temporal indigence as well as the spiritual affluence, of his host.

It was about six in the evening when the Shaikh rose from his tattered prayer mat. Akbar also stood up and said, 'Revered saint, I crave your leave to return to Agra.' Shaikh Salim, a man of few words, nodded his head in affirmation. Akbar again bent to touch the saint's feet, but the Shaikh restrained him, saying, 'Your majesty, in touching my feet, you will make me a sinner. Touching one's feet may be a mark of reverence, but I am not worthy of it. I bow my head only to God and I do not like anyone to bow his head and touch my feet.'

Shaikh Salim walked with Akbar for about fifty yards, till they came to the roughly-cut stones that made a flight of stairs. The Shaikh paused there and said, 'Your Majesty, I do not know if what I say is worth anything. I have a feeling that God will bless you with not one son, but three sons.'

The Emperor was delighted. He said, 'In that case, the succession to the house of Taimur is assured.'

'It is assured for several generations,' Shaikh Salim said confidently.

'I am obsessed with thoughts of an early death, like my father and his father,' Akbar said.

'You will have a long life,' the saint said.

'I am worried about the consolidation of my conquests,' Akbar confessed. 'I want a strong and united Hindustan, where all live in peace and amity.'

'Your conquests will dazzle the eyes of the world,' Shaikh

Salim replied, with his usual brevity. 'Go in peace, Your Majesty, and God be with you.'

'You have put me under your obligation for the rest of my life. I am afraid this burden is too heavy for me to bear,' said Akbar.

The Shahinshah ordered all the men in his entourage to come and beg leave of the saint. Shaikh Salim raised both his hands and blessed them.

VII

Queen Jodha Bai or Mariam Zamani as she was called, was two months pregnant when Akbar, with his small retinue, had made his pilgrimage to Sikri. On his return to Agra, he recounted to his beloved Queen his successful meeting with Shaikh Salim. The Queen was optimistic. She also believed in the piety of sanyasis and saints. What the Shaikh had said, she felt, would come out to be true.

'Jodha,' said Akbar, 'I have a proposal for you, if you agree to it.'

'What is it, Sire?' the Queen asked.

'I will call the Chief Engineer. I want you to live under the shadow of the Shaikh's hut, until the child is born,' said Akbar.

'But where will I live there?' the Queen inquired. 'The area where the saint lives is all wilderness.'

'The Chief Engineer will be instructed to build a small, but comfortable house, for you,' Akbar replied. 'The best *vaid*, the best *hakim* and the best midwife, will be posted there. They will attend you day and night. You will have your own kitchen and kitchen staff. There will be a daily movement of provisions and medicines. An uninterrupted communication will be maintained between you and me.'

'Sire,' said Jodha Bai, 'your suggestion is a proof of the extent of your caring for me. Yet I feel, you are doing all this, more for your expected successor, than for me. Our twin sons died at infancy. You want the baby to be born safe and healthy and to survive, so that he should be the light of our eyes and the comfort of our hearts.'

'You have reasoned well.' said Akbar. 'All this is possible only if you live under the spiritual umbrella of Shaikh Salim. God willing, you will be the highly esteemed mother of the heir to the throne, the throne that has achieved the exalted status it enjoys today, with the combined efforts of our Rajput and Mughal relatives and friends. Future historians will always remember you, as the brightest jewel in the Mughal crown.'

The Queen felt happy. Her happiness lay in her husband's happiness. No sooner did she give her consent, than the Emperor summoned his Chief Engineer. It took no more than a month to implement the Emperor's plan. The Queen and some ladies of the court, who loved her, went to live at Sikri. On 30th August 1569, she became the proud mother of a bonny, baby son.

VIII

September is a pretty cool month in Gwalior. The monsoon begins to recede. The showers are occasional and of a very short duration. All open spaces and trees turn green and animals and birds have a good day. The pre-winter season is supposed to be one of the best seasons for outings and hunting.

There was peace in the country, and no such news came from any part of the far-flung Empire that would necessitate the Shahinshah's immediate presence in his capital. Akbar needed relaxation. He and his hunting party therefore, encamped at Gwalior, adjacent to Agra. The thick forest there abounded in big game. But the Emperor had hardly spent three days there, when the good news was brought to him that he had been blessed with a handsome baby son.

Akbar's joy knew no bounds. He ordered his men to pack up. There should be no more killing of wild life when a new life had come into existence. 'What is sport for us, is death for these innocent and dumb denizens of the forest,' he thought. He summoned Ahmed Shah Bukhari, whom he had specially invited to keep him company at the hunting camp. This dignitary was a well-known occultist and was also well-versed in astronomy.

The news that the Emperor had at last been blessed with the heir to the imperial throne, spread apace, not only in the royal hunting camp but throughout Gwalior and Agra. Akbar received almost an endless number of congratulatory messages. Ahmad Shah Bukhari entered the royal tent, saluted the Emperor and offered his felicitations to the Emperor on the birth of a son.

'Ahmad Shah,' said the Emperor. 'We are brimming with joy. Let us go to Sikri at once. We are impatient to see our son and compliment our Queen. We wish to leave for Sikri immediately.'

'Pardon me, Your Majesty,' said the occultist-astronomer gravely. 'I would not advise any haste. I would also respectfully ask you to suppress your joy, for the sake of your new-born son.'

'What do you mean, Ahmad Shah?' said the Emperor angrily. 'Keep your advice to yourself. We are dying to see our son and compliment our Queen. We must start at once.'

'Your Majesty,' said Ahmad Shah. 'Have patience. The fruit of patience is sweet. I have served the Mughal throne with loyalty and devotion, and I would not like that anything is done in haste, that could deprive the throne of its future Emperor.'

Akbar calmed himself. The occultist-astronomer had touched the Emperor where it hurt most. 'What, then, do you suggest?' Akbar inquired.

Ahmad Shah Bukhari said, 'Defer seeing your baby for forty-one days. The prevalent belief in this country is, that a son, born after a long period of expectation, proves lucky to the family if the father postpones seeing him, for more than a month. Remember, Your Majesty, your own father Humayun of blessed memory did not set his eyes on you till you were thirty-one days old.'

The argument seemed to pacify Akbar. He had waited for five years and as compared to that, waiting for forty-one more days was simple, though emotionally highly stressful.

IX

At last, the prescribed period of forty-one anxiety filled days was over. To the Emperor, these forty-one days seemed longer than forty-one years. On the forty-second day, Ahmad Shah Bukhari sought an audience with the Emperor and was promptly admitted into his presence.

'Your Majesty,' he said, 'other astronomers and astrologers and I myself, find that the stars are in their auspicious positions. Your

Majesty may leave for Sikri now.'

The Emperor's face brightened with joy. 'What else?' he asked.

The occultist-astronomer answered, 'Sikri is throbbing with life, Your Majesty. The court astrologers, chronogram writers, poets, musicians, religious heads, scholars and the nobility are already there, to welcome you. Even Shaikh Salim expects you. All arrangements for your journey are complete.'

'Ahmad Shah, you have brought a very pleasing piece of news. We can be patient no longer. Let us start for Sikri at once.'

It was in the afternoon that Akbar arrived at Sikri. The October air was cool and refreshing. The monsoon rains had made the wilderness of Sikri luscious green. The tiny village had turned into a small, booming town. It had never seen such a large number of VVIPs and VIPs before.

Akbar decided to pay homage to the Shaikh first. He walked alone to the rough-hewn stone stairs, where he had last met the Shaikh. The saint was there. The meeting between them was a get-together of two great men and their belief that the destiny of nations and individuals lay in the hands of God and that nothing ever happens, without his will.

Akbar said cheerfully, 'Allah is great, revered Shaikh.'

'Praise be to Allah,' replied the saint, 'who has made you see this happy day.'

'Praise be to Allah,' replied the Emperor, 'and to all his prophets and to all his saints. Venerable Shaikh, do me the honour of accompanying me to the little abode, where my Queen awaits me, with her peerless gift.'

Akbar and Shaikh Salim wended their way through the stones and shrubs to the palace of the former Princess of Amber. The courtiers had lined themselves up, on both side of the passage. They shouted, 'Long live the Prince! Long live the Queen! Long live Shahinshah Akbar! Long live the holy Shaikh Salim Chisti!'

After Shaikh Salim returned to his hut, a pretty maid-of-honour led Akbar to the Queen's chamber. Jodha Bai sat reclining against the silk-soft pillows. The baby lay on her lap and she was looking at it, with maternal love and affection. When Akbar entered, he saw a most charming smile on her rose-bud lips, a blend of the pride and joy arising out of the fulfilment.

Akbar greeted his Queen and presented her nine necklaces and nine pairs of matching earrings, valued at more than one million gold coins. Then he picked up his infant son in his muscular arms, pressed him close to his heart, kissed him lovingly on his broad forehead and gently placed him in his mother's lap.

'I have hit upon a name for our darling son, Jodha,' he declared. 'The Prince will bear the name Salim.'

The news leaked out of the chamber almost immediately. A maid-of-honour rushed out and informed the courtiers that the Emperor himself had given the forty-two-day-old Prince, the name Salim.

'There can be no greater honour to the Shaikh than this act of the Emperor,' said Ahmad Shah Bukhari, to which all the courtiers seemed to agree, in near unanimity.

X

Akbar and Ahmad Shah Bukhari were closeted together. Ahmad Shah said, 'Your Majesty, there are two systems according to which the horoscope of Shahzada Salim can be prepared. One is the Greek system and the other is the Indian system. Both systems are ancient and prediction-oriented. In some basic respects, however, the Greek system differs from the Indian scheme of tabulation.'

Ahmad Shah paused to observe the Emperor's reaction to what he was saying.

'Go on,' said Akbar, 'we are listening.'

'As Your Majesty is aware,' said Ahmad Shah, 'the most celebrated among the specialists of the Greek system is the white-haired Maulana Chand. Your Majesty's horoscope, prepared by the Maulana, is the perfection of astrological skill.'

'We will ask the Maulana to prepare our Shaikhoo's horoscope. You know we call our son Shahzada Salim in public and Shaikhoo in private, in honour of Shaikh Salim Chisti.'

'Yes, Your Majesty, I know the Shahzada's pet name. Shaikhoo denotes more nearness and love and sounds sweeter to the ear, though Salim is also an appropriate name,' said the occultist-astronomer. 'It will take Maulana Chand at least three years to study, co-ordinate and interpret the positions of the heavenly bodies, at the time of the Shahzada's birth.'

'The predictions based on the Greek system or the Indian system are surprisingly similar,' said Akbar. 'Abul Fazl is one of the nine jewels of our court. He is a brilliant exponent of the science of astronomy. He was keen to blend the two systems. He calls our Shaikhoo the vermilion mark, on the forehead of Fortune. His analysis and synthesis of our four horoscopes are masterpieces of astronomical exposition. But he is so busy. The duties we have assigned him, are time-consuming. We wonder whether he will be able to prepare our Shaikhoo's horoscope according to a synthesis of the two systems. But we will speak to him. Three days have passed since we have been staying at Sikri. Tomorrow, we propose to move to Agra to celebrate the birth of our son and distribute rewards.'

'As you please, Your Majesty,' said Bukhari. 'The celebrations have a spiritual note. The emphasis here will be on three things – prayers, alms-giving and feeding the poor. They are in keeping with the austerity of the saint. The splendour of the court will be kept aside. The elite of the court also expect their share of the rejoicing.'

XI

As soon as Ahmad Shah Bukhari had left, Akbar went to his Queen's chamber. He found her hale and hearty. The young Prince was sleeping peacefully in his cot, beside his mother's couch. Akbar sat down by the side of the Queen and said, 'Jodha, I am told that the first ninety days are critical for the Prince. You have therefore to stay here. The vicinity of the Shaikh is enough to protect the Prince.'

'Sire, it will be hard for me to be separated from you, for three full months,' said the Queen. 'Had it not been for the good of our darling son, I would not have agreed to stay here, away from you. Indeed, I shall miss you very much.'

'Jodha, my Queen,' said Akbar in a persuasive manner, 'I have to return to the court, tomorrow morning. The birth of our son deserves a celebration appropriate to our status. After all, Salim is a child of many prayers. When the mandatory three months are over, you will enter Agra triumphantly and the entire population of the capital will be there, to welcome you.'

The Queen replied, 'Well, since it is a kind of self-sacrifice for our son, I will have to go through it all, willingly and without protest.'

Akbar stood up. He gave a love pat on the Queen's head, went to his son's cradle noiselessly, gently touched the infant's forehead with his lips and left the Queen's chamber.

XII

On Akbar's return to Agra, the celebrations of Prince Salim's birth commenced on a lavish scale. In a vast, open courtyard of the Emperor's palace, there were festivities for three moonlit nights. The bearers brought goblets of the best wine, in large trays, which was enjoyed by all. The musicians were there and the best dancing girls of Benares and Agra, tried to excel each other, by the enchanting movements of their supple and curvaceous bodies. The ladies of the palace sat on the latticed balconies and thoroughly enjoyed the performance, which was unlike any the palace had witnessed before, in its scale of grandeur. Each musician and each dancing girl accumulated wealth, enough, to last him or her, for at least a year.

On the fourth day, a special darbar was convened, at the Diwan-i-Khas. All the nine jewels of Akbar's court, the nobility, most of the Rajput princes, the governors of various provinces, the commanders of the imperial armed forces and other top dignitaries, sat in their glamorous seats. There was a mass effect of the splendour of rich robes and princely jewellery, worn by people of eminence, who comprised the creamy layer of the Mughal Empire.

Akbar entered the Diwan-i-Khas and all stood up, to pay homage to their Emperor. The choicest gifts were presented to the Emperor. The gifts were carried in trays covered with embroidered velvet and satin, turn by turn. The Emperor touched the cover of each tray with his right hand, as a token of acceptance, and the tray was taken by liveried bearers to an anteroom.

The presentation of gifts being over, Akbar made a sign to his Prime Minister, Raja Todar Mal. The Raja stood up, unfolded a scroll and read in a loud and authoritative voice, each name, in a pretty long list of noblemen and announced the conferment of jagirs commensurate with the status of the beneficiary and the services rendered by him and his family.

Prince Salim's future wife, Princess Maan Bai, was the daughter of Raja Bhagwan Das, brother of Queen Jodha Bai and the adopted sister of Raja Maan Singh. They were Akbar's near relatives. The Emperor proclaimed from his throne, 'Raja Bhagwan Das, we are pleased to raise your rank by two thousand horses. Now your grade is next only to members of the royal family.' A tray containing a set of luxuriant robes was brought by a uniformed bearer. Raja Bhagwan Das stood up, walked towards the Emperor's throne, bowed low and accepted the robes in the tray, which the bearer put down at the foot of the royal dias. The robes with the tray would be sent to the Raja after the darbar.

The Emperor next proclaimed, 'Raja Maan Singh, we are delighted to elevate your rank by another two thousand horses. Now you are also next to the grade of the members of our family. Come and receive your robe of honour.' Raja Maan Singh followed the same procedure as Raja Bhagwan Das, in accepting the set of princely robes and returned to his seat.

'Our gallant Rajput princes,' Akbar addressed Raja Bhagwan Das and Raja Maan Singh, 'we are inclined to tell you that the destiny of our son seems to be somehow linked to you – the two men of renown and valour. Do not ask us the reason why, because we ourselves do not know as yet.'

Akbar had broken his own record of generosity. Everyone among the invitees seemed elated. All of them had received more than what they had expected. There was none who returned empty-handed.

'We thank all our honoured guests for taking part in our joy,' said Akbar. 'We hope that, on your return to your homes, the members of your family will rejoice when you tell them of your experience of the festivities. We convey our best wishes to you. We bid you goodbye, till we meet again.'

Akbar stood up from his seat. The audience also rose as the Emperor descended from his throne, walked down the carpeted passage between rows of seats on which the guests had sat and retired to his own chamber. The darbar and the celebrations were over.

War or Women?

I

Salim was in residence at Ajmer. With him was his top aide Khwaja Jahan, a veteran of several wars. In his early forties, he was a strong and well-built man. Khwaja Jahan was as much a sycophant and a self-seeker, as a warrior. He thought that, by allying himself with the Prince, he could further his own ambitions speedily and perhaps, devise a short cut to power and pelf.

'Shahzada Salim,' said Khwaja Jahan when they were together, 'you know that the Emperor has left for the Deccan and it would take him a long time to complete his mission there.'

'I know, Khwaja Jahan, the subjugation of Ahmadnagar and the impregnable fort of Asirgarh is not an easy task. It may take months, even years. The very fact that my father has himself gone there, is an evidence of the magnitude of the mission.'

'Shahzada Salim,' the Khwaja said, 'you are restless. You have nothing to do. You refuse to fight against Prince Amar Singh of Mewar, for your own reasons. You are frustrated. Opium, alcohol and your fast-growing harem, are no solution to what is troubling you.'

'Yes, Khwaja, they do not offer any solution. They give me only temporary relief. You say, my harem is fast growing. It is and is creating problems. There is jealousy among the ladies in the seraglio. Whenever my wife, Princess Maan Bai, hears of these open secrets, it is natural for her to resent. A Rajput woman is devoted to her husband. She frowns when she learns that the husband she loves, holds other women in his arms. The blame rests entirely with me. Fully knowing all this, I cannot help it. I am attracted towards young women and they are drawn towards me. Instead of allowing such relations to remain clandestine and illicit, I make them legal, by marrying these women. When I am no longer interested in a woman, I divorce her and continue to maintain her, in the comfort and luxury to which she has been accustomed to, in the harem. I do not know whether it is right or wrong, but I do it, thinking that it is the only right thing for me to do.'

'I understand your problem, Shahzada Salim,' said Khwaja Jahan. 'You are the heir to the throne. All eyes are riveted on you. The slightest lapse on your part is blown out of all proportions, which damages your reputation. An Emperor may do what you are doing, but his power is such, that few dare to point an accusing finger at him.'

'Do you mean to say I should declare myself the Shahinshah, taking advantage of my father's absence in the Deccan?' asked Salim.

'I suggest no such thing,' replied the Khwaja. 'The time is not ripe yet. Give me some time to think over it.'

'Khwaja Jahan,' said Salim, 'do you think that, after proclaiming myself Emperor under your guidance and with your help, I should make you the Prime Minister of Hindustan?'

'It is for you, when you are Emperor, to do as your deem fit,' the Khwaja answered.

Salim said, 'To tell you frankly and with no intention to hurt your feelings, it is difficult to replace Raja Todar Mal. He is a genius. He has an inventive brain, boldness of conception and the capacity to visualise every little detail of a major policy.'

'I have great respect for Raja Todar Mal,' said Khwaja Jahan. 'The world cannot exist as it is, because of Raja Todar Mal. It will continue even when the noble Raja dies. Men of genius go, but men of genius also come. However, I am not comparing myself, or claiming to be on equal terms with Raja Todar Mal. He is proficient in his own field, while I specialise in my own area of work.'

'You do specialise, Khwaja Jahan,' said Salim, 'and I expect a lot from you. Think over the matter and then tell me how early I can announce myself Emperor. I don't want to revolt against my father whom I hold close to my heart. It would be unfilial. It would break his heart. I wish he could be persuaded to abdicate voluntarily, in my favour.'

II

Raja Maan Singh was the nephew and adopted son of Raja Bhagwan Das, of Amber. He held the post of Governor of Bengal and Bihar, but he lived in Ajmer, ostensibly for reasons of health, but in reality to keep an eye on the activities of Salim. Obviously, the activities of the Prince were such, that the Raja could not look upon them, with an approving eye.

The Raja had played a gallant role in the campaign against Chittor and was rewarded with high honours. He showed his intrepidity and military skill at the siege and capture of Ranthambor. He displayed extraordinary valour at Sarnal and led a military campaign against Dawood Khan, in Bengal. He was the supreme commander of the expeditionary force for the invasion of Mewar. He was dauntless and daring, at the battle of Haldighat, for which he was entrusted with the defence of Rajputana. He held gubernatorial posts twice – first as Governor of Punjab and then, as Governor of Bengal and Bihar.

One day, on the advice of his playmate and friend, Khwaja Muhammad Sharif, Prince Salim called on Raja Maan Singh, to inquire about his health. The Raja had been waiting for such an opportunity. He greeted the Prince cordially, concealing his resentment against him and talked to him amicably.

'Salim,' he said, 'you know that, by virtue of your mother being my adoptive sister, I am your maternal uncle and you are my nephew. As a nephew is no less than a son, I have all affection and love for you. You are as dear to me, as you are valuable to the Mughal Empire.'

The Prince heard the Raja in respectful silence. He knew that the Raja's words were a preliminary to something else. He was curious to know what would come next. 'Salim,' continued the Raja, 'as my nephew, you should know, what you were in the past, what you are now and what you should be, in the years to come.'

'I know what I am, Uncle.' said Salim. 'I would like to know what I should be in future.'

The Raja said, 'You, my nephew, are a child of many prayers. When your father lost his two children, he ardently desired an heir, who should live to inherit his vast empire. You must have heard of how he prayed to God and sought the blessings of so many saints.'

'I know, Uncle,' said Salim. 'In this very city of Ajmer, my father walked all the way to the mausoleum of Khwaja Muin-ud-din Chishti. I also know that I am named Salim after the holy saint of Sikri.'

'Then you must also be knowing that, after the vow your father made at the shrine of the Khwaja of Ajmer was fulfilled, the Emperor made another journey on foot to this city, to pay homage to the Khwaja.'

'I know all this,' said Salim. 'That is why I consider myself special.'

'You are very special,' said Raja Maan Singh affectionately. 'You are the hope of your family as well as of the people of the country. You were brought up with great care and affection. When you grew up, elaborate arrangements were made for your education at the new capital, Fatehpur Sikri. You are familiar with the lofty palace and the magnificent buildings around it. Your school-going ceremony was performed when you were four years old. A number of tutors were appointed to teach you five languages – Hindi, Sanskrit, Persian, Arabic and Turkish. One of the best literatures of the world is in Sanskrit. The language of the common people is Hindi. The first few generations of immigrants from Iran, Arabia and Turkey, speak the language of the country of their origin.'

'In spite of all this, I am a novice in all the five languages and master of none. I have learnt to compose verses in Persian but I find Hindi songs more delightful,' Salim confessed.

The Raja said in a nostalgic tone, 'Several tutors taught you mathematics, history, geography, and other important sciences.'

'Yes, Uncle,' said Salim, 'but the tutor who most influenced me is Abdur Rahim. He owes his title of Khan-i-Khaanan to the versatility of his genius and his scholarship in Hindi, Sanskrit, Persian, Arabic and Turkish. It was he who taught me how to compose Persian verses and aroused my interest in Hindi songs. At the same time, the Khan-i-Khaanan is a soldier and diplomat of no mean order.'

'You were also interested in botany, zoology, music and painting. This is a happy combination of life sciences and fine arts. The Emperor also saw to it that you got the best physical and military education, including the handling of weapons of offence and defence,' said the Raja. 'I hear that you are a fine shot and a mighty hunter.'

'I used to be,' Salim said regretfully. 'At present, I remain restless and depressed. I try to cope with my depression in ways which perhaps have already reached your ears.'

'You are young, my nephew,' said the Raja. 'The tantrums of childhood sometimes grow into sallies of ill-temper, in youth. The current phase of your life will soon pass, if you have the will to repudiate what you are indulging in. After all, you have been associated with the work of military administration since an early age. You were placed in charge of the Kabul campaign and subsequently, you were employed to conduct independent military operations. You were also given training as a civil administrator. All these experiences should stand you in good stead.'

'They have not done me any good,' said Salim. 'I get fits of depression.'

'I am surprised at your talk of depression,' the Raja argued. 'In military campaigns and civil administration, there are challenges to be met, strategies to be devised and planned and expediency to be followed. Depression runs away, as soon as it comes face to face with danger and challenge. Depression implies timidity and cowardice.'

'It also implies indolence,' Salim said. 'And I am for the time being, an indolent person, which I should not be.'

'That is right. You should not be,' said Raja Maan Singh. 'Usman Khan has raised the standard of revolt in Bengal. The Emperor has ordered me to proceed to Bengal forthwith and quell the rebellion. I am leaving tomorrow morning. I invite you to come with me and deal with this insurrection. You will be able to concentrate only on one thing: how to inflict a crushing defeat on Usman Khan and his mercenaries. You will be doing a filial act in preserving your father's hegemony, in the eastern provinces. I will see to it that the entire credit of victory goes to you. You will rise in the Emperor's esteem. You will be away from your revelries, which will have a beneficial effect on you. It will turn you into the prince that you once were. A prince that your father, your mother, and I - your uncle - had dreamt of. Do not miss this opportunity, Salim. It is knocking at your door. If you do not open the door, the opportunity will go away.'

'Uncle, what you say sounds sweet to my ears,' said Salim. 'But my heart hesitates. I refused to raise my sword against Rana Ammu. I will have to raise it against Usman Khan. Whether it is Ammu or Usman, it comes more or less to the same thing – war, bloodshed, arson, loot, rape, widows, orphans, injury and bereavement. Those who die get peace, but those who survive the war, suffer.'

'Salim, my nephew, a war is a war. The man who goes to war has to turn his heart into one of steel. War is a necessity, my son, an evil necessity. If you remain here at Ajmer and make no attempt to put down rebellions with an iron hand, the Empire will be fragmented. Would you like to inherit a truncated Empire?' the Raja asked.

'Uncle, I cannot refute what you say,' Salim answered. 'I shall send you my yes, or no, in the evening. Give me a few hours to think over it.'

'All right,' said the Raja. 'You want to think when there is nothing to think about. You have already hinted at what your answer will be. However, I shall wait for it. My preparations are complete and I shall proceed to Bengal directly.'

III

On his return to the Governor's palace, Prince Salim was not surprised to find Khwaja Jahan waiting for him. The Khwaja stood up as the Prince entered, and bowed. The Prince asked him to take his seat and said, 'Well, Khwaja Jahan, you have come in time. I was just thinking of sending a messenger to call you.'

'Shahzada,' said the Khwaja, laughing, 'the devil, though invisible, is everywhere. Think of the devil, and he is there before you in the person of Khwaja Jahan.'

The Prince smiled at the Khwaja's pleasantry and said,

'Perhaps you know where I have been.'

'It is my duty, as your trusted aide, to keep myself informed,' the Khwaja said. 'Now tell me, what transpired between you and the clever Raja.'

Salim related the pith and substance of his meeting with Raja Maan Singh, saying, 'He monopolised the conversation. I had to listen. After all, he is older than I and also my maternal uncle. He was trying to read me and I was trying to read him. But he spoke so affectionately, so persuasively, so sincerely that I was more than once, inclined to give in. I have no doubt that, in spite of our differences in thought, speech and action, he has a soft corner for me, in his heart. Some of the points he made, appealed to me. He put them in such a logical way that they seemed irrefutable. I wished to avoid saying anything that could leave a bad taste.'

'Did he invite you to join him in subduing Usman Khan's rebellion in Bengal?' the Khwaja asked.

'He did,' replied Salim. 'He did so emphatically, but politely.'

'Did he talk about your son, Khusrau?' asked the Khwaja.

'No, he did not,' said Salim. 'Khusrau's name was not mentioned even once, contrary to what I had expected. What is your reaction to our conversation?'

'Shahzada Salim, your son Khusrau, is now thirteen. He is handsome in appearance and pleasing in manners. He spends most of his time with the Raja. Of course, the approval of his mother and of the Emperor, his grandfather, must be there,' said Khwaja Jahan. 'The Raja is trying to mould your son according to his own standards. Khusrau looks upon the Raja as his real guardian. There are close, personal relations between Khusrau and him. Disappointed with you, his mother, aided and abetted by Raja Bhagwan Das and Raja Maan Singh, he may one day, put up Khusrau as the successor to the throne. What is your right by birth may be snatched away from you and bestowed upon your son, on the basis of what is called merit. The so-called merit is nothing but astute and ceaseless publicity, lauding the virtues of Khusrau. Such propaganda is followed by shrewd stage-management. You know, some people in the Emperor's court as well as in his harem, are adept in manoeuvring, being skilful chess players. Abul Fazl is one of them.'

'If I have alienated my son from me,' said Salim, 'the fault lies with me and you. It is you, your friends and your retainers who have been maintaining an uninterrupted supply of wine and women, far in excess of the demand, wherever I happen to be.'

'We will talk about this, if necessary, at some other time,' said Khwaja Jahan. 'What is important for the present is a thorough analysis of Raja Maan Singh's move, to try to allure you into joining him in the expedition aimed at putting down Usman Khan's insurgency in Bengal. His motive may not be as pious as he makes it seem.'

'What could his motive possibly be?' Salim inquired anxiously.

Khwaja Jahan said, 'The Raja wears a thick mask of affection and courtesy. The fact is, as I understand, he is totally disenchanted with you. Your refusal to fight Rana Ammu has strengthened his belief, that in the guise of being anti-war, you are aiming at something else. He may be harbouring plans of your ouster from succession. It is an open secret among those who know both you and Raja Maan Singh, at close quarters, that there is mutual distrust and near-hatred between the two of you.'

'I asked you to tell me the motive which may have prompted the Raja to invite me to accompany him to Bengal.' Salim said. 'While what you say is true, you are going off the point.'

'Be patient, Shahzada,' said Khwaja Jahan. 'I am coming to that. There may be, as far as I understand, two reasons for the Raja to entice you away, into the perils of hostilities in a distant land. Both these reasons are founded on the theory that he wants to remove the major obstacle in the way of Khusrau's succession. You are that major obstacle. One way of eliminating you is, to have you murdered in some jungle on your way to Bengal. The other is that he may put you in such a position during the actual fight that, without providing you reinforcements and supplies, you will be either killed, or captured by Usman Khan and his mercenaries. In either case, you will be doomed forever.'

'What, then, would you suggest?' asked Salim. 'Going by what you say, the whole thing looks terrible. If this is a conspiracy against my life, the Raja is a villain and cannot be trusted at all. If he really cares for me and allows me to win the credit of quashing the uprising, then you, my top aide, are the villain for weaving such a horrible fantasy.'

'If you really want to know who the villain is – I, or the Raja – ascertain yourself.' said Khwaja Jahan. 'Go with the Raja to Bengal.'

'No, I will not go,' said Salim. 'You have created doubts in my mind. I do not want to lose my life by falling into a trap. Everybody wants to live, as long as he can. I am not a mouse to be enticed by bait, to a trap.'

'In that case, do you want me to draft a polite reply, expressing your inability to join the Raja, in his expedition against Usman Khan? Your reason will be – you cannot leave Ajmer and join the Raja unless you receive orders from the Emperor himself to this effect,' said Khwaja Jahan.

'Under the circumstances, this is the only proper course,' said Salim. 'Let the letter be written. I will sign it. You may put my seal and send it to the Raja, so that it reaches him before evening.'

'I am always at your service, Shahzada,' said Khwaja Jahan, bowing. 'I am always ready to sacrifice my life to preserve yours.'

When the Shahzada left, Khwaja Jahan felt triumphant in his heart of hearts. He had succeeded in widening the wedge between Prince Salim and Raja Maan Singh on one hand and between Prince Salim and Abul Fazl, on the other. He was a good player at the chessboard of power politics. He had already made the next move in his ingenious mind.

IV

What Prince Salim had discussed with Khwaja Jahan, he wanted to discuss first, with his old playmate Muhammad Sharif. But the Khwaja happened to be in the palace, when the Prince returned, after visiting Raja Maan Singh. Now having called Sharif, he told him about the possibility, not only of Khusrau's candidature to succession but also of a powerful lobby among the ladies of the court, as well as among those noblemen who disapproved of his (Salim's) ways.

'Do you think my father-in-law, Raja Bhagwan Das, will go against me and favour my son?' asked Salim.

Sharif answered, 'Raja Bhagwan Das is your father-in-law. As such, he cares for you as much as a father-in-law cares for his son-in-law. He is likely to see that no harm comes to you, for the simple reason that any harm to you directly affects his daughter, Princess Maan Bai. He has not opened his heart yet. He is unhappy to hear of your conduct which, in his opinion, does not become a future Emperor. He is waiting patiently, in the hope that time will bring about a change in you. He has not even tried to wean you away from your aides and companions because, till now, you pose no threat to the throne. Raja Bhagwan Das is the Emperor's man. He will stand by him, through thick and thin. If he sees that your affairs continue to be what they are, he will definitely side with the Emperor, taking care that no harm comes to you.'

'I see,' said Salim pensively. 'What about Maan Singh, my uncle?'

'Raja Maan Singh is with you,' Sharif assured the Prince. 'Khusrau and the Raja are close to each other. But the Raja has a sense of fairness. If he observes a change for the better in you, he will appreciate it, while continuing to shower his affection on your son. But if he discerns no change in you, then Princess Maan Bai and the two Rajas may form a strong lobby, in support of Khusrau.'

'The Raja wanted to lure me away from Ajmer to Bengal, where he is going under my father's orders, to deal with Usman Khan, who has risen in rebellion.'

'Raja Maan Singh has no ulterior motives, as far as I understand him,' Sharif said. 'The Raja is a man of honour. He offered you an opportunity to prove your value and worth. This would have been a clear proof of the change in you. It would have been appreciated by one and all – the Emperor and the court. You have missed a rare opportunity.'

'I have my father's orders to stay at Ajmer,' Salim defended himself. 'In accompanying the Raja, I would have violated his order. This is what I mentioned in my letter to the Raja, while declining his offer.'

'You are still infringing the orders. He sent you here to contain the growing ambition of Rana Amar Singh. But you have not done anything so far,' said Sharif. 'This does not add glory to your office, as Governor of Ajmer. Everybody knows it.'

'Yet,' argued Salim, 'my father's orders are necessary for me to leave my headquarters. Had I gone with the Raja, without my father's permission, I would have been technically branded a deserter.'

'No,' said Sharif, 'Raja Maan Singh is an influential man. He would have secured the Emperor's permission sooner or later, on your behalf, by convincing him of your reluctance to wage an arduous war in the difficult terrain of the Aravalli hills, which is more suitable for guerrilla hit-an-run tactics, surprise ambushes and nocturnal skirmishes, in small and isolated army camps, when most of the tired soldiers are asleep. As an alternative, the Raja would have conveyed your willingness to participate in the open warfare against the rebels in Bengal.'

'Yours is an entirely different point of view,' said Salim. 'You suggest possibilities, evading the factual position, or the legal viewpoint.'

Sharif said, 'Yes, Salim. Analysis is an exercise in both facts and possibilities.'

'The rough-and-tumble of a never-ending guerrilla warfare in the narrow passes and jungles, suits neither my temper nor my military training,' said Salim. 'I would like you to advise me, on how to get out of this predicament.'

'Salim, you have so many advisors. This is a good thing. A good judge listens to every side of the case and then comes to a conclusion. I feel you should also act like a judge. Man is a rational animal and if he does not use his powers of reasoning, he sinks deeper into the mire of folly. Any advice that aims at unifying and strengthening the Empire, is good and must be acted upon. On the contrary, any advice that aims at weakening and disintegrating the Empire, is bad and must be rejected with disdain,' said Sharif in a tone of finality. 'Your father, the Emperor, has carved out an Empire for his successors by dint of hard work, sagacious planning and the co-operation of his generals, princes and the people of all religions and castes. He likes its continuation and solidarity, through his successors. For this reason, Salim, the Empire is above self-interest. I hope you understand what I am driving at.'

'I asked you for advice,' said Salim impatiently. 'You have delivered a harangue. Give me some good, practical advice.'

'This is not a harangue, Salim. It is the reality; the reality you do not want to face,' said Sharif, with his usual calmness. 'Listen to me. Seek an audience with your father, the Emperor, in private. Unbosom your heart to him. Explain your difficulties and diffidence in campaigning in the Aravalli Hills. The Emperor will make alternative arrangements. He has senior generals in his military staff, tried and tested men, who have abundant experience of fighting at Haldighat. Do not suggest any names. Leave everything at the Emperor's discretion.'

'What next?' asked Salim.

'Tell your father, the Emperor,' Sharif advised, 'to post you to some province nearest to Agra, so that your wife and son will remain with you. The presence of your wife and interaction with your son, are likely to bring about a change for the good in your conjugal relations, in your relations with your son and in your own self.'

Muhammad Sharif paused to study the reaction of the Prince. It seemed to him that his suggestions were unpalatable to his old friend.

'Well,' said Salim, 'what else?'

'Before seeking an audience with your father, the Emperor, pension off the surplus women in your harem,' said Sharif. 'Keep only your wives, women relatives and their maids.'

'This is too much,' said Salim. 'You are going to the extreme.'

Sharif said, 'If the Emperor declines to transfer you, then remain at Ajmer. Bring your wife and son here. Win back the confidence of your wife and the love of your son. Raja Maan Singh will be away in Bengal for about six months and during these six months, you can set your house in order. If this is done, there will be no question of Khusrau's candidature for succession, no lobby to back him up and no rancour in the Emperor's heart.'

'My courage fails me, when I appear before my father,' Salim admitted. 'I feel like a prodigal son before him.'

'Your father loves you,' Sharif tried to assure the Prince. 'He will listen to you with patience and sympathy. Few sovereigns are as understanding and generous as the Emperor is to you. It would be better if he rebukes you and thus lets off the steam pent up in him. If he sees a penitent son before him, his heart will melt. There beats in his breast the heart of a father, not that of a butcher.'

'What you say, Sharif, appeals to my head, but not to my heart,' Salim confessed. 'I want short cuts and not long and cumbersome procedures. I want to assert my rights and not beg for them.'

'There is a saying of great significance applicable universally, and that saying is: first deserve, then desire,' Sharif retorted.

V

It was a pleasant evening. All the lamps in the Governor's palace had been lit. An air of peace pervaded Prince Salim's chamber. He was relaxing with Anarkali by his side. This sweet girl, 'the pomegranate bud,' was beautiful, and her Mughal dress, ornaments and light make-up, added much to her natural loveliness. She did not look like an ordinary girl. She seemed to come from noble blood. Reclining her head on Salim's hairy chest, she looked like a veritable princess. Salim played with her long black hair and sometimes tickled her, in one of her armpits.

The Prince said, 'I had a very busy day – meeting Uncle Maan, Khwaja Jahan and Muhammad Sharif, besides looking into the routine affairs of this largely desert province. I declined Uncle Maan's invitation to join him in the Bengal expedition. I think it is good I did so. What do you say? Did I do the right, or the wrong thing?'

'I have never been good in chess,' said Anarkali. 'I do not understand the intricate game of politics. If you had gone and brought Usman, dead or alive, before the Emperor, you would have risen higher in his esteem. As it is, you will stay here, which for you means one girl or the other. There are so many fruits in this world, each of a different flavour that you cannot taste all of them in the brief operational span of your life, my philanderer Prince.'

'You naughty girl,' said Salim, pinching one of her cheeks lovingly. 'I do not eat forbidden fruit, as Adam and Eve had done.

I do not want to lose my little Garden of Eden. Yes, I remember now. A pearl-trader from Samarqand brought a girl he wanted to sell. I was in a hurry to go to Uncle Maan's. I liked the girl. I told you to negotiate the price and buy her. Did you do so?'

'I did,' said Anarkali, 'but I do not like buying and selling of girls. It is flesh trade. When a man is tired of a slave girl, he sells her to another man, at less price, who again sells her to a third man at a lesser price and this goes on, until the girl is encumbered with a few children. This is utterly inhuman. It robs the girl of her dignity and individuality. Instead of calling a halt to this immoral traffic in women, in the province of which you are the Governor, you seem to encourage it by your personal example.'

'You are ahead of the times, Anar,' said Salim. 'There is slave trade over more than three-fourths of the world. A young boy fetches a high price, but a young girl fetches even higher, depending on the symmetry of her figure, the complexion of her skin, her age and her health. I alone cannot stop this practice almost all over the globe.'

Anarkali said suavely, 'You believe in the saying popular in hot countries: So long as the river flows, jump into it and have fun. You always get hot at the sight of a girl.'

Salim paid no heed to what Anarkali was hinting at. He said, 'What is the name of the girl from Samarqand, Anar?'

'She seems to be a Caucasian, not of Samarqand, and the girls of Caucasia are known as fairies, on account of their matchless beauty,' said Anarkali.

'I asked you her name,' Salim reminded her.

'God knows what her real name is,' replied Anarkali. 'The pearl-trader said her name was Gul Afshan.'

'The name sounds sweet,' said Salim. 'Now get up and send her to me. I want to ask her a few questions.'

Anarkali took her own time in getting up. She said, 'I had been expecting this order from you. Your excessive fondness for women will never be satiated.'

She directed her steps towards the ladies' quarters in the palace and as she walked, her gait looked highly graceful.

VI

A pretty girl, in her late teens, entered silently and stood boldly before Salim. The Prince appraised her from top to toe. She was tall and graceful. Her hair was black and long, almost falling to her hips, her forehead was about a span broad; her eyes were big and deep and her eyelashes were black, thick and pointed. Her nose was shapely; her face well-chiselled and her mouth small. She had pink lips and pearl-white teeth. There was a dimple on each of her rosy cheeks, which was a valuable asset to her beauty. She had a long, swan-like neck and a well-proportioned body.

The Prince said, 'What is your name, pretty girl?'

'My real name is Firdaus Khanum. The first man who bought me, named me Gul Afshan, and ever since, I have been called by this name.'

'Do you belong to Samarqand?' the Prince inquired.

'No, I come from somewhere in Caucasia. When my parents died, I was brought up by my maternal aunt, who lives in Samarqand.'

'Why did she sell you?'

'She was offered one thousand gold coins. It was enough to make her live comfortably for the whole of her life.'

The Prince said, 'Both your names are significant. Firdaus means paradise. Gul Afshan means one who sheds flowers when she speaks. To explore you is to explore the fragrant regions of paradise. To listen to you is to think of flowers.'

'I have heard my praises so many times that I do not feel flattered at all,' Gul Afshan said.

'How many times have you been bought and sold?'

'You are my third master.'

'Who was the first?'

'He was a fur-trader in Kabul.'

'How did he play with you?'

'He was a middle-aged man, but his heart was young. He wanted to re-live his spent youth with me. Sometimes he would suddenly enter when I was washing or dressing myself. He was a strong man. He would lift me in his arms, toss me high up in the air as if I were a little child and catch me again in his arms.'

'Did you ever fall down?'

'He always took care to prevent me from falling down and breaking my bones.'

'Who was your second master?'

'He said he was the heir of a small, tribal principality in Baluchistan, near the sea coast.'

'How did you find him?'

'He had a villa near the sea shore. He lived there, with a few retainers. His father sent him an allowance. He was younger than the fur dealer. He was unmarried. He told me it was no use keeping a cow, when one could buy fresh milk in the market.'

'What did he teach you?'

'He taught me a lot of love tricks such as locating the sensitive spots in one's body, where one feels most thrilled.'

'What did he do with you?'

'He was fond of swimming. He swam like a fish. He also taught me swimming. We used to swim in the Arabian Sea, during moonlit nights.'

'How did you feel during and after swimming?'

'We got excited during swimming and we cooled ourselves afterwards.'

'How do you like life in the harem?'

'I am a fresher. There are too many women here.'

'Should there be less?'

'Not more than two or three.'

'Why?'

'To prevent jealousy and rivalry.'

'You seem to be quite experienced. You are a good girl. You may go now.'

The Caucasian beauty departed, without bowing. She had yet to learn courtly manners. 'Anarkali will teach her,' said the Prince to himself.

The God-Gifted Kingdom

I

Next morning, Khwaja Jahan was back again. The Prince had passed the early hours of the night with the vivacious Caucasian beauty, Gul Afshan. Anarkali was personally present to instruct and help the obliging slave girl, in the ways of pleasing the Prince. With the departure of these two stimulating girls shortly before midnight, the Prince slept soundly for six or seven hours. When he was ready to receive visitors, his body was relaxed, but his mind was not at perfect ease. Khwaja Jahan had asked for some time, to think about the Prince's future plans. When the Khwaja was announced, the Prince hoped that his top aide had come with a well-thought-out plan.

After the usual ceremonial greetings, when the Khwaja was seated, the Prince looked at his visitor's face. The expression on the Khwaja's countenance predicted heartening news. 'Well, Khwaja Jahan,' he said. 'It seems to me that you have something nice to tell me.'

'At the moment, your prospects are bright,' said the Khwaja. 'The Emperor is in the Deccan. Raja Maan Singh has left for Bengal. Both of them will be engaged in their respective army operations, for many months. I see for you no better opportunity than the present, to make a bold bid for the throne.'

The Prince said, 'I want to be the Emperor. At the same time, I do not want to hurt my father and my relatives at court.'

'The hurt is a part of the game. The choice before you is Emperorship now, or uncertainty after your father's demise,' said the Khwaja.

'What will happen when my father is no more, I cannot predict. My son Khusrau, is in the fray. His lobby may win. I would like to exert all the pressure I can, to persuade my father to abdicate in my favour. I would like him to place the glittering gem-studded Mughal turban on my head, with his own hands and take a pledge from his courtiers and his princely allies that, in serving me as Emperor, they should feel as if they were serving my father himself. I shall keep my father, my mother, my stepmother and all the other relatives, in unmitigated luxury. The only difference is: let my father give me willingly now, what will ultimately devolve on me, when he is no more. I shall also continue all my father's major policies and alliances and thus fulfil his cherished dreams of a glorious Hindustan.'

'Very well said, Shahzada,' the Khwaja said suppressing a smile of derision. 'But you overlook one thing: where persuasion fails, coercion succeeds. Are you prepared for this?'

Prince Salim said, 'Yes, coercion is the last resort. Show of force is different from use of force, just as barking is different from biting. I shall use intimidation, but do no physical harm.'

'You are right, Shahzada,' said Khwaja Jahan. 'You have also the means to do so. On the death of Shahbaz Khan Kamboh, you seized all his effects, including his cash, amounting to over one billion *asharfis* or gold coins. That money is sufficient for the expenses of a gigantic showdown exercise. If you authorise me in writing, I shall start the recruitment drive in those areas of Rajputana that are not unfriendly to us. I shall order all blacksmiths in several cities, to engage more artisans and skilled labour to mould cannons and make swords, daggers, and lances, as well as all farriers to make horseshoes. I shall send knowledgeable officers on a buying spree, to procure weapons and the best war horses. I shall summon all tailors in Ajmer and other cities to prepare uniforms for our officers and the men under their command. I prefer cavalry to infantry, because of speed and mobility. What is most important in warfare is speed and surprise. I will have the order written and send it through one of my confidants, for you to sign and put your seal on it.'

'What then, shall we do?' Salim asked.

'The showdown preparations will take some months. I will utilise this time in identifying and sounding some of those who may be disgruntled with the Emperor. I will tantalise them, with mouth-watering rewards. If they support us with whatever armed forces they have, we will be economising on our expenses. With or without them, whatever be the case, we will proceed directly to Agra and see that the Governor, Quli Khan, opens the gates of the city. When this is done – by threat, or by greasing his palm – we will enter the city with all our troops. We will proclaim you Emperor. You will have an excellent opportunity to ingratiate yourself with your mother and relatives in the palace. On his return, the Emperor will find an accomplished fact. It would then be easy to bring him round to the idea of stepping down from the throne. Diplomacy demands that you accept whatever conditions he is pleased to lay down.'

'What will happen if he refuses to climb down?' asked Salim anxiously.

'We have to move with caution. Remember, this is a showdown, not a fight. Our thirty thousand, well-equipped troops, are sufficient to inspire awe. Some of the courtiers and the nobility might like to worship the rising sun, forsaking the Emperor's – the setting sun,' the Khwaja replied.

Khwaja Jahan was aware of Salim's ambition of becoming Emperor through some short cut. The scheme therefore, did not seem to be entirely new. The confiscation of Shahbaz Khan's huge wealth by Prince Salim may have germinated the idea in the Khwaja's intriguing brain. The fact that a large part of the imperial forces were busy in the Deccan and in Bengal, may have been responsible for an early ripening of the idea of revolt.

II

Muhammad Sharif was waiting in the antechamber when Khwaja Jahan left. Prince Salim called him in. He did not tell his old friend what the Khwaja had proposed to him. He thought it necessary to keep Sharif in total darkness. If Sharif stays at Ajmer, he will come to know of the preparations of his (Salim's) revolt, against his own loving father.

Salim said, 'Sharif, my old friend, when you are with me, the good old childhood days flash across my mind – how we read and played together and indulged in boyish pranks.'

Sharif smiled and said, 'I have not come here to be reminded of our childhood days. That golden period of our lives is dead and gone. Why remember it? We live in the present and the present is beset with its own problems. What is important is, how to tide over the crisis caused by your unwillingness to take up arms against Rana Amar Singh. You seem to be frightened of Mewar. You forget that the present Mewar is not the Mewar of the immediate past.'

Salim said, 'We have already discussed the peculiar situation I find myself in. I want you to go to Agra and explain my predicament to my mother. She understands me. This does not mean that my father, the Emperor, does not understand me. He does. When you explain to the Queen, the near impossibility of waging a guerrilla war, in which I am not adept, she will persuade the Emperor, when he returns victorious from the Deccan, to relieve me of this arduous duty, because my heart does not go with it.'

'This is better than acting as the Chief Negotiator between you and Prince Ammu, without the Emperor's authority to validate whatever terms are settled, if they are settled at all,' said Sharif.

'You have been helpful to me many times,' said Salim. 'I am always asking you to do one thing or the other, for me.'

'Last evening, an urgent message came from my mother. She feels I have stayed too long, at Ajmer. She wants me to return to Agra. My packing has been done. My armed escorts are ready. I had come here to take your leave for my departure.'

'The letter from your mother recalling you to Agra and my desire to send you there, are happy coincidences, though their purposes differ,' said Salim cheerfully.

The Prince stood up and so did Sharif. This meant an end to the interview. Salim said, 'I wish you a comfortable journey. God be with you.'

'God be with you,' said Sharif.

III

For several months, Ajmer was buzzing with ceaseless activity. Employment was just for the asking. The manufacturers and their staff were busy night and day, working in three shifts, producing every article of a full-scale war. There were frequent traffic jams in almost every road, street and lane. Ajmer had become a boom town, all of a sudden. It had never been so prosperous before. Money was pouring in daily, out of the coffers of Prince Salim. It was the money that once belonged to Shahbaz Khan Kamboh. It became difficult for most people to exchange gold coins for smaller units of currency. The indigenous bankers were collecting silver and copper coins of various denominations, from nearby towns. The money exchange rate went up, according to the law of demand and supply. Enhanced currency exchange rate meant an enormous amount of profit, within a few months, for the money-changers. Khwaja Jahan was happy; but Prince Salim was happier. It took about four months for the military outfit to be ready. Khwaja Jahan believed in speed and the pace with which things were done, was proof of speed.

At last, the troops were ready and so were Prince Salim and the Khwaja. About sixty ladies of the harem, including Anarkali and Gul Afshan, were to accompany the Prince. They were the means of the Prince's relaxation at each campaign place, after a fatiguing journey. Salim wanted to take more than a hundred women, but the Khwaja dissuaded him from doing so.

The Khwaja remarked, 'There may be trouble on the way. There may be skirmishes with hostile elements. The protection of a hundred women will distract our attention from the forces that may oppose us, on our way to Agra. These women specialise in the tactics of bed and not in the tactics of the battlefield. They cannot fight, except among themselves. They are not trained in weapons of war but in the weapons of blandishments. As a matter of principle, I am against the harem forming a part of a military expedition. It is ridiculous. The pleasure of the flesh has nothing to do with war, where the principle is, do or die. In the harem, on the other hand, the motives are relaxation and sleep.'

The Prince said nothing. The Khwaja was right. But it had become a common practice for the harem to move with the army. The idea behind it did not have sensual significance alone, but also exposure of the women to the realities of danger and death.

The day of the proposed march to the capital had arrived. The way was long – through desert and hills, jungles and fertile land, streams and rivers. The common soldiers were in high spirits because of the prospects of plunder on the way, in case any town or village resisted their passage. There was no danger from dacoits because they wore the uniform of Prince Salim's armed forces.

'Shahzada Salim,' said Khwaja Jahan, 'I have already sent a large, advance party for reconnaissance. It will clear our way and identify safe and convenient encampment places, where plenty of water and fodder are available.'

'Good,' said the Prince. 'Your foresight is admirable.'

'I have had detailed discussions with many chieftains,' the Khwaja added. 'Some of them chose to remain neutral, while a few will join us with their contingents, on our way. All the combined forces will be under a single, high command.'

'Whose?'

'Yours.'

'Very good,' said Prince Salim. 'This is also laudable.'

'Some of the chieftains have also volunteered donations. The money is in the custody of your Treasurer.'

'They are not donations,' said the Prince. 'They are investments which will yield much higher returns than is usual, on account of the risk factor. These so-called donations are speculative investment, a gamble. If I win, they get back not only their principal, but also returns exceeding their principal, by several times. If I lose, they lose all – their investment in terms of money, manpower and equipment.'

'No, Shahzada, this may not be so,' said Khwaja Jahan. 'It is a case of sinking, or swimming together.'

'Well our coffers are full and our troops are ready,' said the Prince. 'Why wait any longer?'

'I am waiting for you to give the marching orders.'

'Let the marching orders be given,' said the Prince. Khwaja Jahan bowed and left the Prince. He wanted to proclaim the Prince's orders for the long march, in correct formation, to Agra.

IV

Prince Salim and his troops halted outside the city walls of Agra. All the gates of the city were shut and guarded. The Prince, dressed like an Emperor, was seated in a regally decorated elephant. Behind him, dressed in the outfit of a general, Khwaja Jahan was seated on a similar elephant. On all sides were well-equipped cavalry. All had arrived at Agra, without any major, untoward incident. None had offered them the least resistance, on the way. Wherever they encamped, crowds of people gathered to watch from a distance.

Half a dozen soldiers, however, had tried to molest some women at a village well and strip them off their silver ornaments, and Khwaja Jahan not only foiled their attempt but also severely admonished them. He distributed a handful of coins to every woman and her family, at the well as compensation, besides tendering an apology on behalf of the erring soldiers.

On hearing the news of the rebel Prince, the citizens of Agra showed no surprise. News of the revolt of the prodigal Prince had reached them much earlier. The people had complete faith in their Governor, Quli Khan, who had already summoned additional troops from neighbouring provinces, to reinforce the defence of the city. Provisions had been stored in the city as well as the fort, in case the Prince decided to besiege the city. The defence was so foolproof that besieging the city would be futile. The river Jamna was accessible both to the Prince and Quli Khan. The besiegers would themselves be besieged, if imperial troops from adjacent provinces were summoned. But Khwaja Jahan thought otherwise.

Business was going on as usual in the city. No production, commercial, or trading establishment was closed. But small groups of people gathered in the streets and discussed among themselves, what would happen next. The Governor's men patrolled the streets, to inspire confidence among the masses.

In the palace, Queen Jodha Bai was filled with a feeling, in which anger and anguish were mixed together – anger at her son's disobedience and anguish at his uncertain fate. The feelings of Princess Maan Bai, Salim's wife, were more or less similar. Khusrau was too young to understand the deeper implications of the revolt. He longed for Raja Maan Singh's return. The other ladies of the palace were also much concerned. Only the pro-Khusrau faction was happy. It felt that the revolt would be crushed and Salim disinherited. This would clear the way for Khusrau's succession. Khwaja Jahan insisted upon Salim launching an attack.

'Not yet,' Salim cautioned. 'Let us try other ways. Contact Quli Khan. Let us talk to him.'

The intrepid and loyal Governor was contacted soon. He appeared before Salim. The Prince still sat on his elephant. He said, 'Quli Khan, you see we have a large army. Open all the city gates to enable our troops to enter the city quickly, from every easily accessible side.'

'Shahzada,' said Quli Khan. 'I am entrusted with the task of looking after the fort and the city, by orders of the Emperor. We have enough men to match yours. Your men are tired, while ours are fresh. Most of your men are raw hands, hastily recruited; ours have seen the rise and fall of fortunes in several bloody battles. You have been given evil advice by your short-sighted counsellors. Return in peace and after disbanding your troops enter the city with all honour and dignity and meet the Queen Mother, the Princess and Prince Khusrau.'

'Nonsense!' exclaimed Khwaja Jahan indignantly. 'We will attack and make mincemeat of you and your troops. You were not talking to the Prince just now but to the new Emperor. Prince Salim is your Emperor now, by virtue of conquest. His word is law and disobedience to him is punishable with death. Save your skin and open the city gates. We do not want unnecessary bloodshed.'

'Khwaja Jahan, I know you well,' replied Quli Khan. 'Your voice is loud, but what you have said, lacks logic. Where is the conquest of which you speak? The mighty Akbar is Emperor still. News of his successes in the Deccan reach us daily. I am his subject and perform my duties in his name and by his orders. Prince Salim is our Prince, the Emperor's eldest son. Wishful thinking cannot make him Emperor. As for avoiding bloodshed, avoid it by retracing your steps from here. We are also equally strong, perhaps stronger. God knows what may happen if there is a fight. The Prince may be killed; you may be killed; I may be killed; the Prince's mother, wife and son, may be killed. Think of this before you take any rash step.'

Prince Salim said, 'Quli Khan, we learn there are over two billion asharfis stored in the vaults of the fort. If you allow us to get hold of this immense wealth, we shall give you fifty million asharfis. This much money will last you for generations. You and your family, along with this huge wealth, are free to leave this country and go and settle in Iran, Afghanistan, Turkey or anywhere. We personally give our word as guarantee for your safe passage, up to the border. Or, you can stay here and serve us and we will reward your loyalty by raising you higher than the office you occupy now.'

'Shahzada,' said Quli Khan firmly. 'The man who can purchase me is yet to be born. My allegiance to the Emperor is wealth in itself. Dismiss this man,' Quli Khan pointed his finger towards Khwaja Jahan. 'He is your bad angel. Your reliance on him spells your ruin. You are the son of the Emperor I serve. I respect you as I respect the Emperor, Queen Jodha Bai, Princess Maan Bai and Prince Khusrau.'

Khwaja Jahan could control himself no longer. He drew out his sword. Quli Khan also unsheathed his. The Prince made a sign to the Khwaja to put his sword back into the scabbard. When the Khwaja did so, Quli Khan also followed his example. The Prince remembered his childhood days in the palace. He was familiar with every nook and corner of the magnificent buildings. Many tender memories were associated with them. He thought of his mother, his wife, his son and the other relatives in the palace. They had rejoiced at his birth. They showered their love and affection on him. They still celebrated his birthdays. He had been breastfed by his mother, the Queen. He had passed the most intimate moments with Princess Maan Bai. He had fondled Khusrau in his arms and played with him. Quli Khan was right. He could be neither bribed nor intimidated. He will give a tough fight. Who knows who may be killed? The Prince lost his nerve. He said, 'Khwaja Jahan, order the troops to cross the river. We will encamp there and discuss the matter tomorrow.'

The Khwaja looked at the Prince with scorn. He saw Salim's courage deserting him. He compared Salim in his mind, to the cat who would like to eat fish, but was averse to wetting her feet.

V

Tents had been pitched expeditiously across the Jamna. The river flowed calmly, unmindful of what had been going on since centuries, in the lives of human beings who had lived and who were still living in the towns and villages, through which it flowed. Khwaja Jahan was in his tent, brooding over the unexpected turn the events had taken, on account of the caprice of the Prince. He was, however, not plunged in total despair. The Prince would call him the next morning and hold discussions with him. Perhaps Prince Salim had an alternative and a more feasible outline of a plan in his mind.

As compared to the tents of the others, Prince Salim's tent was more commodious and stately, carpeted and curtained, well lit and well guarded. Behind his tent was a still more spacious tent, divided into rooms, to accommodate the sixty selected ladies of his moving harem. The Prince felt frustrated. Anarkali consoled him, 'Shahzada, what has been done is done and cannot be undone. Just as every cloud has a silver lining, so out of the present situation, something better will emerge. Let us therefore hope for the best.'

'True,' said Salim. 'I feel a tenseness all over my mind and body. The events have been too much for my nerves. I want to relax. Send me some hakim. He may prescribe something to ease my tension.'

'There is no need to call a hakim. The goblet and the cup are before you.' Anarkali filled a cup and took it to the Prince's lips. 'Drink, Shahzada, and the tension will disappear like a ghost at cockcrow. This is the first time I have heard you asking for a tension-curing hakim. Earlier, you drowned your tension in the winecup and the cosy bosom of a woman. Sometimes you used me, as your tranquilliser.'

After a couple of drinks, Salim felt at ease. He said, 'Anar, what is the name of the lovely, long-legged girl with a ruddy complexion and a happy-go-lucky air about her? The one who set the wine and winecups here?'

Anarkali replied, 'She has been useful to you once. You easily forget names. With so many women in the harem, you are likely to forget both their names and their individuality. Keeping women in the harem is like keeping poultry. You choose the bird you like and a delicious dish is there before you, in the evening.'

'What is her name and what are her antecedents?'

'I do not know all her antecedents. No records of the women's bio-data are kept in the harem. All I know is that she comes from Azerbaijan, near the Turkish border. Her name is Mahnaz which perhaps means the envy of the moon.'

'Would you send her to me?'

'Now?'

'At once.'

'Am I your procuress?'

'No. You are a very, very naughty girl,' Salim said, pulling Anarkali into his lap and caressing her hair and cheeks. 'Now get up and fetch Shahnaz.'

'Not Shahnaz, but Mahnaz,' said Anarkali rising up and smoothing her hair with her hand.

In about fifteen minutes, the *Azerbaijani* girl stood before the Prince. She was under twenty, voluptuous and exuding sensuality from every limb. A faint, but pleasant odour, spread all around her.

'Sit down,' said Salim.

The girl sat down provocatively, deliberately exposing part of her legs above her ankles. The Prince saw her shapely feet and legs. He seemed to scrutinise her as a painter scrutinises his model. He sized up her narrow waist and said, 'Beautiful, indeed.'

'What?' asked Mahnaz. 'I do not understand.'

'Nothing,' said the Prince. 'I was wondering whether you wear undergarments.'

'No.'

'Why?'

'It is too hot in this country. I often perspire.'

'What do you do to look fresh and sweet?'

'I take a bath twice daily – once when I get up in the morning and once before going to bed.'

'Do you bathe alone, or is there someone to help you?'

'I have never taken a bath alone in this country. I prefer running water. I need a helper to massage me and pour bucket after bucket of water over me.'

'Who is your helper?'

'My friend, an Afghan girl from near the Khyber Pass.'

'What is her name?'

'Zaitoon.'

'Zaitoon means olive.'

'She is like a ripe olive – sweet, very sweet.'

'How do you know?'

'We sleep together. Neither she nor I can sleep alone. Togetherness makes us feel secure.'

'You mean one and one make eleven.'

'I lie with her feet close to my face, and she lies with her feet close to my face.'

Salim understood the nuance. He asked, 'Do you love each other passionately?'

'There is no other way. The harem is full of so many women. The eunuchs guard us. No man can enter the harem. We cannot leave the harem except on rare occasions and that too, under heavy vigilance. It is all because of you. Many of us feel like swans in a huge, golden cage. We swans love to fly in the air. We love to float in water. We love to choose our own mate, build our own nest, lay our eggs, hatch them, look after the fledglings and teach them to fly and seek for food on their own.'

'A pair of swans are exceedingly devoted to each other. One cannot live without the other.'

'So are we – Zaitoon and I.'

'You must be.'

'It is hot here. Shall I...?

'No,' said Salim. 'Bring your other swan Zaitoon and lie together here, embracing each other with your wings. I have never seen the amorous behaviour of a pair of swans.'

'As you wish,' Mahnaz said. She bowed and went in to fetch her friend Zaitoon.

VI

Next morning, Prince Salim appeared fresh and cheerful. It seemed that watching the feats of Mahnaz and Zaitoon had stimulated him to deal with both of them alternately, in his own way. Khwaja Jahan sat silent, waiting for the Prince to speak.

'Khwaja, you must have been surprised at the sudden somersault I did yesterday. Frankly speaking, my courage failed me at the crucial moment. I was also nostalgic about the palace, my mother, my wife and my son,' the Prince said.

'I need hardly remind you, Shahzada that war is war. In war, we can neither beg nor give any quarter,' said the Khwaja.

'I was also impressed by the unflinching loyalty of the redoubtable Quli Khan. He refused to be bribed or menaced. But what I regret most is: we could not grab the estimated two billion gold coins reported to be stored in the vaults of the palace.'

'What do you propose to do now?' asked the Khwaja.

'Let us now move to Allahabad. A number of dissidents will welcome us. I want to carve out a sizeable kingdom for myself. Bihar is weak and without adequate defence. It is an easy target for conquest. We shall have to add more, to our thirty thousand armed men. The conquest will furnish us plenty of money. The men will also have ample opportunity to enrich themselves by the spoils of war. The conquest of Bihar will wash out the stigma of timidity, from me.'

'Let us see how you do it,' said Khwaja Jahan indifferently. 'But if all this has to be done, it must be done with the utmost speed before the Emperor and Raja Maan Singh return.'

Salim said, 'I propose we should rest ourselves, our troops, our horses and elephants for about a week before the marching orders for Allahabad are given.'

'Why don't we, when the period of rest is over, attempt to attack Agra again and capture the town and the fort?' Khwaja Jahan suggested.

'This is out of the question, Khwaja,' said Salim. 'A message must have been sent by Quli Khan to my father by now. He will expedite the fall of Asirgarh and return post haste, to Agra. The imperial forces are loyal to him. His army is much superior to ours in training, discipline and experience. Our army is at present a motley crowd of ill-assorted people, mercenaries and dacoits. They need proper training. My father's army is patriotic; ours adventurous. We cannot be successful against the experienced imperial forces. Our safety lies in being as far away from them as we can. For this, Allahabad seems to me the best place.'

'There is a point in what you say. The strategy has to be worked out, but it will delay your Emperorship,' the Khwaja said.

'I would rather rule over a chunk of the Empire as an independent sovereign, than face the might and main of my father.'

'The Emperor, as long as he lives, will never allow an inch of his territory to go to any one. You will either have to meet him on the battlefield, which is beyond your courage and capability, or beg his pardon, like a repentant son,' said Khwaja Jahan.

'I am afraid that in a military confrontation with my father, my two inveterate foes – Raja Maan Singh and Abul Fazl – will see to it that I am killed. I do not want to die in disgrace. I want to live. The world is a lovely place and the loveliest things in this world are wine and more than wine, women. In fact, young and beautiful women are themselves strong and heady wine. Their beauty enters through the eyes, then goes to the heart and from there, it circulates in the blood, to reach the head. The head then sends command to the body to clasp a woman in a tight embrace.'

'You are poetical, Prince. This comes out of your composing Persian verses,' said the Khwaja. 'First, a territory has to be gained. Next, you have to be proclaimed King or Emperor, or whatever be the appellation by which you would like to be addressed. Wine and women come afterwards.'

'Why not simultaneously?'

'Never, Prince, never,' said the Khwaja. 'Without territory, there can be wine and women, but no Kingship or Emperorship. You want to butter your bread on both sides.'

'Well,' said Salim, 'let the debate remain inconclusive. We shall chalk out details of our strategy at Allahabad.'

'As you wish,' said the Khwaja. 'I hope Allahabad proves more fruitful than Ajmer.'

VII

Prince Salim and his troops had settled at Allahabad. The dissenters had accorded the Prince a warm reception. He held a darbar, sat on a throne, with his elite assembled there. Khwaja Jahan was the acting Prime Minister. The Prince said, 'Khwaja Jahan, in your capacity as acting Prime Minister, read out the proclamation.'

The Khwaja stood up, unrolled a scroll and read aloud, 'We, the nobility assembled in this darbar, on our behalf and on behalf of the people, do hereby solemnly affirm that we renounce our allegiance to Emperor Akbar, who has neglected our welfare and the welfare of the people of this part of the country and that we acknowledge with our heart and soul, the Emperor's eldest son, Sultan Muhammad Salim, our rightful King or Sultan who is from now on, an independent sovereign in our hope and belief that the Sultan will establish a truly welfare Sultanate, in which no one shall have occasion to complain. Our illustrious Sultan is renowned for his sense of justice and fair play, and should there be any legitimate grievance to anyone – whether rich or poor – he shall have the inalienable right to ring the bell, installed outside the palace, during daylight hours and demand justice, which Sultan Muhammad is under obligation to administer speedily.'

The courtiers were so pleased at this innovation that they shouted in jubilance, 'Long live Sultan Salim.' When the jubilant voices had calmed down, the Acting Prime Minister said, 'You have acclaimed Sultan Muhammad Salim as your sovereign with unanimous consent. There is more in the proclamation, which I shall read out now. Listen attentively.'

All ears turned to the Khwaja who read out, 'Be it known to all that by virtue of having been acknowledged an independent sovereign by the agreement of all, the Sultan stands legitimately invested with the powers of having gold, silver and copper coins of all current denominations bearing his name, minted; of issuing *farmans* or decrees; of granting titles and jagirs or landed estates; of collecting and disbursing revenues; of sending and receiving ambassadors; of promoting industry, trade and commerce; of patronising the arts and culture of the country under his rule and of performing all functions necessary for an efficient administration, either himself or through his deputies, for the welfare of this distinguished land of the Ganga and the Jamna.'

Khwaja Jahan, having read the proclamation, took his seat. Sultan Salim said, 'Acting Prime Minister, read out the other scroll.'

The Khwaja stood up, opened another scroll. 'It is a *farman* or royal decree,' he said. There was an air of expectancy in the court. The Khwaja read out, amidst pin drop silence, 'By virtue of the authority vested in us as an independent sovereign, we, Sultan Muhammad Salim, are pleased to announce and ratify that:

'One: The post of Prime Minister is assigned to Khwaja Jahan until a suitable incumbent is found;

'Two: Khwaja Jahan is hereby appointed *Sipah Salar* or the Chief Commander of the Sultan's armed forces, the Sultan himself remaining Supreme Commander, with powers to overrule, at his discretion, the orders of the Chief Commander;

'Three: Raja Nirmal Singh is hereby appointed Diwan or Controller of the Mint, Chief Treasurer and Chief Collector of Revenue;

'Four: Raja Anand Khatri is hereby appointed Minister of Industry, Trade, Commerce and Civil Supplies;

'Five: Raja Jai Kishan, Raja Chandra Bhan, Raja Mohan Das, Mirza Aslam Khan, Saiyyid Bashir Ahmad and Turkman Khan, are hereby elevated to the rank of Generals, accountable to the Chief Commander;

'Six: Amin Sarhadi is hereby appointed Mir Bakhshi or In-charge of the Military Establishment, with the rank of Minister;

'Seven: Shaikh Ali Haider is hereby appointed Khan-i-Saamaan or High Steward, with the rank of Minister;

'Eight: Thakur Tomar Singh is hereby appointed Superintendent of the Artillery, with the rank of Minister;

'Nine: Janbaz Khan is hereby appointed Superintendent of Intelligence and Posts, with the rank of Minister;

'Ten: A copy of the list of jagirs, together with maps showing demarcation lines, conferred on the officials in this darbar, will be available in the acting Prime Minister's office. The jagirs have been conferred on the recipients and their heirs in perpetuity and are near their hometowns or villages.'

'Read out the third scroll,' Sultan Salim said.

Khwaja Jahan, who had taken his seat, stood up again and read out, 'Be it known to all that we, Sultan Muhammad Salim, are pleased to announce that the next darbar will be held after twenty days, in which the officials appointed in today's darbar will furnish a brief, progress report of the work assigned to them. It is also hereby ordered that Raja Nirmal Singh, our Diwan, should send an invitation, in polite language, to the famous sanyasi of Allahabad, Bairagi Ram Das, to attend the darbar and enlighten us with his vast spiritual knowledge.'

The Sultan descended from his throne and walked down the carpeted passage between the rows of the seats. The courtiers stood up and bowed. Prince Salim was now an Emperor in miniature.

VIII

The second darbar was more spectacular than the first. The Sultan and the courtiers were dazzling in appearance, dress and jewellery. The newly appointed officials had an air of authority that goes with the attainment of power. Each official had to start from scratch. It would take more time to get things going in a near-smooth manner. However, the major policy decisions had been taken by them on their own and they had come prepared to report on whatever progress they had made.

Sultan Muhammad Salim sat on his throne. Two pretty girls stood on either side of the throne, holding large, fancy fans in their hands. The fans moved so slowly as to be noiseless, not because the Sultan needed circulation of air around him, but because the pretty girls and their fancy fans formed a part of the paraphernalia of the court and added lustre to the great man, who sat on the throne, with several strings of pearls studded in his turban. Salim said, 'Acting Prime Minister, let the proceedings begin.'

Khwaja Jahan stood up, bowed, and said, 'Your Majesty, as Sipah Salar, I have undertaken the exercise of establishing some training centres for Your Majesty's fighting forces, to make them equal to, if not better than, the Emperor's. Further, in apprehension of a face-to-face confrontation between the imperial army and Your Majesty's, I have taken some measures to consolidate our armed strength both from the offensive and the defensive tactical standpoints.'

When the Khwaja had taken his seat, Raja Nirmal Singh stood up and said, 'Your Majesty, as the Diwan of this God-gifted Kingdom, I have yet to set up a mint, with the capacity of large-scale production, to meet the needs of the people. I have so far summoned most of the smiths of Allahabad and nearby towns. I had designs of the various coins prepared. The designs which met Your Majesty's approval were retained, while the others were rejected and the artists were paid their remuneration. A fairly good proportion of the coins have been minted. I have the honour and the privilege of presenting Your Majesty a dozen sets of the new coins. I seek your permission to send two sets of these coins to Agra – one set for Her Exalted Majesty the Queen, your mother, and the other, to the honourable Raja Todar Mal, as a proof of Your Majesty's independence and sovereignty.

'Meanwhile, I have issued orders that both the currencies – Your Majesty's and the Emperor's – will continue to remain valid, until further orders. I have in mind the gradual withdrawal of the old currency and its replacement by the new.'

Raja Nirmal Singh walked to the Sultan's throne and placed into his hands four sets of gold, silver and copper coins. Each set was packed in an attractive velvet-lined case. The Sultan opened one of the cases and cast an appreciative look at the lustrous coins. Reading his names on the currency, fresh from the mint, strengthened his belief of really being a ruling sovereign. He said, 'The Diwan has my permission to send two sets of coins to Agra. Let an attendant show the Diwan's achievement to each nobleman present here.' A set of new coins was shown to each dignitary, who marvelled at the glitter and purity of metal.

It was now the turn of Raja Anand Khatri to rise. Curtsying before the Sultan, he said, 'Your Majesty, as your Minister of Production and Supplies, I have provided certain incentives to the producers and workers. I have granted them, a one-year tax holiday, subject to a certain quantum of mandatory production in each unit. If production in the unit falls below the specified level, or is inferior in quality, the tax holiday stands cancelled. If production achieves or exceeds the target, the tax concession is renewable for another year. The agreement with the producers contains a clause that, in addition to their normal wages, the workers will be disbursed one per cent of the profits of the unit, at the end of the production year.'

Sultan Muhammad Salim nodded approval. Among the six Generals, the senior most among them in age, Raja Jai Kishan, stood up, made his obeisance to the Sultan and said, 'Your Majesty, my colleagues – the valiant Generals sitting here – and I, have despatched scouting missions to Bihar to identify areas where defence is the weakest. On receipt of their reports, I shall discuss with the Sipah Salar the action to be taken, to extend our territories and increase our revenues.'

Amin Sarhadi now rose to speak. Bowing before the Sultan, he said, 'Your Majesty, as Mir Bakhshi, my department is working in co-ordination with the Chief Commander and the Generals. They have sent me a preliminary requisition list and I am making efforts to see that they get their initial, military supplies as early as possible.'

Shaikh Ali Haider stood up, bowed and said, 'Your Majesty, in my capacity as Khan-i-Saamaan, I have drawn an inventory of what the palace needs, together with the estimated cost of each item. Some of the articles are locally available. For some, orders can be placed with the manufacturers of this God-gifted Kingdom, while some others have to be imported from the provinces, under the Emperor's control. To make the palace and the court as resplendent as befits Your Majesty's exalted status, I have been in touch with the Diwan, for allocation of funds.'

Thakur Tomar Singh, rising and bowing to the Sultan, said, 'Your Majesty, as Superintendent of the Artillery, I need huge funds, which may be borrowed from professional moneylenders and indigenous bankers, at a negotiable rate of interest. In view of the possibility of the Bihar invasion I believe in light weapons, including cannons, so that they can be moved with greater rapidity.'

Janbaz Khan rose from his seat, curtsied to the Sultan and said,

'The Emperor's relay posts are superbly conceived and planned. The convention of each mail-carrying rider, covering a distance of fifteen miles by day and ten miles by night, has been retained. I have ordered a survey all over this God-gifted kingdom, to explore measures to reduce the distance between one relay post and another. As and when we enter Bihar, similar short-route posts will have to be established.

'As for intelligence collection, I need adequate and undisclosed funds for which I am holding discussions with the Diwan.'

Sultan Muhammad Salim said, 'We are delighted at the originality of conception and the ingenuity of your planning, in such a short time. All your proposals are acceptable to us. There is, indeed, a crunch of resources in this infant kingdom. Infancy, as we all know, has its teething troubles. We are proud to have such a scintillating galaxy of loyal, diligent and innovative officials as are present in this distinguished gathering. We hope that with your combined efforts the teething problem will soon be over. Now let the court listen to what the venerable Bairagi Ram Das has to teach all of us.'

The saffron clad ascetic stood up and said, 'Pardon me, Your Majesty. I am not in touch with the world. I have nothing common with this august court. I find myself a misfit. I have listened patiently to what each of your ministers has said. My heart does not go with it. I have meditated, among other things, over good and evil, virtue and sin. I can tell you only what comes straight from my heart. I do not know what politics and diplomacy are. If what I say may incur your displeasure, let me remain tongue-tied and be allowed to go in peace.'

The Sultan was stunned. He had never expected this. He had forgotten that sanyasis and saints are not sycophants. He said, 'Venerable sanyasi, we have cordially invited you to our court. How can we allow you to leave, without giving you an opportunity to speak out your mind freely and fearlessly?'

The Bairagi said, 'Your Majesty, it is a sin for a son to make an enemy of his father.'

The Sultan, grasping the insinuation, said curtly, 'Tell God that it is a greater sin for a father-king to live so long, as to make his son despair of wearing the crown.'

The Bairagi said, 'Your Majesty, you have commanded me, in the presence of everybody here, to speak out my mind freely and fearlessly. I say, man should not arrogate to himself the repulsive role of a carping critic, in relation to his Creator. In this context, allow me to recite an old Hindi hymn:

> Man is higher than all living creatures,
> But the highest is He who created them.
> To blame the Lord
> Is to blame our own selves.
> To cast aspersions on Him
> Is to smear ourselves with dirt.
> God is to mankind
> What a father is to his sons.
> Both God and father
> Are to be held in the highest esteem.
> Do not violate this rule,
> Else the sun and the moon and the stars
> Will fall down,
> And the cosmos will turn into chaos again.

The Sultan felt outraged. The courtiers anticipated that the Sultan, fickle and temperamental as he was, may order some stringent punishment for the innocent sanyasi. But the Sultan did not do so. To everybody's surprise, he invited the holy hermit to sit on his right hand side.

'Revered Bairagi,' he said, 'I implore you to visit me everyday, for an hour and explain to me the full significance and import of your hymn.'

The Bairagi called on the Sultan for eleven days. He explained in detail the implications of the father-son relationship, on the spiritual as well as the temporal plane. He succeeded, to some extent, in mitigating the Sultan's hostile feelings against the Emperor.

IX

A few days later, Salim and Muhammad Sharif sat together in the garden of the Allahabad palace. Sharif said jocularly, 'Should I address you as Your Majesty?'

Salim laughed and said, 'We do not have to observe ceremonies in private.'

'Well, Shahzada, you must have guessed by now that I have not come on my own. I have been sent by the Emperor himself. You must have received my letter. I will remind you of its contents, in case you have forgotten them. I had a heart-to-heart talk with the Queen, your mother. She is not ready to subscribe to the idea of your revolting against your father. I also had a heart-to-heart talk with the Princess, your wife. She is furious at your openly flouting the authority of your father. I had a fatherly talk with your son. He says you do not love him as much as his Uncle Raja Maan Singh does. I tried to soften all three of them. They all wish you to keep out of harm's way. The Queen and the Princess prevailed on the Emperor to send me to you believing that, for the sake of the good old days, I might be able to bring you round.'

'I had guessed that,' said Salim. 'My father has sent you to persuade me to crush my ambition; to demobilise my army; to beg his forgiveness and promise to remain his dutiful son. Bairagi Ram Das took about a dozen hours, harping on the same string.'

The Conquest of North Bihar

I

It was past midnight. Emperor Akbar was not in his bed. He was profoundly perturbed. He paced in an adjoining chamber, engrossed in deep thought. He was restless as a fish out of water. He taxed his brain, but in vain. There seemed to be no solution in sight, to the problems created by his Heir Apparent – problems for the Empire and problems for the preservation of Babar's dynasty. Had there been any rebel other than his own son, there would have been no emotional element and no lacerated heart. Akbar had humbled many proud and firmly established principalities and, compared to them, Salim's rebellion was nothing.

Queen Jodha Bai, not finding the Emperor in bed, entered his chamber. She was no less disturbed, but she maintained her equanimity. The Emperor and the first lady of Hindustan, were co-sharers of joys and sorrows. She laid her hand gently on her husband's shoulder, saying, 'Try to sleep, my lord. Do not strain your mind further. What you need is rest, complete rest. I shall sit by you and soothe you, to sleep.'

'Jodha, Shaikhoo has snatched away sleep from my eyes. His treachery has wounded me here,' Akbar said, placing his hand over his breast. 'Treachery from others is understandable and appropriate punishment can be meted out. But treachery from our own son, flesh of our flesh and bone of our bone, hurts like an arrow, piercing the heart.'

'Relax, my lord, relax,' said the Queen in a comforting voice.

'Jodha, Shaikhoo is foiling all my plans. I had to conclude the siege of Asirgarh to be here. I could have gone straight to Allahabad and, with my troops flushed with the recent victory, humbled into dust Shaikhoo, his misguided followers and his hotchpotch of an army. I could have exterminated him from the face of the earth forever. He would have been rotting in his grave by now. But this heart, Jodha, this heart was not willing to do so.'

'It is good you did not go to Allahabad', said the Queen. 'Putting Shaikhoo to death, in a moment of wrath, would have been easy, but the qualms of conscience, the sense of guilt, the feeling of having slain your own son, would have tormented you for the rest of your life.'

'At your and our daughter-in-law Maan Bai's instance, I sent Shaikhoo's old playmate, Muhammad Sharif, on a goodwill mission. Instead of listening to reason, the errant Shaikhoo tried to win him over with the bait of the dubious post of Prime Minister, in his nebulous kingdom. Sharif had to return with his head down. Shaikhoo is tiring my patience. He is incorrigible. He must be taught the lesson of his life. The battlefield is the only remedy. But I know how chicken-hearted he is. He will take to his heels. He lacks the qualities of a leader. I am ashamed to call him my son. He is a disgrace to me, to you, to Khusrau's mother and to the Empire.'

'Use restraint, my lord,' urged the Queen, while trying to calm him down. 'Shaikhoo is a gift of God in answer to uncounted prayers. He may be killed in the battle. I did not give him birth to have him murdered by his own father.'

'I am also as much concerned for his safety as you, Jodha,' said Akbar. 'I do not want our daughter-in-law to be a widow and Khusrau an orphan. Shaikhoo and his so-called army are not in Allahabad. They are camping at Etawah, near Agra. Their purpose is to attack the capital, depose or kill me and usurp the throne.'

'Send Shaikhoo a letter,' the Queen suggested. 'Word of mouth may enter by one ear and slip out by the other ear. The written word is repeatedly read, weighed carefully for what it is worth, debated in the mind and is more effective.'

'Well,' said Akbar, heaving a sigh, 'I will also try that. At least the letter will be discussed by his advisors. Somebody may speak the voice of sanity. The letter will be sent tomorrow. A special messenger will take it.'

The Queen led the Emperor to his bedchamber. She wanted to allay the turbulence in his mind and she thought that sleep would be the best remedy.

II

While Akbar was passing an uneasy night at Agra, worried about his son, Salim was relaxing himself at his Etawah camp. Anarkali lay resting her head in his lap while a young girl named Nilofer was serving him wine. She was from Teheran. She was the perfection of Iranian, womanly beauty. Nilofer is the name of a lovely flower and she was as fragrant and welcome to the eye as the flower whose name she bore. Anarkali had made her wear a thin décolleté dress, resembling a nightie – something rare in the harem. Her bare neck was white and long as a swan's and her bare shoulders and arms were indices to what the rest of her body would be. Her bare feet were shapely. One could see her beautiful toes, her smooth heels and the golden chain around each of her ankles. In candlelight, she seemed an exotic creature, more like a fairy, than a pretty young girl. The eyes saw much of her artistically moulded body and what the eyes could not see was supplied by the imagination.

Salim enjoyed the sight of both the pretty girls. He found his sensuality in a dilemma. The choice before him was between the two – Anarkali or Nilofer. It was a difficult choice; like placing two delicious apples before a man and asking him to pick up only one. Salim decided to warm himself up, as well as both the girls. He brought a cup of wine to Anarkali's lips, saying, 'Drink Anar, and soar in the high regions of the moon and the stars.' Anarkali sipped from the cup leisurely. She said, 'I am not in the habit of drinking. I am doing this only for you.'

Salim's eyes were riveted on Nilofer's graceful movements as she filled the cup and presented it to the Prince. As she bent her head and neck to pour wine into the cup, Salim fixed his eyes below Nilofer's neckline. The beauty of her form excited him. Anarkali was quick to perceive that the Prince was fully warmed up. Wanting to delay the inevitable, she said, 'Shahzada, talk to the girl. Niloo must be thinking you are dumb as a bull.'

'How old are you, Niloo?' the Prince asked.

'Past seventeen, going eighteen. About half your age.'

Anarkali said, 'Shahzada, I compared you to a bull. I had a stud bull in mind. Now you seem to be a bull that talks.'

'What is the difference between a dumb bull and a talking bull, Anar?' said Salim in a voice rather hoarse with rising passion.

'A dumb bull is rather tame. A wild bull is beyond control. A bull that bellows wants something. Whom do you want now – Niloo or me?'

'You naughty, naughty girl,' said Salim, patting her cheek. 'Have one more drink. Niloo, give her one.'

Nilofer did so. Anarkali sipped it in her leisurely fashion.

'Niloo,' said Anarkali, 'do you have any conscientious objection to drinking?'

'No,' Nilofer replied.

Salim said, 'If so, have a drink or two yourself. Do not hesitate. Here everyone is free from inhibitions.'

When the Prince insisted, Nilofer also sipped from a cup, which Anarkali had filled for her. Her lips were so tantalising that Salim had difficulty in restraining himself from pulling Nilofer towards him and crushing her dainty mouth with his.

Anarkali said, 'Niloo, do you have any inhibitions?'

'Before others. Not here.'

'Is there any other word for inhibition?' the Prince asked mischievously.

'Decency and decorum. If inhibitions are shed off, social decency and decorum are also off,' Nilofer said.

'What about private decency and decorum, as opposed to public decency and decorum?' Salim asked.

Nilofer said, 'An individual, away from society, can do what he likes. There is no one to call him decent or indecent, decorous or indecorous.'

'Are you in society at present?'

'No, I am not exactly in society. We three are not a society in the sense in which the word is commonly understood. In the common *hamaam* (Turkish bath), all are nude.'

'Are we three in the hamaam?'

'In the figurative, not in the literal, sense,' said Nilofer.

'Well, Anar, what do you say?' said Salim. 'Is Niloo right?'

'All of us are born nude,' Anarkali replied. 'It is others who make us wear clothes.'

'What if no one wears clothes?' Salim asked.

'There would be some disorder at first, then things will settle down. Nudity would be accepted as natural. Animals do not wear clothes.'

'The natural clothes of animals are their hides and skins, their hair and fur,' said Salim.

'The natural clothes of animals do not hide everything.' Anarkali said. 'Man-made clothes do.'

'How do you feel when you are nude – when you take a bath or change your apparel for instance?' Salim asked.

'There is hardly any woman in the whole world who has not, at some period of her life, seen her nude reflection in the mirror from all perceptible angles and not admired her body and fallen in love with herself,' Anarkali said.

'Have you ever done that Niloo?' Salim inquired.

'Almost every day,' said Nilofer. 'What is admirable must be admired. What is loveable must be loved. What harm is there?'

'There is no harm,' said Salim, 'and all inhibitions are out of place where there are wine and women and a handsome man.'

'You are certainly a handsome man, Shahzada,' said Nilofer.

'We are beautiful young women,' Anarkali added.

'Let us have a couple of drinks more,' said Salim, 'all three of us.'

Nilofer intentionally bent low to fill the cups, and Salim had a brief glimpse of a beautiful valley, laden with fragrant flowers and ripe golden fruit.

III

Sultan Muhammad Salim summoned Khwaja Jahan and Raja Nirmal Singh to his Etawah camp, for secret consultations. They sat in the Sultan's closely guarded tent. The Sultan said, 'Prime Minister Khwaja Jahan, a special messenger has delivered in our hands a very important letter from our father. We have gone through it very carefully. Here it is. We want you to read it out to our Diwan, Raja Nirmal Singh, so that you and he may know its contents. The matter is so confidential that it must not leak out to others, otherwise rumour mongers will have a field day.'

The Khwaja took the letter from the Sultan and unrolling it, read it aloud slowly and distinctly, so that each word could be clearly understood:

Our beloved son Shaikhoo Baba,

We are solicitous about your health and welfare.

We have been keeping ourselves posted about you, although a distance of many miles separates us. We feel that a change in the geographical and social environment will do you good. We therefore appoint you Governor of Bengal and Orissa and advise you to assume charge of this high office forthwith. If you cannot wind up your affairs expeditiously, we would ask you to depute a sufficient number of men of proven integrity and tolerant outlook, to take charge of Bengal and Orissa on your behalf, until you reach there.

Reports of your activities are rampant in some of our provinces, including your attempt to obtain military assistance from the Portuguese. It is good that the foreigners rejected your entreaty outright. They know they cannot gain lasting advantage from a Prince whose political position is precarious.

We further advise you, in your own interest, to dismiss your followers and return to Allahabad to settle your affairs there, without delay, before proceeding to your new place of posting.

We finally advise you to learn to obey, so that you may know how to rule. It is not our intention to humiliate you. But we will consider it our finest hour, if we have to take up arms against our beloved son, in defence of values sacrosanct to the house of Babar.

By order and bearing the seal of
Shahinshah Akbar

'Prime Minister Khwaja Jahan,' said the Sultan, 'read the letter again and then pass it on to our Diwan, Raja Nirmal Singh. Let both of you try to read between the lines to detect the meaning not expressed in the letter.'

Khwaja Jahan read the letter again with deep concentration and made some notes. He handed it over to Raja Nirmal Singh, an experienced man in statecraft, who read it twice and jotted down his own comments on a piece of paper. When this was done, Khwaja Jahan said, 'Your Majesty this letter says more than meets the eye. The Emperor knows much more than we suppose. His intelligence service is much superior to ours. The mission to Goa to seek armed assistance may have been leaked out by someone in our delegation, or by the Portuguese themselves.'

Raja Nirmal Singh said, 'Your Majesty, I wish to invite your attention to the expression "your own interest". It suggests that the Emperor supports you and would like to make your succession secure. It also implies a pre-condition – your public image and conduct must conform to the Emperor's entire satisfaction.'

Khwaja Jahan said, 'Your Majesty, your appointment as Governor of Bengal and Orissa is aimed at keeping you away from Allahabad and Agra. This amounts to the demolition of your God-gifted kingdom, which is your stronghold.'

Raja Nirmal Singh said, 'Your Majesty, I wish to draw your attention to the expression "dismiss your followers". This means the disbanding of our armed forces and the dismissal of the Ministers and the other State functionaries appointed by you.'

Khwaja Jahan added, 'There is also an unambiguous threat, that if his orders are not obeyed in letter and spirit, the Emperor is prepared to settle with you in the arena of war.'

'The letter and its import are ominous,' said the Sultan. 'What is your advice?'

Khwaja Jahan said, 'Your Majesty, let us improve our intelligence services, so that in the final war against the Emperor, we know the number of men comprising his divisions, including the number of artillery, as well as the movements of his troops.'

Raja Nirmal Singh added, 'Your Majesty, we have gone so far as to reach a point of no return. The demobilisation of the army and the dismissal of the Ministers will spread dissatisfaction, leading to the destruction of our public image. Some of the chieftains and the officials may cross over to the Emperor.'

The Khwaja added, 'Your Majesty, let a letter be drafted and despatched to the effect, that you accept all the Emperor's terms and conditions, both expressed and implied. Let us withdraw to Allahabad, where we are stronger. This will postpone the present crisis.'

The Sultan said, 'The special messenger of my father is

enjoying our hospitality. We will send our reply as soon as both of you, in consultation with each other, draft it and get it approved by us. It is true we have advanced as far as Etawah but, as Khwaja Jahan says, our supply lines are not as safe and uninterrupted as they should be. If the Emperor cuts off our supply lines, an attack on Agra would be no more than an exercise in futility. Yet we have to undertake an assault on Agra, one day or the other. How and when can we do that?'

Raja Nirmal Singh said, 'Your Majesty, do not go to Bengal and Orissa, nor send your men there. Prepare an all-out attack on Bihar and show the Emperor proof of your strength. With additional money and manpower, plus the tactical experience gained in Bihar, let there be an ultimate trial of strength on the battlefield, between Your Majesty and the Emperor.'

Sultan Muhammad Salim was not fully convinced; but he had no other option. The reality was harsh. He could not face it alone. He let his Ministers tackle this difficult problem. After all, their fortunes were intertwined with the fortunes of their Sultan.

IV

Emperor Akbar held a special darbar at the Diwan-i-Khas. The nobility knew that Salim was determined to upset the Emperor's applecart. They also knew that besides the Emperor and his stalwarts, Salim and his sycophants were mere pigmies. They, however, shared the Emperor's concern for his son. They themselves had been present at Salim's birthday celebrations and were recipients of the Emperor's generosity.

The Emperor said, 'We are pleased to announce that Raja Maan Singh had the courage and the single-minded resolution to proceed to Bengal alone. He brought Usman Khan and his rebels to their knees, in less than six months. He has added another feather to his cap. This is no mean achievement. We therefore bestow upon him the rank of the command of seven thousand men.'

The court looked at the Raja with admiration. The Raja stood up and said, 'Your Majesty, your appreciation of my humble services is a reward in itself. Perhaps I do not deserve the high rank you have conferred on me. It is an unprecedented honour, reserved for a few members of the royal family. The only other recipient of this high distinction is my colleague here, Abdur Rahim Khan-i-Khanaan.'

Abdur Rahim stood up and said, 'Raja Maan Singh, what you accomplished in less than six months perhaps, I could not have achieved in a year. Yours was one of the most remarkable displays of military genius. I heartily congratulate you, on your acquitting yourself so creditably.'

The Emperor praised the Khan-i-Khanaan's modesty. But he had to lay bare the anguish of his heart. He said, 'Our woes, however, have not come to an end. You are all aware that our beloved son, Salim, is fomenting trouble after trouble, for us. We sent him a conciliatory letter, but we are not satisfied with his answer. His words do not match his deeds. He promises to do whatever we advised him to do. But we hear he has not done anything so far. He is surrounded by evil companions. He has not gone to Bengal and Orissa. He has not even sent his men there. What is the use of appointing him Governor of these provinces? He seems to be readying himself for a final showdown. We know we can defeat him in battle, but we do not wish to humiliate him publicly.'

The Emperor paused, to see if anyone in the court offered a constructive suggestion. When all sat mute, the Emperor said, 'Abul Fazl is at Burhanpur in the Deccan. We need him at this crucial hour. We propose to send for him immediately. He is an expert in crisis management. Perhaps he can be helpful to us.'

The court knew that Salim was recalcitrant to any move of reconciliation. No amount of goodwill and persuasion could round off his angularities. But no one dared to open his mouth. They knew that, however much the Emperor tried to tame Salim, he was not likely to succeed. They also knew, that there was no love lost between Salim and Abul Fazl.

Raja Todar Mal stood up and said, 'Your Majesty, if you permit me, I will send an immediate message to my colleague Abul Fazl, on your behalf. The way, however, from Burhanpur to Agra is perilous for a person of the stature of Abul Fazl. Some of the Bundelkhand chieftains are notorious for their treachery and bribe taking. With Your Majesty's permission, I would like to caution my colleague Abul Fazl, to make adequate security arrangements for the long journey from Burhanpur to Agra through Bundelkhand territory. I know what is tormenting Your Majesty's mind. The hostility between Your Majesty and Prince Salim is nothing new, in history. It is the hostility between two generations. It is visible when it surfaces up; it is invisible when it is repressed. The sons are apt to feel themselves wiser than their fathers.'

The Emperor did not say anything. He knew that the more a child is pampered, the more headstrong and arrogant he becomes.

V

Sultan Muhamad Salim had convened an in camera meeting with his Sipah Salar, Khwaja Jahan and his Diwan, Raja Nirmal Singh. News had reached Salim that the Emperor was recalling Abul Fazl for consultation on his (Salim's) flagrant violation of the Emperor's authority.

Three people had endeared themselves to the Emperor on account of their honesty, intelligence, loyalty, learning and scholarship. They were Shaikh Mubarak and his two sons, Abul Faiz and Abul Fazl. Shaikh Mubarak traced his descent from a darwesh of Yemen. He was born at Nagor, a small town north-west of Ajmer. Akbar chose him to explain Din-i-Ilahi (the religion of God), to the people. Din-i-Ilahi was a synthesis of the best points of all religions, but the people's response to it was cold. The Shaikh lived up to a ripe old age, of over one hundred years.

Abul Faiz was older than Abul Fazl by two years. He assumed the pseudonym 'Faizi' and was the author of a diwan (an anthology of his ghazals), a verse tale, a commentary on the Quran and a translation of a Sanskrit book, entitled *Lilawati.* Abul Fazl was the author of *Akbarnama* (The Book of Akbar), and *Aina-i-Akbari* (The Mirror of Akbar), both written in simple Persian, purified of Arabic words and expressions, besides several other books.

Salim said to Khwaja Jahan and Raja Nirmal Singh, 'Our

intelligence service reports, that Raja Todar Mal has despatched an urgent message on behalf of our father, to Abul Fazl at Burhanpur, to return to Agra. We would like to inform you, if you do not know it already that we hate Abul Fazl as much as he hates us. He disparages us for what he calls, our loose morals and we do not love him because he wants to ensure the succession of our son Khusrau, which will deprive us of our own right. We seek your advice on this sensitive issue.'

Khwaja Jahan said, 'Your Majesty, Abul Fazl is an intellectual giant. His learning is vast and his vision far-reaching. The Emperor has implict trust in him.'

Salim replied, 'We hold Abul Fazl in the highest esteem for his erudition and breadth of vision. But we cannot encourage him to continue being a thorn in our way. If he reaches Agra, he will advise our father to disown and disinherit us and also proclaim us an outlaw.'

Raja Nirmal Singh said, 'Your Majesty, knowing that all attempts to make you give up your inimical attitude towards him have failed, the Emperor is likely to accept such an advice, whatever reluctance he may show initially.'

Khwaja Jahan said, 'Your Majesty, there are ways and means of preventing Abul Fazl from reaching Agra.'

Raja Nirmal Singh said, 'Do you suggest he should be liquidated on the way?'

Khwaja Jahan replied, 'Exactly, but in such a way that no suspicion falls on His Majesty.'

Salim said, 'Yes, I have got it now. Abul Fazl will have to pass through Sironj. Raja Gopal Das is known to me. The whole area, extending over several hundred miles, prospers on plunder. An oral message, together with a sum of money as advance, should be sent to him through a person whom he knows. He will deal with Abul Fazl properly. He will not do it himself. He will devise his own strategy and hire the most capable man, to do the rest.'

Raja Nirmal Singh said, 'Your Majesty, I have such a man in my pay. He is thoroughly reliable. He is Dhoom Bahadur. He and his armed escort party, will leave for Sironj this very day. The treasury has enough funds for this purpose.'

Salim cautioned, 'Remember, this is top secret. If it leaks out, it will have grave repercussions on us all. Abul Fazl has got to be eliminated. We are sure Raja Gopal Das will take care of it.'

VI

The lives of the members of a common soldier's family is miserable after his death. There is little gratuity and less family pension. The family, if it wishes, could either get an eligible son employed in the army, or manage to live on its own. Dallan Rai was an ordinary soldier in Salim's army. After Quli Khan refused to open the city gates, Salim's troops had to cross the Jamna and encamp there. There were about twenty men, besides two oarsmen, in the small boat. The current of the river was strong, in the middle of the river. The overcrowded little boat tilted towards the left side and gradually capsized. Those who could swim, saved themselves. Some were rescued. However, one man was drowned. He was Dallan Rai. He had only one child from his wife, whom he affectionately called Nannoo. He had remarried a woman nearly half his age.

Nannoo was a good-looking young man. He was interested in composing and singing Hindi songs. He had a flair for elementary arithmetic. He was good in addition, subtraction, multiplication and division. He wanted to work as *munim* or accountant, for any businessmen; but he had no experience. His stepmother kept body and soul together by entertaining Salim's soldiers. Most soldiers paid, while a few walked away, twirling the tips of their moustaches, as if their profession had bestowed upon them the right to use helpless, female flesh.

Nannoo was disgusted with such visitors who stepped in and out of his dilapidated house, even at odd hours. His ambition was to seek employment, support his mother, marry the girl he loved and rear a family of his own. It was his misfortune to fall in love with a young girl Bibbo, who sympathised with him, but did not believe in loving him for his own sake. One evening, Nannoo saw her shopping in the main bazar of Allahabad. He knew that his heart-throb was encouraging Sohani, the bachelor son of a grocer, who worked as a helper in his father's shop and had access to his father's cash-box. Nannoo was filled with jealousy. When Bibbo had done her modest shopping he accosted her in the corner of the bazar and said, 'Who gave you the money?'

Bibbo said, 'It is no concern of yours who gave me what. You have nothing to give. You are penniless.'

Nannoo asked, 'Is it Sohani?'

'It is Sohani.' said the girl in a bold voice. 'Why do you not enlist yourself in the Sultan's army? I hear the recruitment drive is going on. You will get preference, because your father died in the Sultan's active service.'

'I do not want to follow my father's profession,' said Nannoo. 'It is like butchering, or being butchered.'

'Now get out of my way,' said Bibbo. 'I want to reach home early.'

'Why did you take Sohani's money?' Nannoo queried again. 'What did you give him in return?'

'Nothing.'

'Nobody gives any girl money for nothing.'

'This is none of your business. I will give what I like to anybody,' said Bibbo, asserting her independence.

'For money?'

'Yes, for money.'

'What about love?' said Nannoo. 'You know I love you from the core of my heart.'

'Love is not everything in the world,' said Bibbo. 'We do not eat love, but bread. We do not drink love, but water. We do not wear love, but clothes. Our feet need shoes, not love. Love does not protect us from the wind and the rain: a house does. It is money and not love that can buy anything available in the bazar.'

'What nonsense you talk!' said Nannoo. 'Love is the be-all and end-all of life. The poets say so.'

'Go to the poets,' said Bibbo. 'Leave me to myself. The correct order of precedence is: money for running the home, love for mutual happiness.'

'So you distribute your favours for money?'

'Love is an abstraction. You are in love with your own idea of love. Had you loved me, you would have sought some employment, or run some business to earn enough to marry me and keep me in comfort. Doing all this for a girl means loving that girl.'

'I want to marry you,' Nannoo pleaded.

'I will not marry a man who is good-for-nothing.'

'Am I a good-for-nothing?'

'You are, until you start earning.'

'Will you wait for me?'

'I will not wait. I will marry the first man who wins my heart and is economically well off.' said Bibbo with determination.

The girl moved on. Nannoo did not stop her. 'I will redouble my efforts to find a job. I will marry no other girl but Bibbo. She is fair and frank. She will lend me immense moral support. Her advice will make me practical,' Nannoo said to himself.

VII

Sultan Salim had convened a meeting of his cabinet in the darbar hall of his Allahabad palace. The members of the cabinet were to apprise him, of the latest developments in his infant kingdom. The Sultan said, 'Begin the proceedings.'

Khwaja Jahan said, 'Your Majesty, in my humble opinion, the time is now ripe for an assault on Bihar. The military training centres have been doing some good work. Our men are now more competent than before. They comprise a stronger and more efficient fighting force. With the conquest of Bihar, we will be in a more advantageous position, to wage war with the Emperor.'

Raja Nirmal Singh said, 'Your Majesty, much of the old currency has been withdrawn from circulation. The old coins have been melted down and their purity tested, to cast new ones. The people are happy at the gloss of the new currency. It is exchanged freely in the provinces, under the suzerainty of the Emperor, on account of its greater percentage of purity. The literates read and bless your name. There is enough in the State Exchequer to fund the Bihar campaign.'

Raja Anand Khatri said, 'Your Majesty, the incentives to producers and workers have shown some results. Production has increased and the workers are happy with the one per cent bonus. Most of the smithies have switched over to war production. The boom in the industries, on account of the gathering shadows of war, has yielded handsome dividends to the producers. The industrial barons say, Sultan Salim is more lucky for them than Emperor Akbar.'

Amin Sarhadi said, 'Your Majesty, we are rushing supplies to the army. Almost all demands have been met with, to their satisfaction.'

Shaikh Ali Haider said, 'Your Majesty must be pleased with the new look of the palace and the court as well as the ampleness of provisions for the royal kitchen. The Diwan was generous enough, in the allocation of funds.'

Thakur Tomar Singh said, 'Your Majesty, the moneylenders and indigenous bankers have responded well to the target we set for our borrowings. Our cannons are light and mounted on wheels, to increase their mobility. Their firing range has also been made longer.'

Janbaz Khan said, 'The intelligence services and relay posts are functioning well. The reduction in the distance of the mail-carrying riders make them and their horses less tired and consequently, more speedy. The collection of intelligence has been made more dependable. We have identified and mapped out the most vulnerable points in Bihar, north of the river Ganga.'

Sultan Salim said, 'We appreciate your capacity to work under pressure. Now fix a date for our march to Bihar. We do not believe in astrologers, though we do not interfere with those who do. The astrologers have also a right to earn their living. The date should be fixed when all is ready. The day we achieve success is by itself, auspicious for us. Similarly, the day we suffer a setback, is by itself inauspicious for us.'

Khwaja Jahan said, 'Shall we set out in a couple of days?'

Raja Nirmal Singh said, 'A fortnight from today.'

Sultan Salim said, 'Then our march begins on the morning, a fortnight from today.'

The cabinet meeting was over.

VIII

It was the penultimate night of Salim's departure for Bihar. He lay on his stomach on the carpet, his head resting on a downy pillow. Anarkali ran a peacock feather gently and slowly from his neck down to his heels, each time in a straight line. Salim turned over and Anarkali repeated the exercise from his cheeks to his neck, then downwards to his breast and abdomen and then over each side of the thigh to his toes. Salim felt hot. Two young women of the harem, scantily clad, were gently moving their fancy fans. They felt a current of excitement all over their bodies and Anarkali could see desire beaming out of their eyes.

Anarkali covered Salim with a golden silk sheet and asked. 'How did you like it?'

'Wonderful,' said Salim. 'Where did you learn this?

'Look, Shahzada,' Anarkali said, pointing to the two girls with fancy fans, with naughtiness in her eyes. 'The peacock feather ran over you, but it seems it tickled Talat and Raeesa simultaneously.'

'Sit down, Talat,' Salim said. 'Sit down Raeesa. Put away your fans and sit down before me. Where do you come from, Talat?'

'I come from Badakhshan, Shahzada,' said Talat, revealing to the Prince as much of her smooth and shapely legs as she thought fit.

'How did you come here?' Salim inquired.

'I have been in your harem since the last three years. I was seventeen then. Now I am twenty. Several weeks after my arrival here, you had sent for me and taught me all sorts of tricks, in your bed. But now you seem to have forgotten me.'

'Did you know any of them before?'

'No. You were my first teacher.'

'And who is your second teacher?'

'Raeesa, here. She taught me a few more.'

'How?'

'By exchanging roles. Sometimes she had to feign she was a man. Sometimes the roles were reversed. I had to pretend I was the man.'

'Did you like this role enacting?'

'There is nothing else to do in the harem, We, Raeesa and I, often pass our nights together in this way.'

'Would you like a real man?'

'I like you. I have never been intimate with any other man. Tonight may perhaps be my second round with you.'

'You are a pretty girl, Talat. You are as pretty as Raeesa.'

'Raeesa's body is more developed than mine.'

'Is it, Raeesa?'

'Explore it,' Raeesa said invitingly.

'Before you ask me, I would like to tell you that I come from Samarqand. I have also been in your harem for the last three years. Talat and I came here together. I had to wait for nearly a year since my arrival, to enjoy the cosiness of your arms. You appeared mightily pleased, but then I felt myself being receded into the background.'

'How did you come here?'

'My family was travelling with a caravan and so was Talat's. Our families had heard of Hindustan and opportunities of high-salaried appointments. Talat's father was a scholar; mine a diplomat. We camped for the night at Herat. The master of the caravan took a bag of asharfis and in exchange, allowed some men on the Afghan-Iran border to raid tents and abduct ten young girls by force. They raised a lot of hue and cry to frighten the inmates, but left the families untouched and did no harm to the whole caravan. The abductors thought we are beautiful. They came to Ajmer and sold us as slave girls to your Harem Keeper, assuring us that our families are safe at the court of Shah Abbas of Iran. But we have no news of them.'

'I will find out about your families. Shah Abbas is known to my father and me and, if you wish, I will arrange to send you to Shah Abbas's court. Reunion with your families will delight both of you.'

'When will you do this?' Talat asked.

'Tomorrow. I am taking only a dozen ladies of the harem with me, to Bihar. This offensive will not last beyond two or three months. I had asked Anar to select twelve girls. It seems she wanted to include both of you. But you are such pretty girls and your story is so convincing, that I shall not ask you to be in my harem in the Bihar campaign. I will ask the Prime Minister to arrange for a well-armed contingent to conduct you to the Shah's court. The leader of the contingent will also carry a letter from me, to Shah Abbas. If your families are prepared to accept you, well and good; if not, you are free to return to me with the contingent that will escort you there.'

'Shahzada,' Anarkali queried, 'Why are you reducing the strength of the harem?'

'I want to create an impression on my father, the Emperor that I am more interested in battle tactics, than in bedroom frolics.'

'I see,' said Anarkali.

Salim said. 'These pretty young things from Badakhshan and Samarqand have had a taste of the manhood of Hindustan. Let them rejoin their families and their parents will perhaps find handsome grooms for their pretty daughters.'

'Should Talat and Raeesa be allowed to retire to their rooms now?'

'No,' said Salim. 'I want them to re-enact the roles before you and me that Talat was talking about.'

'As a gesture of acknowledgement to your generosity in sending us back to our families, we will gladly do so, Shahzada,' said Talat. 'Later, if you like, you can play the role of the man, you really are and we will play the role of women, we actually are.'

'Agreed,' said Salim.

IX

Sultan Salim returned in triumph from Bihar to Allahabad. He was a happy man. He felt he would be the happiest if somehow, the Emperor could be persuaded, by means fair or foul, to step down from the throne. He was even willing to use force, if necessary, for the throne. He called a meeting of his cabinet to take stock of the achievements in Bihar and to discuss the future course of action. The Sultan said, 'It gives us great pleasure to announce before this distinguished assemblage, how proud we are of all of you, who have co-operated with us, in the conquest of Bihar. All of you deserve rich rewards. But greater rewards await you, when you get us seated on the throne, as Emperor of

Hindustan.'

Khwaja Jahan said, 'Your Majesty, this will take some time. For the present I, on behalf of all present here and on my own behalf, consider it a special privilege to offer our heartiest felicitations to Your Majesty, on your brilliant victory.'

Raja Nirmal Singh said, 'Your Majesty, the Emperor's forces in Bengal and Orissa, did not stand in our way. Perhaps they were under the Emperor's orders to distance themselves from us. Had they intercepted us, our advance to Bihar would have slowed down, if not totally halted. I believe the Emperor does not want to imperil your precious life.'

Raja Anand Khatri said, 'Your Majesty, we are in possession of three million rupees, which we found in the Bihar treasury. This sum is now in Your Majesty's coffers. It will help in repaying a very large part of the money, which we had borrowed from moneylenders and bankers. Thus, the burden of our debt will be considerably lightened.'

Amin Sarhadi said, 'Your Majesty, we have about sixty distinguished prisoners of war. They are petty chieftains, rich landlords and wealthy moneylenders. They are to be released, if their ransom is paid to us. Assuming that each of these prisoners fetches us an average of one thousand asharfis, we will have more than sixty thousand asharfis – an asset, if we have the conquest of South Bihar, or a confrontation with the Emperor, in mind.'

The Sultan said, 'As you all know, we have appointed Najeeb Khan, the veteran of Afghan wars, our Governor of Bihar. He has served in Bihar before. He has a large jagir there. He knows the place and the people and is an able administrator. He will negotiate the settlement of the ransom of our war prisoners, with their relatives and friends. Orders to this effect will be despatched as soon as you have fixed the ransom amount of each prisoner.'

Shaikh Ali Haider said, 'Your Majesty, we have allowed every soldier to take home whatever booty he could lay his hands on, in Bihar. It is their customary right.'

Thakur Tomar Singh said, 'Your Majesty, according to our strict instructions, no soldier has touched any place of religious worship. Many people – men, women, and children – had taken refuge there. We did not enter any of these places. On the contrary, we arranged for free supply of provisions to those who were in want. We assured them, that they could return to their homes when the fighting was over.'

Janbaz said, 'Your Majesty, we fought the combatants and those who resisted us. The civilian population was left unharmed and for that, we earned immense goodwill.'

Khwaja Jahan said, 'Your Majesty, the number of casualties on both sides have been much less than anticipated. Our estimate is about two hundred deaths and eight hundred injuries on our side, and between four to five hundred deaths and over one thousand injuries, on the other side. We have given a decent burial and cremation to all our friends and foes.'

'Good,' said the Sultan. 'It was proper and necessary.'

Khwaja Jahan added, 'Your Majesty, I propose that according to tradition, an eligible son from the family of each deceased be taken into army employment. I also propose something that will sound new to everybody's ears. It does not conform to tradition but will bring us, not only a good name, but also the loyalty of the people.'

'What is it?' Sultan Salim queried.

Khwaja Jahan said, 'I propose that a sum of one thousand rupees be paid to the next of kin of those who are killed and a sum of five hundred rupees, to the injured.'

Sultan Salim said, 'It is a good proposal. We hope all will agree to this.'

The Ministers nodded in assent.

Khwaja Jahan said, 'Our next target is Agra. Let our men and horses rest. Let our training centres offer refresher courses for the veterans, besides providing intensive training to fresh recruits, as well as to those whose performance was below the mark. The Generals will ask their next in command to prepare such a list – a list of those whose performance, according to their observation and experience – needs further improvement. We have to meet the Emperor's much more superior army.'

'What the Prime Minister has suggested is decreed,' said the Sultan. 'Any further suggestion?'

None spoke. This meant that the meeting had come to an end.

X

An attractive looking man, in Kashmiri dress, over which he wore a loose embroidered cloak, was admitted into the premises of Sultan Salim's palace. He had an appointment with the Darogha-i-Harem or Superintendent of the Seraglio and was escorted into his office. The Superintendent was a middle-aged eunuch, who shaved his face clean each morning, wore women's clothes and jewellery and spoke like a woman, though his voice was distinctly masculine. Eunuchs, being impotent, were usually employed in the women's quarters of the palace, because of their virile constitution. The Kashmiri caller seemed to be in his early twenties. He was accompanied by a servant younger than him and his face somewhat resembled that of Anarkali. The youngster bore something in a round tray, covered with embroidered green velvet.

'Are you Meer Muhammad Theelu?' asked the Harem Officer.

'Yes, Your Honour.' said Meer Muhammad Theelu respectfully, 'and this is my servant Meer Ahmad.'

'What is in this?' the eunuch inquired, pointing to the tray.

'A little gift from my homeland Chahalgam, Your Honour,' said Meer Theelu. 'Ahmad, place the tray at His Honour's feet.'

The eunuch lifted the green velvet cover, picked up a thin pashmina shawl and seemed to admire its floral embroidery. He felt the texture with his two fingers and said, 'Very light in weight and exquisitely designed.' He unfolded the second shawl and looking at it appreciatively, said, 'I like the colour and pattern of both. Are they warm?'

'Very warm in winter, Your Honour,' said the Kashmiri visitor.

'How much does each one cost?' the Darogha inquired.

'Your Honour's appreciation is enough for me,' Meer Theelu said humbly.

'What is your business with me?' the eunuch queried.

'Your Honour,' said the visitor, 'I have two teenage Kashmiri girls to show you. They are fit for an Emperor. They are the masterpieces of God's creation.'

'We have not purchased any girl since the last six months or so,' said the eunuch. 'You will have to show them to the Chief Lady of the Harem. If she approves, she will negotiate the price. Where are the girls?'

'They are awaiting Your Honour's pleasure outside the palace gate.'

'You stay here. I will fetch the Chief Lady.'

The big and burly eunuch went inside, and soon Anarkali entered the eunuch's office. She stared at the visitor and his boyish-looking servant in wonder, mixed with delight. The Kashmiri visitor put his fingers to his lips as a signal to Anarkali, that she should remain silent. He quickly passed a piece of paper into her hands, which she immediately hid in her bosom. The hefty eunuch re-entered, with an air of authority.

Anarkali said drily, 'Darogha-i-Harem, the Sultan wants no more girls. He is reducing the size of the harem. He will be busy in affairs of the State for several months. Ask this man to call again, before six months are over.'

Anarkali walked away. The big-boned eunuch said, 'I am sorry. You may go. If you like, take back the shawls with you.'

'No, Your Honour. They are a humble gift for you,' said the visitor. 'If I could not make any deals, it is because of my bad luck. I paid quite a fabulous sum for the Kashmiri beauties. I thought they would adorn the harem, please the Sultan and exalt Your Honour, in the Sultan's esteem. I shall try my luck elsewhere. As the Chief Lady ordered, I shall call again in about six months.'

Saying this, the visitor and his servant bowed to the Darogha and departed, saying, 'God be with you, Your Honour.'

XI

Back in her room, Anarkali took out the bit of paper, looked about her to see if anyone was near and finding none, read to herself:

Farhat Afza,

I travelled almost a quarter of the world in search of you. When I learnt that you were at the Sultan's harem, I put on the disguise and devised a stratagem, in the hope of meeting you.

Your family is at Chahalgam, thriving in the shawl and carpet trade. I live with your family and manage the marketing of shawls and carpets to Tibet and China. Your family seems to regard me, as the future son-in-law.

I remember the good old days when we played together in Pasandad. You might perhaps be recollecting, in your vacant hours, the scenic beauty of the Turkish side of the border of Azerbaijan. I am so deeply in love with you, that if you cannot marry me, I will give up the world and live with some darwesh, in Tarbez, as his disciple.

Idrees Pasha

Note: Burn this letter as soon as you have read it.

In the evening, when the candles were lit, the letter turned into ashes. Anarkali said to herself, 'Idrees is as perfect as before. He brought my younger brother Jahan Qadar, who has grown so tall and so handsome. I shall sound the Shahzada on this rather sensitive subject. He has sent Talat and Raeesa back to their families in Iran. Had I not been so close and so useful to him, he would have also allowed me to be reunited with my family, at Chahalgam. Now it may take some months to obtain his consent to my marriage with Idrees. The dashing fellow shows his constancy. He is prepared to marry me, knowing fully well, that I am a virgin no longer.'

The Murder of a Renowned Scholar

I

Allama Abul Fazl was seated in a meeting hall of the Burhanpur mansion, studying some official documents. The title Allama stands for learning and scholarship. An attendant announced, 'Your Highness, an emissary from the Emperor craves admittance.'

Abul Fazl put down the papers and said, 'Usher him in, with honour.'

The messenger entered, bowed before the Allama, saluted him three times and said, 'Your Highness, I have a letter for you.'

'Give it to me,' said the Allama.

'Here it is,' said the emissary.

The messenger handed over to Abul Fazl the Emperor's letter, in a very respectful manner.

'The royal messenger is our honoured guest. Attend to him and his horse.' Turning to the emissary Abul Fazl asked, 'Do you want an answer?'

'Yes, Your Highness,' said the emissary suavely. 'The Emperor would not like me to return empty-handed.'

'All right,' said the Allama. 'I shall study the letter and give you a reply tomorrow morning. You may be tired. Have rest and refresh yourself.'

As soon as the messenger departed, the Allama opened the Emperor's letter and read it:

> *Be it known to our friend and philosopher Abul Fazl that our beloved son Salim, is adamant. All attempts at persuasion have been in vain. He refuses to obey us. His intentions are dangerous to the Empire and to himself. He has proclaimed himself King of the territories around Allahabad. He holds his own court and behaves as an independent sovereign. His hostility towards us increases day*

by day. We cannot brook two governments, running parallel to each other; one headed by the father, the other headed by his break-away son.

We want you to report to us at Agra, without unnecessary delay. We would like you to ensure your safety and be escorted by well-seasoned troops. The treacherous territory of Bundelkhand lies between Burhanpur and Agra.

May God keep you under His protection.

By order and bearing the seal of
Shahinshah Akbar

Abul Fazl deliberated in his mind, again and again, how to extricate the Emperor from this quandary. He knew that Salim, considering his character and conduct, was unfit to succeed to the Mughal throne. Salim's son Khusrau, was by contrast, a fit person to administer the growing Empire. He knew that Salim was dead against him (Abdul Fazl). He knew that the Emperor needed him in his difficult plight, as he valued his advice highly. He made up his mind.

Abul Fazl would advise the Emperor to give up his policy of leniency towards Salim, once and for all. A man like Salim could not be reformed. Engineering trouble for the aging Emperor meant drawing his attention away from the other duties and obligations towards the Empire. The only way to deal with an unmitigated rebel was to defeat him and his army, in open conflict and put him and his abettors to death. Such an advice might be a bitter pill for the Emperor to swallow, but it was, as far as Abul Fazl could envisage, the only way out. With Salim killed in the war or executed for treason, the way for Khusrau would be clear.

The Allama thought that he must hurry to Agra. The Emperor advised him to take a well-equipped contingent for his security, during his perilous journey. He called General Najaf Khan and said, 'I have been ordered by the Emperor to return to Agra without delay. My presence is urgently required there. The way lies through Bundelkhand, whose potentates are notorious for their wiles.'

'True, Your Highness,' said Najaf Khan. 'You can bypass

Bundelkhand, although the bypass will take more time to reach Agra. I would advise you to avoid the Bundelkhand territory.'

'Najaf Khan,' said the Allama, 'the Emperor would be unhappy if we reach late. I would like you to arrange a well-disciplined and armed escort party of seasoned warriors, capable of repulsing any attack. Let me know as early as possible, when you have done so.'

'I will provide you a hundred men, the best in my fighting force,' said Najaf Khan. 'After all, the Emperor's orders have to be obeyed. In your absence, I will look after the affairs of Burhanpur which is the gateway to the Deccan. For this, an order to this effect is necessary. Distances between one part of the Empire and the other are so great, that verifiable news does not reach us on time. We want the genie of Alladin's lamp. He could transport us and our troops on the flying carpet, within minutes. This would give the enemy the surprise of their lives. They would be humbled even before they would have started preparing for war.'

'The genius of Alladin's lamp and flying carpets are figments of imagination', the Allama said. 'Yet, if there were flying carpets to transport our artillery and our cavalry, we could conquer the world. If a flying carpet, laden with heavy boulders, is made to fall on Salim, he would be pulverised beyond recognition. But these are all fables, not the harsh realities of life.'

Najaf Khan saluted the Allama and walked out of the meeting hall of the Burhanpur mansion, to select one hundred trustworthy men, mature in facing sudden dangers. Abul Fazl set about penning a reply to the Emperor's letter which, through the messenger, would reach the Emperor a few days earlier than his own arrival:

Your Majesty,

In prompt compliance with your orders, I shall be leaving Burhanpur for Agra, tomorrow morning. General Najaf Khan will look after the routine affairs of Burhanpur, during my absence. He is providing me an armed escort of one hundred, hand-picked men. I can well visualise Your Majesty's state of mind when confronted by none else but a beloved son. I share your Majesty's anxiety and will endeavour to do my best to put down this unwarranted hostility and needless confrontation, between a loving father and an unfilial son.

Your Majesty, I do not deserve such encomiums, as being regarded as your friend and philosopher. I am content to remain

Your Majesty's
Most humble and most loyal servant,
Abul Fazl
Son of Shaikh Mubarak

II

It was late in the evening, when a hermit called on Abul Fazl. He was a septuagenarian. A halo of innocence surrounded his face. Abul Fazl did not know him. The elderly man had come on his own. He lived in a hut in the Burhanpur forest. Abul Fazl wondered why he had come at such an unusual hour. He told an attendant to send the holy man in.

The hermit entered and stood before the Allama. 'Who are you,' the Allama queried, 'and what is the purpose of your visit?'

The holy man said, 'Do not ask my name. Every name betrays the bearer's religion. People do not know my name. They call me Baba. The word Baba is used to address an elderly person of any religion, in this part of the country. My purpose in coming to you, exclusively concerns you.'

'What reward do you expect?'

'I am a faqir. I neither expect nor take rewards. I happened to hear of your intention of leaving Burhanpur for Agra. I have come, of my own accord, to put you on guard that you should take another, though a longer route, shunning Sironj and Vidisha.'

'Why?'

'Before I became a hermit, I was a worldly-wise young man, in the service of Gopal Das, now Raja of Sironj. He is a crafty man and revels in pillage and plunder. His right-hand man is Bir Singh, younger brother of the infamous marauder, Ram Chand. Both brothers are Bundelas. Bir Singh calls himself the Chief of Orchha. He murders mercilessly, for love of money. He is a rebel.

Akbar and his nine jewels of the court are an anathema to him.'

'I don't understand,' said Abul Fazl. 'Elaborate your point.'

'When enemies join hands against a common enemy, they become friends. Common sense tells me, that Salim is hand in glove with Gopal Das as well as Bir Singh. While Gopal Das does the brain work, Bir Singh and his ruffians wield muscle power. I suspect trick, treachery and cold-blooded murder. Your life is not safe. I respect scholars of all religions. There are plenty of men in the world to translate their muscle power into action, if they have anything to gain. But real scholars like you, are so few in our country, that one can count them on the fingertips. Hindustan would lose a very liberal man if something happens to you.'

'Is it your instinct or intuition?' the Allama queried.

'Instinct is some inner power. You might call it the sixth sense. It forewarns you of danger. When you see a bird picking grain from the ground or perched on the branch of a tree and you advance stealthily to catch it, it flies away. A bird has neither mind nor reason. Its instinct tells it there is danger and it flies away and saves itself.'

'Are you, or am I, a bird?'

'Neither you, nor I, are a bird. There is intuition in human beings, particularly in women. There is also intuition in hermits, who live among wild beasts in the forest.'

'So your intuition tells you I will be killed at Sironj or Vidisha or Orchha? Is intuition always true? Is there no such thing as false intuition? If what you are told, by what you call the sixth sense, does not occur, is it not a false intuition?'

'I never used the word instinct or intuition in your case. I have presented facts based on common sense, which is nothing but, putting two and two together. I am not a scholar like you. Intuition has nothing to do with reason and logic. I have never taken part in hair-splitting discussions. To be forewarned is to be forearmed is an old saying. I wanted to forewarn you. I thought it was my duty to do so. I am your well-wisher, Allama, not your enemy. My duty is done. I must go now.'

'Holy Baba,' said Abul Fazl, 'Pardon me if I inadvertently offended you. It has never been my intention to hurt anybody's feelings. I appreciate the sincerity of the sentiments behind your advice. General Najaf Khan's advice was almost the same. You have first-hand knowledge of Gopal Das and Bir Singh. Your advice rests on solid foundations. I would have gladly acted on your advice, had my summons to Agra not been so urgent. I hope my escort of one hundred men, the best among Najaf's warriors, would be protection enough, against all perfidy.

'Holy Baba, I thank you very much for the pains you have taken in coming on foot, from your sylvan abode, to caution me against possible peril. May God always keep you under His protection.'

'Allama, God helps those who help themselves. Be wary at every step.'

The aged Baba went away, disappointment writ large on his hallowed countenance.

III

Sironj in Central India was a petty principality in the sixteenth century. It was a haven for freebooters and dacoits. Once these men entered Sironj, they were safe. In return, they had to surrender half of the loot. Goverdhan Tabela was the treasurer of Raja Gopal Das. He was a cunning man, on whom the Raja reposed full trust. He did not take the dacoits and thieves at their word. Each day, he had the entire loot brought before him. He weighed cash and jewellery. He rubbed the gold coins and gold ornaments on his black touchstone and assessed them at one-third of the prevailing market price. The largest part of the State revenue was derived from this fifty per cent cut of the assessed value of plunder. No man dared to cheat the Raja and his Treasurer. The punishment for cheating was death.

Raja Gopal Das was a kind of modern don, in his small State. Besides the fifty per cent cut, his State had other sources of revenue. Professional killers were in his pay. The amount payable for murder depended on the paying capacity of the client and the social status of the victim. Goverdhan Tabela was also the head of the intelligence service, the information gatherers being the plunderers, the dacoits and their informers. Each piece of information was paid for, in cash, depending on its immediacy and utility. After all, there is also honour among thieves.

Raja Gopal Das called for Goverdhan Tabela. 'Munimji', he said, 'I gave you two big bags, each containing one thousand asharfis. They were sent to me, by Sultan Salim, as advance payment for severing the head of Abul Fazl. Have you placed them in safe custody?'

'One thousand two hundred and fifty asharfis are in the big iron chest in the vault of your palace, Maharaj,' said Tabela, 'and one thousand two hundred and fifty asharfis are in this bag, as you ordered.'

'Place the bag here and tell me the latest news of Abul Fazl's progress, towards Sironj.'

'Our informers tell us that the Allama is likely to arrive on the third day from today. It is also reported that his escort consists of a hundred chosen veterans, several of whom have scars, as a result of wounds received in war. It will not be easy to overcome them.'

'Leave all this to me. My courtiers and I will be present at the city gate to welcome Abul Fazl. Reserve for him two of the best rooms in our palace. Accommodate his warriors in the best tents outside the palace. Arrange for an uninterrupted supply of water, grain and green fodder, for their horses. Most of the men are Afghans. They are non vegetarians and have their own cooks. Give them ten of the best goats we have in Sironj and whatever else they need. Feed their horses well. Place ten farriers at their service, in case their horses need new shoes. See that they are made comfortable. Spare no expense. Have Abul Fazl's room decorated in the Mughal style. Some of his bodyguards will perhaps be in his room and some in the adjacent room. Extend to, all of them the courtesy to which they are entitled.'

'Maharaj, all this will be done by tomorrow evening.'

'How many young and able-bodied Pathans do we have, in the town?'

'More than six hundred, Maharaj.'

'Choose one hundred and fifty from among them. They should be aged between twenty and twenty-five. Pay them one hundred rupees each and tell them they are in our army. Give them weapons from our armoury. There is no need to train them. One hundred rupees is an enormous sum these days when the pay of a soldier is only a few rupees a month.'

'Maharaj, this will also be done before the Allama arrives.'

'Has Raja Bir Singh Deo come from Orchha?'

'The Raja was not at Orchha. We found him in Vidisha. He is in the palace and his personal servant is helping him in putting on his princely dress.'

'Invite him here, for a tête-à-tête.'

When Goverdhan Tabela was out of the room, Raja Bir Singh Deo walked in. He was about six feet tall, with a broad chest and a vigorous, well-built physical constitution. His moustache and beard were like those of a ferocious dacoit. He wore a four-string pearl necklace round his neck and pearl-studded tops, in both his ears. His turban was after the regal, Rajput fashion. His towering personality exuded masculinity, from every limb of his robust body. He and his men were known for their ruthless muscle flexing.

Raja Gopal Das stood up and advancing towards Raja Bir Singh, embraced the princely visitor. 'Welcome, Maharaja,' said Gopal Das and led his guest to a seat at his right hand. When both were seated, Gopal Das picked up the bag of gold coins and, presenting it to Bir Singh, said, 'Maharaj, this is for you.'

Bir Singh seemed to weigh the bag, placing it in both his hands.

'How many?' he queried.

'One thousand two hundred and fifty.'

'Who is it?'

'Abul Fazl.'

'When is he expected?'

'On the third day from today. Do not touch him here. He is yours, when he crosses our border. My courtiers and I will see him off at the border with full honours.'

'How much when the deed is done?'

'Another one thousand two hundred and fifty.'

'Done,' said Bir Singh. 'Have you made the other arrangements?'

'I have,' said Gopal Das. 'Don't worry.'

'I hate the Emperor. The slaughter of Pathans gives me immense pleasure. Each Pathan killed, is revenge for each martyr of Rajputana.'

'The money is your fee,' said Raja Gopal Das, 'and the pleasure in the massacre is the bonus. The deed should be done in such a way that not an iota of suspicion should fall on me. You know my ostensible loyalty to the Emperor.'

'I know,' said Bir Singh. 'Keep up this show of loyalty. I shall receive much more, if and when, Sultan Salim becomes Emperor. My liking for Salim is a kind of forward trading. Sometimes I feel I am in the wrong. We have to coexist with the Mughals. We can neither defeat nor drive them away.'

'Maharaj,' said Gopal Das, laughing. 'Make hay while the sun shines. The glitter of gold is more dazzling than fighting an unequal war with the imperial forces.'

Raja Bir Singh stood up and, taking the bag of asharfis in his hand, said, 'I must be off now. I have to make arrangements to welcome Abul Fazl. This jewel of Akbar's court will be my most coveted prize.'

IV

Around noon on the third day, Raja Gopal Das and a handful of his courtiers, dressed in their finery, stood outside the gate of Sironj town, waiting for Abul Fazl and his escort party. The road from the city gate to the palace had been swept clean and sprinkled with water. It was a special occasion for the Sironj nobility. A renowned dignitary of the Emperor was coming and they were all curious to have a glimpse of this grandee. They had all lined up behind their Raja, each man bearing a garland in his hand.

A cloud of dust was visible on the dirt road, leading to Sironj. This was an indicator of the speed with which Abul Fazl wanted to be with his Emperor. As the dust cloud drew nearer, Goverdhan Tabela could see the faint outline of a number of horse riders. The men were in a formation of three in each horizontal row. The leader of the escort party, Aslam Beg, was in the middle of the first row. About a dozen rows behind, was Abul Fazl, seated on a white horse, with two stalwarts on either side of him. Towards the rear, were the rest of the men. As they neared the city gate, they slowed down to an easy pace.

Raja Gopal Das saw that fine grains of dust had settled on the riders and their horses and they seemed to be nearing exhaustion. When the city gate was reached, the riders halted and eyed the men standing at the gate, with suspicion. But their rich apparel and a garland in the hands of each person brushed aside their suspicion. They presumed it was a reception party, headed by the Raja of Sironj himself.

Aslam Beg alighted from his horse. He was an Afghan warrior. His face, his headdress and his weapons were awe-inspiring. Shaking off the dust from his clothes and wiping his face with a piece of cloth, he advanced towards the welcome party.

'My name is Aslam Beg,' he said, 'and I am the leader of Allama Abul Fazl's escort.'

'Welcome; heartiest welcome to all of you,' said the Raja. 'I am Gopal Das, the Raja of Sironj. Where is the revered Allama?'

'Wait a moment,' Aslam Beg said. He turned round and walked back, the riders making a passage for him. He returned soon, leading the white horse of the Allama by its bridle. 'Here is the Raja of Sironj, Your Highness,' he said to the Allama. He helped Abul Fazl in getting down from his horse. The Allama extended both his arms to embrace the Raja, who put a garland of flowers round the grandee's neck. 'These are my courtiers,' the Raja said, pointing to his nobles. 'They beg to be allowed to garland Your Highness.'

The Raja's courtiers came forward one by one, bowed before Abul Fazl and garlanded him. The Allama took off each garland, as soon as it was put on and handed it to Aslam Beg.

'Your Highness,' said the Raja, 'as a humble servant of the Emperor, I feel honoured to have you as my guest. My nobles and I, are your faithful servants. They were keen to have a look at one of the brightest jewels of the Emperor's court. Honour me with your company. I shall lead you to your rest rooms.'

The Raja and his noblemen mounted their horses. Aslam Beg and Goverdhan Tabela rode in front, followed by Abul Fazl and the Raja. The escort party was behind the Raja and the Allama. Raja Gopal Das's courtiers comprised the rear.

The party halted at the palace gate. Goverdhan Tabela guided the escorts to their tents. The Raja and Abul Fazl, followed by Aslam Beg and nine others, rode through the palace gate. On reaching the palace, Aslam Beg and the Raja dismounted. Aslam Beg assisted Abul Fazl in alighting from his white horse. The Raja guided the Allama and his ten armed men to two of the most spacious interconnected rooms of his palace, already reserved for the distinguished visitor.

The formalities being over, Gopal Das said, 'Your Highness may refresh yourself. I should now leave you alone. I wish you and your gallant men to rest here, for a couple of days. The pleasure will be entirely mine.'

'We intend to continue our journey tomorrow morning,' said Aslam Beg gravely. 'Thanks for your hospitality.'

'Allow me to present myself again before Your Highness to inquire if all is well with you and your men,' the Raja said to Abul Fazl, folding both his hands.

'See me after my evening prayers,' said Abul Fazl.

'As you wish,' said the Raja humbly. 'May I go now?'

'Yes, you may,' Abul Fazl replied.

The Raja walked towards his chamber, where he found Bir Singh waiting for him.

'All is well so far, Maharaj,' said Gopal Das. 'He leaves tomorrow morning.'

'The other arrangement?' asked Bir Singh.

'I will work it out,' said Gopal Das. 'His men are too tired. This will make it easy. Leave by the back door. Nobody will notice you. My attendant will guide you.'

'I could muster seven hundred and fifty men,' Bir Singh said.

'This is five times more,' Gopal Das said.

Bir Singh stood up to go.

'The back door, Maharaj,' Gopal Das repeated his caution.

'Leave the attendant alone,' said Bir Singh, in a voice of the utmost caution. 'I know my way.'

V

When he felt Abul Fazl's evening prayers must have been over, Gopal Das went to meet him. He met Aslam Beg outside the room. 'I have come to inquire whether you and your men are comfortable,' the Raja said.

'They are quite comfortable,' said Aslam Beg.

'Is the Allama in?'

'He is waiting for you.'

Along with Aslam Beg, Gopal Das stepped in and saw Abul Fazl in the best of spirits.'

'Raja Gopal Das,' the Allama said, 'we are obliged to you. You are a good host.'

'Your Highness,' said Gopal Das with folded hands, 'to have you and your men here is my good fortune. I wish for more such opportunities, so that I could serve the Emperor.'

'I will tell the Emperor that you had placed even barbers and washermen at the service of our men.'

'This is nothing, Your Highness. Your men are weary and tired. They need rest. I have arranged a fresh escort of able-bodied and reliable men. They are all Pathans. They have the same weapons and horses as your men have. They are well-trained and fully experienced. I have lined them all, for your inspection. I have provided my own horse for Your Highness.'

'Aslam Beg knows much more about sentries, guards and commandos than I,' said Abul Fazl.

'Your Highness,' said Aslam Beg, 'we are thankful to the Raja, but we cannot trust his guides and guards because we do not know them.'

Abul Fazl stood up and said, 'Inspect them yourself. Ask them questions if you like. Let us go with Gopal Das. We are all human beings. The blood that runs in the veins of our soldiers is of the same colour as that circulating in the Raja's armed men. The Raja has done so much for us. If you are satisfied, let us send our men back to Burhanpur. The long distance to Agra with our men will fatigue them and their horses further. A change in the escort is not only desirable but also necessary. If tired horses can be changed for fresh horses after having covered a certain distance, why not men?'

The Raja led Abul Fazl and Aslam Beg outside the palace building. They saw a pretty large contingent before them, larger than Abul Fazl's. The men stood in six rows, each row consisting of twenty-five men. Aslam Beg inspected all the rows. He asked one of the young men. 'Who is your leader?'

'None.'

Aslam Beg frowned. He turned to Abul Fazl and said, 'I do not like any of these men. They seem to be herded together, in haste. They do not look like soldiers. They do not have any leader.'

Gopal Das said, 'Your Highness, it is for you to choose from among them the person you like best and appoint him leader.'

Abul Fazl uttered no word, but Aslam Beg said, 'I disagree. Our men will go with us.'

'Aslam Beg,' said Abul Fazl. 'We are in Bundelkhand territory. Raja Gopal Das is also a Bundela. What harm has come to us? Our fears have been baseless. The Raja's men seem to be as good as our men. If we have faith in the Raja, we should have faith in his men.'

'Your Highness, General Najaf Khan would not like this.'

'Leave Najaf Khan to me,' said Abul Fazl. 'Gopal Das will feel hurt, if we turn down his offer.'

Aslam Beg said, 'Your Highness, since you have made up your mind, it is useless to argue any further. Your heart overflows with the milk of human kindness. But never mind. I will lead the Raja's escort. But first I must see my men out of Sironj, on the road to Burhanpur, early in the morning.' Aslam Beg left Abul Fazl and the Raja to talk and went outside the palace to inform his men of the change in the schedule.

VI

Everybody was up early, next morning. Abul Fazl's men trooped out of Sironj town, their safe exit being supervised by Aslam Beg. The troops were unwilling to leave Abul Fazl under an unknown escort. But orders were orders and had to be obeyed.

When Aslam Beg returned, he saw Abul Fazl seated on Gopal

Das's horse. He went round the horse and, scrutinising it keenly, seemed to be satisfied. The Raja and his courtiers, in ceremonial dress, were ready to see off the Allama, at the border of Gopal Das's principality.

Aslam Beg rearranged the formation of the Pathans, three men in each successive row. Abul Fazl asked the Raja to give the order for the onward march. The courtiers rode ahead of the Raja and Abul Fazl, who were in the middle and behind them, was Aslam Beg and the Pathan squads.

It took them an hour or so to reach the frontier. The Raja and his courtiers dismounted. Aslam Beg got down from his horse and stood near Abul Fazl with his hand on the hilt of his sheathed sword. 'Your Highness,' said Gopal Das, 'here is a little present for you, as a token of the remembrance of your visit to Sironj.'

'No presents, Gopal Das,' said Abul Fazl. 'Your hospitality is enough.'

The Raja said, 'The nobles have also brought some souvenirs for Your Highness. Their hearts will break, if their pleasure is denied to them.'

'Their goodwill is enough for me,' said Abul Fazl. 'Skip over the ceremonies and let me hasten to the Emperor.'

Tucking away in their pockets the gifts they had brought at Gopal Das's behest, the courtiers came to Abul Fazl, turn by turn, and wished the Allama a happy journey.

Aslam Beg re-formed the Pathans, placing the Allama in the middle. The formalities cut short at Abul Fazl's order, the Allama bade farewell to the Raja and his courtiers, by waving his hand as a gesture of friendliness. The convoy moved on the dirt road, through a dense jungle.

Fifteen minutes later, Goverdhan Tabela saw Raja Gopal Das riding furiously on his steed and disappearing into the thick forest. Tabela understood that his master had gone to join Bir Singh and warn him to beware of Aslam Beg.

VII

Abul Fazl and the new escort crossed the forest village of Barki Sarai and advanced towards the next village Atari, when there was a movement among the leaves and shrubs. The party found itself surrounded on three sides, by several hundred men.

'They seem to be robbers,' said a Pathan, riding next to Aslam Beg.

'They are not robbers. Their vast numbers show they are an army. They seem to be Rajputs. We will have to give them a tough fight.'

'We have no experience of fighting against an army.'

'We fight only among ourselves,' said the Pathan, 'but we will have to fight for our lives. There is something fishy about all this. Some of our Pathans saw Bir Singh, the marauder, entering and leaving Gopal Das's palace, through the back door.'

'There seems to be a vicious nexus between Gopal Das and Bir Singh. We are betrayed. You have been deliberately chosen as ignoble animals for sacrifice. Well, try to save the Allama and yourselves. How much did they pay to hire you?'

'A hundred rupees each.'

'The life of an able-bodied Pathan is valued at a hundred rupees. This means that the slaughter of one hundred and fifty Pathans at a cost of fifteen thousand rupees, is the price of the Allama's murder.'

'We do not know all this. We were told we were in the Raja's army. We were hired only two or three days earlier. They also gave us the weapons,' said the Pathan. 'Look, Bir Singh is heading towards us.'

Aslam Beg shouted at the top of his voice. 'Fight, Pathans, fight for your lives. You are betrayed by your Raja. Look, the enemy is advancing to attack us.'

The Pathans were highly incensed at their Raja's faithlessness. They had to save the Allama, as well as themselves. Though untrained, they were no cowards. They had Pathan blood in them.

As the freebooters came near, the Pathans rushed forward to meet them. Aslam Beg and three Pathans encircled Abul Fazl, like a wall of steel. Around them, blow after blow was dealt with, on either side, The Pathans soon found that the Rajputs were in armour. This made the task more difficult for the armourless Pathans.

As the fighting intensified, Aslam Beg discovered they were heavily outnumbered. For one Pathan, there were five Rajputs. Aslam Beg tried to lead Abul Fazl out of the scene of action. The Allama saw death staring him in the face, when a Rajput came galloping with a lance, aimed at Abul Fazl and tried to rush past him. The lance pierced the Allama's body and came out from the other side. The Allama fell down and so did his killer. Aslam Beg put his foot on the fallen Rajput's chest, loosened his facial armour and plunged his dagger deep into his face. The Rajput winced in great pain, rolling over the dusty ground.

Four other Raiputs rushed to attack the four men protecting Abul Fazl. The Pathans and Aslam Beg dismounted from their horses. With the speed of lightning, they pushed their horses away and ducked and drove their spears into the sides of the horses of their assailants. The Rajputs dropped down from the bleeding horses. Aslam Beg and the three Pathans pressed the bodies of the fallen assailants with their feet, untied their armour at whatever part of their bodies they could lay their hands on and thrust their daggers there, with all their might. Meanwhile, the three Pathans and Aslam Beg found themselves confronted by several armed Rajputs. The members of the Raja's escort were overwhelmed, by sheer numbers.

Abul Fazl was bleeding profusely. To pull out the lance from his body would have meant more pain, more bleeding and a sooner death. To make matters worse, his horse rolled over him. It was surprising that he did not succumb, under the weight of the animal. Amidst the din and commotion of the combatants, Raja Gopal Das and Raja Bir Singh came galloping towards Abul Fazl. Both the Rajas dismounted and walked briskly towards the dying man of letters. Raja Bhagwan Das took out a piece of cloth from his pocket and wiped off the blood, pouring out of the mortal wound.

Abul Fazl was pale and weak. He mustered whatever strength was left in him and said, 'Gopal Das, this is treachery.' This angered Bir Singh and he flashed out his sword and cut off Abul Fazl's head, from the neck. He said to a Rajput, 'Carry this head and this blood-soaked piece of cloth. They will be sent to Salim.'

With Abul Fazl wiped off from the face of the earth, the

Raiputs scampered away. Aslam Beg came galloping towards the headless body of Abul Fazl. Gopal Das and Bir Singh had departed, leaving behind more than half the Pathans dead and many wounded. The casualties and injuries were few, on the Rajput side. Kites and vultures flew overhead to feast over the corpses, whether of Pathans or Rajputs. But Aslam Beg and a handful of survivors, dug a grave for the Allama, buried him and put a stone to mark the spot. Another mass grave was dug for the slain. Wood was collected from the forest and the handful of Rajputs who had died, were cremated. Meanwhile, some of the Pathans succumbed to their grievous wounds.

It was nearing evening when bullock carts were brought from the village Atari and the wounded, who were still alive were transported there, where the village Vaid, the village Hakim and the village barber-surgeon, assisted by the elderly men and women, tended to the wounds, with herbal pastes and medicines.

VIII

Akbar, with his elite, sat in the audience hall. He said, 'We sent Abul Fazl an urgent message. Almost a fortnight has passed since we received his reply. He has neither come himself, nor has he sent any news. He is not a procrastinating man. He should have been here by now. We are worried over Salim and now there is the additional worry over Abul Fazl's inordinate delay. He shall have to answer when he reaches, for keeping us waiting so long.'

'He will be here soon, Your Majesty,' said Raja Todar Mal. 'Let us be patient. The way is long. He may have fallen ill.'

'If so, he should have sent a message,' said Akbar. 'We would have sent him our own Hakim.'

Presently, Asad Beg, a close associate of Abul Fazl, entered the audience hall. A blue scarf was wrapped round his neck. He bowed in the customary way and stood speechless before the throne. Those who were unfamiliar with this custom would have thought that he was a convict, waiting for the Emperor to pronounce his doom. The fact was that none dared to break the tragic news of Abul Fazl's death to the Emperor, knowing how dear the deceased was to Akbar. The Taimurid tradition was that, when any Prince or a close friend of the reigning Emperor was no more, his death was not announced in plain language. A representative of the departed, presented himself before the throne, with a blue scarf around his neck.

Akbar gazed at Asad Beg for a few moments. It took him some time to comprehend the symbolism of the blue scarf. When he fully understood the full import of Asad Beg's presence with the scarf, big drops of hot tears welled forth from his eyes and flowed down his cheeks. The members of the court began to wail in genuine sorrow.

It was too much for Akbar to bear. The man he expected to be near him had gone afar, never to return, to comfort and console and sustain him. The assassin's lance and Bir Singh's sword had sent the scholar and philosopher much before his time to a region, mysterious and unmapped, where there is eternal one-way traffic. Those who go, are detained there forever.

'Have patience, Your Majesty,' said Raja Man Singh. 'We will always miss Allama Abul Fazl. It is the will of God.'

'The unexpected demise of Allama Abul Fazl has left a vacuum in Your Majesty's court,' said Raja Birbal. 'May God bestow Heaven's choicest blessings on his soul and give his family and friends the patience to bear this heavy burden of grief.'

'The unexpected passing away of Allama Abul Fazl is an irreparable loss to his family, to all of us and to the Mughal Empire,' said Mirza Aziz Kokaltash. 'We pray to the Almighty to rest his soul in peace.'

'The demise of Allama Abul Fazl has come to all of us as a great shock. We will always remember him for his learning and loyalty,' said Abdur Rahim Khan-i-Khanaan. 'We pray that God may assign to him the paradise, where only the blessed go.'

'Your Majesty, a man like Abul Fazl is born in a thousand years. His loss is immeasurable. But we have to submit to the will of God,' said Meer Hamam.

'God recalls early, from this earth, those who are dear to him, Your Majesty,' said Mulla Dopiaza. 'For us, time is the healer.'

Akbar said in a mournful voice, 'If Salim wanted to be Emperor, he should have spared Abul Fazl and killed me.'

IX

Every morning, the majority of people of all communities at Fatehpur-Sikri, gathers below the window of a room in the upper storey of the Emperor's palace, where he appears and shows himself to the public. It is considered an auspicious sign by the public, to have a morning glimpse of the Emperor. For the last three days, they had been going there, crowded below in the open space, but had returned disappointed.

'The Emperor is ill,' said an old man. 'May God restore him to good health.'

'The Shahinshah is out of Agra. He has gone to crush his son Salim's rebellion. The present age is the age of sin and sinners. In the past, the sons obeyed their fathers. Now, they take pride in disobedience.'

'The Emperor is within the palace,' said a third aged man. 'He is tired of showing himself to us. We are too poor to present him any gift except our prayer that he may have a long and prosperous life.'

'The Shahinshah has a heart so big that it contains within itself both the worlds – the lower world where we live and the upper world beyond the sky, where God and His angels have their seats. He is tolerant to all and, as the saying goes, the lion and the goat drink water in peace at the same river bank.' said another superannuated man.

'I have some inside information from the palace sources that Shahinshah Akbar is now a broken-hearted man. The death of Allama Abul Fazl has broken his heart. May God give him enough patience to bear this grief! He will mourn the Allama's death for three days. He has not declared public mourning for three days, because it would have caused losses to wage earners, factory owners and shopkeepers.'

Akbar learnt all the details of Abul Fazl's death from Asad Beg. He appeared at the window on the fourth day. The people were delighted to see him. It was a good omen for them.

That day, the Emperor summoned the Governor of Agra. He said, 'You know, Abul Fazl was brutally slaughtered by mercenaries. It was an act of treachery. We want vengeance. We want you and the contingents of the Mughal army to search every nook and corner of Bundelkhand and capture Bir Singh. Bring him to us alive, so that we can have the satisfaction of cutting off his head with our own sword. In case he dies before being captured, bring his corpse. We will have it filled with straw and have it hung upside down at the main public road, so that kites and vultures may pick out bits of his rotting flesh. Send as many contingents as you like and use every device to track down Bir Singh.'

'This will be done, Your Majesty,' said the Governor. 'Bir Singh is cunning as a fox. He may have gone into hiding somewhere outside Bundelkhand.'

'Arrest Gopal Das and if he does not reveal Bir Singh's whereabouts, torture him, until he does so.'

'I learn, Your Majesty that Bhagwan Das has already absconded.'

'We want no excuses,' said Akbar. 'We want action. Bir Singh must not live to enjoy Salim's favours.'

'The sad and sudden death of Allama Abul Fazl is no doubt a severe blow not only to Your Majesty but also to the Empire,' said the Governor. 'We shall leave no stone unturned to apprehend the assassin.'

'Would you like to know what Abul Fazl did for us and the Empire? Abul Fazl's influence on the present age has been immense. It was he who led us to a true appreciation of our duties. From his very induction into our court, he has guided us in tackling successfully the knotty problem of ruling over a nation of mixed races, castes and creeds. He taught us the policy of tolerance. He taught us that the ruling sovereign is the father of his people. He had a sharp mind, an undimmed vision and a very broad outlook. He saw the past, the present and the future, not as isolated compartments of history, but as an almost endless continuum. This was something bold in conception and it was Abul Fazl alone, who could correct mistakes in its execution.'

'Yes, the Allama was a pillar of strength to Your Majesty's expanding Empire.'

'Faizi is no more. Abul Fazl has passed away. Their father, Shaikh Mubarak, has left for his heavenly abode. We are left solitary and helpless. Who will replace these great men?'

'Your Majesty,' said the Governor, 'the moment produces its own man. If the phoenix dies, its successor is born of the deceased's ashes.'

The Governor departed. His words did not comfort Akbar. The Emperor felt a void in his heart. He wondered if he could, alone and unaided, maintain a united Empire, with the undivided loyalty of the people. It distressed him that his eldest son was bent upon the fragmentation of the Empire, in his own father's lifetime.

Joy and Sorrow

I

Something in Salim seemed to have given him peace. He was no longer worried at present. The days passed in affairs of the State. The evenings were his own. His ministers seemed to be doing well, strengthening his position in his little kingdom. He was free for the rest of the time. The bell that hung at the palace gate for redressal of wrongs had been a publicity stunt. Perhaps no common man was allowed to approach the palace even if he had a grievance, so well protected had Salim remained.

News of the going-on in the Emperor's court reached him regularly. Sometimes he felt he was doing wrong and should have been with his father, his mother, his wife and his son. But at Fatehpur-Sikri he would have to live under vigilant eyes. No exotic beauties would be there at his beck and call, such as Anarkali, Gulshan, Gul Afshan, Talat and Raeesa. There would also be quota restrictions on his drinks. Instead of being surrounded by a bevy of lovely girls, he would find himself besieged by his mother, his stepmother, his grandmother and the other elderly ladies of the Emperor's palace. Instead of uninhibited relations with the young beauties of his own harem, he would have had, only an occasional go with a slave girl or two in a clandestine manner, without the knowledge of his wife. He knew his wife strongly disapproved of the extramarital relations of her husband. He, therefore, preferred to remain at Allahabad.

He lay on his rich Persian carpet, his head resting on a big round pillow. The goblet and the cups were beside him. The wine was called the 'red fairy' and it was imprisoned in the goblet. The 'red fairy' reminded him of the red pomegranate bud which, in turn, evoked the image of Anarkali, who lay on her side, moving her legs up and down. Her shapely feet and toes, and her beautiful bosom, stimulated Salim to sit up and run his finger over them.

'What are you doing, Shahzada?' Anarkali said. 'I get tickled.'

The Shahzada now began to run his finger between each of Anarkali's toes. Having done so with one foot, he repeated the exercise with Anarkali's other foot.

'Your ways are inscrutable, Shahzada,' said Anarkali, getting up. 'Shall I send a girl from the harem to cool your blood if it is too hot? Name any of them.'

'No Anar, I want no other girl,' said the Shahzada. 'I want you. I hardly remember the names of the girls, except a few.'

'Whose names do you remember?'

'Gul Afshan, Mahnaz, Talat and Raeesa.'

'Talat and Raeesa must be with their families. Their escorts have returned. They say the families of the girls were glad to have them back again.'

'Would you also some day ask me to send you back to your family?'

'I will certainly ask you, not some day, but just now. My family is at Chahalgam in Kashmir in the shawl and carpet trade.'

'They say many good things about Kashmir. One of them is: if there is paradise on earth, it is here, it is here, it is here. I love Kashmir. On becoming Emperor, I shall make Kashmir my summer capital.'

'On becoming Emperor, Shahzada,' said Anarkali, 'you will not need me. You withdraw old coins.'

'I cannot say anything at present about what I shall do in future. But you have always been good to me. I shall often remember you. Why do you wish to leave me, Anar?'

'Shahzada, I will be frank with you, as I have always been. Your mother named me Anarkali on account of my exotic beauty. I am a Turk. My real name has been forgotten by everyone in the palace and even by you. My name is Farhat Afza.'

'A very suggestive name,' said Salim. 'It means one who refreshes, and you have refreshed me time and again.'

'Shahzada, Sharif is your old playmate and you have great regard for him. I too have an old playmate and I have as great a regard for him as he has for me. His name is Idrees Pasha. He lives with my family at Chahalgam and helps my father in exporting shawls and carpets with peculiar designs popular in Tibet and China. My parents would be delighted to marry me to him. He has taken a vow that he will remain a celibate if I refuse to marry him.'

'Anar,' said Salim, 'it is your frankness that touches my heart. For me, one girl is as good as another if she is beautiful and young. But you have made for yourself a soft corner in my heart. It is not because of your youth, beauty and responsiveness, but because of your devotion and loyalty. How often you have been serviceable to me, I can hardly recount. If you wish to, go. I will not detain you against your will. After all, you will have to lead your own life some day. You have to look at your own future. Why at some other day? Why not now?'

'Shahzada,' said Anarkali, putting both her arms round his neck, 'you are so good to me. I knew you will say *yes*. You have never said no to me.'

'I could have said *no* to you, Anar, and I can still say so, but then it will be too late. Beauty and youth are like a wave: here they come and there they go. Beauty and youth are like fragrance that does not last forever. Beauty perishes: the rosy cheeks lose their fragrance. The gleam in the eyes fades away and hair turn white. Old age is wrinkled: the skin hangs loose; the gait is unsteady; the voice loses its melody. Youth is a prop to the old, who were once a prop to others. Go, my Anar, go at your leisure. What name did you say was your lover's?'

'Idrees Pasha.'

'Will Idrees Pasha accept you as you are – a girl who has already experienced what Idrees will want you to experience with him?'

'Idrees does not believe in the disease which people call modesty. He knows it can be cured. He knows that a Prince, the future Emperor of Hindustan, has cured me.'

'All right, my Anar,' said Salim. 'Write to your brother to come and take you, any day that suits your convenience.'

'Shahzada,' said Anarkali, rolling him on his back and sitting on him astride, 'you are unique in your generosity. You are a liberator of girls you like most. Is it not a contradiction?'

'It is not contradiction,' said Salim. 'It is reciprocity.'

II

Sultan Salim and his Prime Minister Khwaja Jahan were seated in the Sultan's chamber. Salim said, 'Have the twenty-five thousand asharfis gone down the drain? We have had no news of Abul Fazl. He may be somewhere near Agra, if not at Agra itself, by now?'

'Your Majesty, Gopal Das is our man. The lure of money is his chief weakness. He will do what we asked, to get the other twenty-five thousand gold mohars we have promised him.'

Salim was about to say something, when an attendant entered and announced, 'Your Majesty, Raja Gopal Das of Sironj and Raja Bir Singh are here. They seek an audience.'

Salim and Khwaja Jahan exchanged glances. Salim said, 'Bring them in, with proper courtesy and respect.'

Soon there entered the two Rajas, with an attendant bearing a silver tray covered with velvet. When the Rajas had paid their respects to the Sultan, Gopal Das said, 'Your Majesty, we have brought a present for you.'

The Sultan understood. He said. 'Let us see him.'

Raja Bir Singh made a sign to his attendant to take the round tray near the Sultan and take off the velvet cover. When the attendant had done so, the Sultan had a look at what was in the tray and said, 'It is he. Well done, Gopal Das!'

'Your Majesty, the plan was mine. Its execution was in the hands of my friend Bir Singh Deo, the Raja of Orchha.'

Khwaja Jahan also had a look at Abul Fazl's head and the blood-soaked piece of cloth. He asked, 'Why this bloodstained kerchief?'

'It is the blood of the wounds of the man whose head you find in the tray,' said Bir Singh. 'Would you like to hear the story?'

'We are interested in eating the mango, not in counting the trees,' said the Sultan.

'Your Majesty, the Emperor's army contingents are searching for us everywhere,' said Gopal Das. 'They are after Bir Singh's blood. We have no place to go. If we return to our palaces, we shall either be captured and skinned alive or hounded from pillar to post.'

'You are our honoured guests,' said the Sultan. 'You are safe in our kingdom. You may move here freely until the heat is off.'

'Thanks, Your Majesty,' said Gopal Das. 'It is said that Sultan Salim is the umbrella that protects everyone from the sun and the rain.'

'Raja Bir Singh.' said the Sultan, 'you have done us meritorious service. You will live to enjoy more of our favours.'

The Rajas bowed in gratitude.

'Prime Minister,' said the Sultan, 'pay Raja Gopal Das the balance of twenty-five thousand asharfis. How they distribute it between themselves is their business.'

The two Rajas were happy. They had caught the biggest fish in their net. The Sultan said to an attendant. 'Take the head and the kerchief in a bag and bury them at some obscure spot, outside the city. The Ganga and the Jamna will be polluted if you throw this stuff in either of these sacred rivers.'

The Rajas were surprised to hear the Sultan talk of the holiness of the rivers. The Sultan's remark displayed the extent of his abhorrence for Abul Fazl.

Salim said to another attendant, 'Conduct our guests to our Diwan. Raja Nirmal Singh will make arrangements for their stay. Let their comforts be such, as those they are accustomed to.'

The Rajas were more than satisfied and left the Sultan's chamber with their own attendant as well as those of the Sultan.

'Prime Minister,' said Salim, 'you wanted to say something. Say it.'

'Your Majesty, one thorn in our flesh has been removed. Another remains.'

'Maan Singh?'

'Yes, Maan Singh,' said Khwaja Jahan. 'He cannot be liquidated so easily.'

'We will think of Maan Singh at some other time. At least one man who could poison our father the Emperor's ears against us, has been effaced. He was the most vociferous in espousing Khusrau's cause.'

'Your Majesty, the Emperor is furious. He will not spare you if you happen to go near him now. His wounds are still green. Abul Fazl was very dear to him.'

'Why should we go now?' said Salim. 'We will go when we are

fully ready to meet him in the battlefield. We have deflated the Emperor by taking out the wind that was Abul Fazl. The less the number of our antagonists, the better it is for us.'

'Quite,' said Khwaja Jahan. 'Quite.'

'Tell the Rajas when you happen to meet them that they should ask their brave accomplices to join our army secretly and one by one.'

'Your Majesty, this would be indiscretion at this juncture,' said Khwaja Jahan. 'The news that the Rajas are here will leak out at Sironj and Orchha. Wait till the dust settles down. It will take some time. But we have certainly made the Rajas our staunch allies. They dare not go outside our State. They are wanted men. They will do what we ask them to do. They have no other option.'

'Indeed,' said Salim, standing up, 'they have none. You may go now. This meeting has been most fruitful.'

III

Sohani blatantly refused to be a helper in his father's grocery store. He said to his father, 'I have no heart in this ancestral business. I do not like weighing and giving out short measure. Counting coins and giving out short change to illiterate customers, goes against my grain. I am good at simple arithmetic. I have told you times without number, I want to be a *munim* or accountant. However, I do not want that you should dismiss your munim and take me in his place. First, because our old and faithful munim will lose his job. Secondly, a son working as a munim under his own father does not lead to efficiency, because of the father-and-son relationship. The best you can do for me, is to let our munim give me practical training. Without experience, nobody will give me a job. As an apprentice to our munim, I can say I have some experience.'

'All right,' said Sohani's father. 'Have your own way. Work under munimji from tomorrow. But do not loiter about aimlessly.'

Sohani asked, 'How will you manage without a helper?'

'I will engage Nannoo in your place. He is a poor widow's

son. His ambition is also to be an accountant. He will be more useful to me than you are. He came to me yesterday to buy grocery on credit. I will make him work as long as what his mother owes to me is not cleared off, together with interest. The debt will go on increasing. It will never be paid off, because of the dexterity of our loyal munimji. This is the way I have thought of making Nannoo my bonded servant. When I die and you succeed me, you will have Nannoo's son as your bonded labourer. How will you like that?'

'I do not like the idea of bonded labour,' said Sohani, 'but I will not interfere. Perhaps you are more interested in the mother than in the son.'

'Shut your big mouth,' the elder Sohani said. 'Do not talk nonsense. You have yet to learn the tricks of the trade.'

Sohani left his home and went to roam about on the banks of the river. He liked solitary places. He avoided pilgrims and devotees and bathing ghats. Walking on the bank, he saw two young people bathing in the shallow waters. They were not swimmers and seemed to be afraid of deep water, away from the bank. On approaching nearer, he received the shock of his life. He saw his sweetheart Bibbo and her paramour Nannoo, laughing and throwing water with both hands, on each other. They were thoroughly enjoying themselves. Their clothes and an empty earthen pitcher were lying on the sand.

At first, Sohani thought he should run away with their clothes. His second thought was that he should not do so. Bibbo and Nannoo would not be able to return to their homes. It would be such a shame to go without apparel. His third thought was that the young lovers had previously fixed this sequestered spot as their tryst and that Bibbo had left her home, on the pretext of fetching water from the river.

The sight was nauseating to him. Without disturbing the young lovers, he left them to their flirtatious play and wended his way to the main market, to lie in wait for Bibbo and Nannoo. He thought to himself, 'Strange are the ways of the young girls of today! What sort of a girl is Bibbo? She is after money which I have and Nannoo has not. Everyone knows what Nannoo's mother does. Respectable people avoid him, because of his unabashed mother. It is essential I should speak to Bibbo and give her a piece of my mind. I cannot tolerate this brazen face for long. Yet she is luscious and lovely and I love her.'

Sohani arrived at the main bazar of Allahabad and stood at a turning. He saw a pretty little girl, hardly twelve, selling flower garlands, hung from a stick in her hand. His heart was moved to sympathy to see little children earning their keep. He thought it was the poverty of their parents that deprived children of their childhood.

Soon a soldier of the Sultan's army came and said, 'How much for the whole lot, sweetie?'

'A quarter rupee,' said the little girl.

'I will give you half a rupee. Follow me to my house. It is just round the corner. Nobody is there. My wife has gone for a month to her parents' village, with all my four children. Come every day and I will give you a half-rupee coin each time.'

Sohani overheard what the soldier had said. The little flower girl replied, 'I am not what you think me to be. A quarter-rupee by honest work is better than a half-rupee by dirty work.'

The soldier was impatient. He wanted to grab her by the arm and drag her away when Sohani stepped forward and intervened. 'This is child abuse, sir,' he said. 'You said just now you are a married man with four children and yet you are trying to seduce a minor girl who, in age, is like your own daughter.'

'Mind yourself,' the soldier said harshly. 'Do you know whom you are talking to?'

'I know whom I am talking to,' said Sohani with firmness in his voice. 'You are a common soldier of the Sultan, not the Sultan himself. Sultan Salim does not accost minor girls in the streets and ask them to follow him home for a half-rupee coin.'

'You will regret for talking to me like this,' the soldier said in a threatening tone.

'It is you who will regret your impertinence,' said Sohani. 'Tell me your name and who your commander is. My father supplies grocery to the troops under Raja Jai Kishan, Raja Chandra Bhan, Raja Mohan Das, Mirza Aslam Khan, Saiyyid Bashir Ahmad and Turkman Khan. I will report your misbehaviour with this girl child, to my father, who will take up the matter with the higher-ups.'

The bluff worked. 'Sorry,' said the soldier in a placating tone, 'we soldiers can lay our hands on any girl, minor or major, during the war, in enemy territory, with impunity. In peace times, it is a heinous crime to do so. The top brass inflicts heavy punishment. Let the matter rest here. No harm has actually been done to the girl. Forgive and forget. Here, daughter, take this half-rupee coin. Buy anything you like. I admire your negative attitude to people like me, who make indecent proposals.'

'Keep your half-rupee coin with you,' the flower girl said. 'When your wife returns with your four children, buy sweets with this coin and give it to them.'

Meanwhile, a few passers-by had collected round the flower girl, the soldier and Sohani. Some of them cried, 'Shame: Shame!' to the soldier, who strode away hastily. A few among them bought some of the girl's garlands with small coins. 'Bravo, little girl!' one of them said. Unnoticed, Sohani slipped away to where he had stood, at a corner of the bazar.

Hardly had a few minutes passed when a woman of about forty, in shabby make-up, eyed Sohani standing alone. She strolled leisurely towards him and said with a smile, 'Young man, do you know the difference between old rice and new rice?'

'I am a grocer's son,' Sohani answered. 'The older the rice, the tastier it is. Old rice costs more than new rice.'

'I do not cost more,' the woman said. 'Only one rupee. I should taste better than the new rice. Try me.'

'You have come to the wrong man,' said Sohani. 'I am not interested.'

'You seem to be raw and young. Have you ever been with a woman?'

'No,' said Sohani. 'Never.'

'I have some big ones to show you,' the woman said, pointing to her low neckline. 'They are sweeter than mangoes.'

'I am not interested,' said Sohani emphatically.

'You seem to know nothing, young fellow. How will you manage when you marry?'

'I will manage somehow,' said Sohani.'Go away.'

'Perhaps you do not have a rupee in your pocket,' said the

woman with another smile.

'I have two rupees with me,' said Sohani, 'but as I told you, I am not interested.'

'I will make you interested,' she said. 'Unless you learn, how can you teach? Unless you receive pleasure, how can you please your wife? Come with me. I live in a one-room tenement nearby.'

'Go away,' said Sohani. 'I do not want to lose my morals.'

'What are morals?' the woman said. 'Morals are made and unmade. What is morality in one section of society is immorality in another section of the same society. There is nothing immoral in getting married or in purchasing pleasure while remaining unmarried.'

'You will tell others and blackmail me.'

'I will not tell anyone and I am not a blackmailer. You are a grocer's son. You sell things that satisfy hunger. I sell pleasure that satisfies hunger of a different kind. You seem to be half-inclined. Follow me, before you change your mind. An hour of enjoyment such as you never had before, will make you come to me again and again.'

'It is a sin and I do not like to be a sinner.'

'A sin is when you feel sinful. If you do not feel sinful, there is neither sin nor sinner. Come, be a good fellow.'

The woman walked from the main bazar, turned into a narrow lane, and entered a blind alley. Sohani followed her, half in fear and half in expectation of the promised pleasure. 'This is my first time,' he said to himself. 'Let me see how it turns out.' The woman stood before a dingy room, turned a key into a rusted lock and opened a creaky door. She asked Sohani to step in. 'I will not even ask your name and your address,' she assured him.

Sohani suddenly changed his mind. If what he was about to do was right, then what Bibbo and Nannoo were doing at the river was not wrong. He had come to the main market in the hope that, in an hour or two, he would spot either or both of them. Nannoo was nothing to him, but Bibbo was everything. He would chastise her, because he hoped he would marry her one day.

'Come out,' he said to the woman. 'Here is your rupee. I have seen your house. I will come some other time.'

The woman took the silver coin in her hand and wondered at the unpredictability of the young man. She was willing to give him lessons for a modest fee of one rupee per one-hour session: the would-be student paid the fee, but would not receive tuition.

Sohani came out of the maze of lanes and bylanes and as he approached the spot where the streetwalker had spoken to him first, he saw Bibbo with a basket dangling from her hand. He greeted her with a smile which was reciprocated by her.

'Vegetables?' he asked her.

'Yes,' said Bibbo.

'Give me the bag and come with me.'

Bibbo relieved herself of the bag and Sohani walked with Bibbo to one of the greengrocer's who had a larger variety.

'Choose what you like,' Sohani said. 'I will not interfere.' Soon Bibbo's bag was nearly full. Sohani paid for the vegetables. The girl was glad to save for herself the little bit of money her mother gave her to buy vegetables.

This tiny sum would go into her earthen saving pot, which she called her 'treasury.'

As soon as Sohani and Bibbo were out of the bazar, Sohani inquired, 'Where had you been in the morning?'

'To fetch water from the river.'

'Alone?'

The girl was no liar. 'No,' she said. 'Nannoo and I decided yesterday we would have some water-splashing fun. He was waiting there.'

'Where were your clothes?'

'We left them on the sand.'

'How would you have felt if somebody had run away with them?'

'Nobody comes there. But we saw you loitering nearabout.'

'Suppose, I had sped off with your clothes?'

'You could not. You are a decent man.'

'Why don't you bathe with your clothes on?'

'With clothes on, it is not bathing. It is simply getting wet.'

'Was there any funny business between you and Nannoo?'

'Nothing. I wouldn't have allowed him if he tried.'

'Did he try?'

'He daren't. I would have pushed his head below the water and drowned him.'

'Whom do you love more – Nannoo or me?'

'You.'

'Then why the water-splashing tricks with Nannoo?'

'Come on, Sohani, don't be jealous,' said Bibbo. 'Why should I grudge Nannoo a bit of fun? It needs two, to throw water on each other. If you like, you and I can try it tomorrow morning. But nothing beyond that.'

'Bibbo,' said Sohani. 'I know you very well. I like your independent nature. You are not submissive, but assertive. You don't believe in gender discrimination. You want equality of the sexes. Two men love you – Nannoo and I. Choose between the two of us.'

'There is no question of choice at present,' said Bibbo. 'Both of you are non-earners. I will marry him, who earns enough to keep me in comfort. The married couple should live in a separate house with a separate kitchen. I won't like living in a joint family. One is not free to do there, what one likes. There is constant surveillance day and night. He who fulfils these conditions will be the partner of my life. It may be you. It may be Nannoo. It may be some other man.'

'I will be the first to fulfil your conditions.'

'Let us see,' said Bibbo. 'I want to watch a competition for success between you two.'

So saying, Bibbo walked homeward. As she walked, Sohani realised she was as sensual from behind, as she was from the front.

IV

While Salim was gradually thinning out his harem at Allahabad, rumours were rife at Agra that he was selling his harem girls at an exorbitant price, to Shah Abbas of Iran and to prosperous traders in Kashmir, to meet the increasing recurrent and non-recurrent expenditure of his nascent kingdom. Rumours tend to get more and more magnified as they pass from one mouth to another, with the result that truth vanishes and only fiction remains. Molehills are made into mountains and mountains are so enlarged as to become many times higher than the highest peak in the world.

The geographical distance that often separated Salim and his wife, the wild stories of the sensuality and infidelity of her husband and lack of face-to-face communication, broke their marriage. To

Princess Maan Bai, or Shah Begum as she was called in the palace at Fatehpur-Sikri, there were little chances of making it up. As a mother, she should have been glad that a powerful lobby was championing the cause of her son Khusrau, to the succession. But she was a scrupulous lady. She knew that if anybody should succeed her father-in-law, it should be her husband. She also knew that the Emperor did not relish the idea of Khusrau's candidature, as the scramble for succession would create a breach between father and son, almost similar to that between Salim and Akbar. Ambition may have also been partly responsible for wounding her psyche. If Salim sat on the throne, she would enjoy the exalted status of Queen. If Khusrau succeeded Akbar, her status would be relegated low to that of Queen Mother. It pained her most that, knowing his father's profound regard for his eldest son, her husband was not amenable to reason and reconciliation.

The Princess found herself depressed. Her depression grew deeper with each passing day. Wagging tongues said Salim was head over heels in love with Anarkali, once a maid-of-honour of Jodha Bai and in order to marry her, he would spurn the throne. Some windbags said, Salim was raising a colossal army to attack his father, kill him and capture all the palace ladies as war prisoners, to sell the young ones to Princes in alien lands, ransom some others for huge sums and send the old ones into the forest, as exiles. Such baseless gossip horrified Princess Maan Bai. What her husband was doing was inexplicable to her. Panicmongers had wrecked havoc on her sensitive soul. In a fit of depression, she took an overdose of opium and went to bed, never to rise again. A beautiful rose had been withered by the scorching winds of rumours and its petals lay dry, in the dust. Her suicide was another emotional blow to Salim, Khursau, Akbar, Jodha Bai and those who loved her and wished her well. The circumstances leading to her death were largely not of her making.

V

'Khwaja Jahan,' said Salim, 'the death of my Maan Bai has come to me as a stunning blow. Had she died a natural death in her ripe old age, it would have been a different matter. But suicide points an accusing finger at me. She took her own life because I was unworthy of her. It is true I have many faults. Everybody has. I am no exception. She disapproved of my harem. This was unfair of her. Even some Rajputs are known to keep concubines. Almost all Princes have more than one wife. It is the order of the day. I can tell you names of Maan Bai's relatives, who have several mistresses. She should not have put an end to her life like this. I loved her and I love my son, even though he has been misled to oppose me, in the matter of succession.'

'Your Majesty, you must not feel guilty. You cannot condemn yourself because Shah Begum has committed self-murder. I was present at Your Majesty's wedding. It was a magnificent marriage, a splendid spectacle. At that time, who would have thought that this innocent bride would take her own life? When your son was born, the festivities were worth seeing. The Emperor felt proud of having become a grandfather. He gifted vast lands to Shah Begum and honoured all her relatives. At that time, it was inconceivable that by taking her own life, she would make her husband a widower and her son motherless. Everyone is overcome with sorrow.'

Salim said, 'She held a place of the highest esteem in the palace. Nothing was withheld from her. She should have been happier under the loving care of my father and my mother. She should have seen Khusrau blossoming into manhood like a true Prince. Perhaps she could not grasp the nature of power politics. But there is power politics in her father's mini court too. It is not anything new. There are cliques even in the courts of Rajput Princes. She ought to have known this.'

'Your Majesty, let us speak nothing but good of the dead. May her soul rest in peace!'

'Khwaja Jahan,' said Salim, 'should I go to attend her last rites?'

'The last rites must have been performed by now,' said Khwaja Jahan. 'The atmosphere in the court is not congenial for you. You have more enemies than friends there. Stay here and send a letter of condolence.'

'I feel guilty, Khwaja Jahan,' said Salim, 'I feel as if I alone am to blame for her death.'

'Your Majesty, death comes to one and all, in various forms – sometimes through suicide, sometimes through the assassin's dagger, sometimes through accident, sometimes as war casualty and sometimes on account of brief or prolonged illness. The bereaved husband or wife, father or mother, son or daughter, uncle or nephew or niece, do not lament the loss for ever. The dead are forgotten with the effluxion of time. Their minus points sink into oblivion. Their plus points remain in memory. Shah Begum had many plus points.'

'I am overwhelmed with sorrow, Khwaja Jahan,' said Salim. 'Being here, I could not even have a last look at her face, before her funeral rites.'

'Your Majesty,' said Khwaja Jahan, 'drown your sorrow in the wine cup. The "red fairy" will cheer you up.'

'A few days from now, Anarkali's brother and her would-be fiancé Idrees Pasha, will come to take her away to her parents. You know, Anarkali is nearest to my heart. But I have to cut down the size of the seraglio. This will abate rumours. If Anarkali had left me earlier, perhaps Maan Bai would have remained alive today.'

'Your Majesty, ifs and buts lead to nothing. Go to your chamber and relax and call for the "red fairy".'

'I suppose what you say makes sense.'

'It does, Your Majesty. May I take your leave now?'

'Yes, you may go,' said Salim. 'The sun has set. Darkness is spreading not only outside but also in my life. The lamps in the palace are being lit, but the lamp of my life has been extinguished forever.'

Khwaja Jahan stood up to go. 'Your Majesty, calm yourself. Put the "red fairy" in a cup and let her touch your lips. You will feel better.'

VI

Chahalgam was a picturesque place in the Kashmir valley. It was a town of freshwater lakes, evergreen hills and wild fruit and flowers. There was no need for man-made water supply. Many natural springs of fresh water, spouting from the rocks of the

Himalayan mountains, flowed down the hills perennially. There was one such spring at the back of the house of Muneer Pasha, Anarkali's father, from where his wife Rahat Afza, fetched unpolluted and crystal-clear water for drinking and other purposes, in her small household. There were also ten trees in the large compound of the house – an apricot tree, two peach trees, three plum trees and four walnut trees. Down below the house, there was a road encircling the lake, dotted with small boats of every kind. For about seven months of the year, it was winter, heavy rain and snow, but during the rest of the five months, it was cool, pleasant and refreshing, as compared to the parching heat of the Indo-Gangetic plains. That is why it was a summer resort for some of the rich, living in the plains. Muneer Pasha had a big shop of shawls and carpets, on the circular road. His business was largely wholesale but for summer visitors he would also became a retailer. There was no fixed price for shawls and carpets. Bargaining depended on two indicators – the customer's preference and his paying capacity. Muneer Pasha had a penetrative eye for both of these. The same shawl and carpet fetched a much higher price from a customer who was class-conscious as well as quality-conscious. Such customers were few and the larger part of the income of shawl and carpet traders was derived from export.

Shawl and carpet weaving was a cottage industry, in which children worked strenuously, under a master weaver. Shawl embroidery was done by women in their own homes. The shawl, or carpet maker, brought the finished product to the trader who had a thorough look at each item. The faultless product was accepted and paid for and the faulty one rejected. The traders were middlemen between the producer and the consumer. They also advanced money on exorbitant interest to the cottagers for productive and non-productive purposes, but ostensibly to buy raw material. The interest was deducted when an approved shawl or carpet was paid for, but the principal remained, to earn more interest. The cottagers therefore remained in perpetual indebtedness. Behind every beautiful shawl and carpet, there was a sordid story of penury, self-deprivation and child labour.

Idrees Pasha was an asset to Farhat Afza's family. He was an energetic man and an unfailing salesman. Muneer Pasha's trade flourished because of Idrees's acumen. The old man openly acknowledged Idrees's industry and assiduity. He said, 'Idrees, we are now as prosperous as we were in Pasandad. The climate here is nearly the same as of our Turkish village. I owe much to you. You are a man of liberal and innovative ideas – ideas that have yielded excellent results. But your impoverished childhood haunts you. You cannot see children working for long hours and being poorly paid. That is why you insisted that I should open a madarsa and offer each child a scholarship, equivalent to the amount he earned every month. The madarsa provides both theological and secular education. The concept was yours. You brought dedicated teachers from Agra. My son Anwar has passed from this school and I am satisfied.'

'Respected Muneer Pasha, you are like my father. You are right that I was deprived of my childhood. I was also part of the pernicious child labour system. I know child labour cannot be abolished unless the socio-economic status of parents is raised to a level, where the children are not compelled to earn their living. No shawl and carpet trader can do what you have done. There is no child labour in Chahalgam. All children attend your madarsa.'

'Idrees,' said Muneer Pasha, 'you have also rendered a service of another kind. You have succeeded in locating Farhat. Her letter tells us that Sultan Salim of Allahabad has condescended to release her from her gilded cage. She asks me to send you and Anwar to bring her home. You say I am like your father. I would like to be your father-in-law.'

Idrees could not believe his ears. He would marry his beloved at last. The Pasha home would be brightened by Farhat's luminous presence. The name Anarkali would be discarded and left behind at Allahabad. The real name, Farhat, in consonance with the girl herself, would bring refreshing breeze in the Pasha home. Idrees was not a relative of the Pashas, but soon he would be one.

'Venerable Sir,' said Idrees. 'I don't know what to say. Words fail me. You have said what I had been cherishing in my heart since my childhood days. When do you want Anwar and me to go? The Sultan is a noble man, indeed.'

'Go, my son, when you and Anwar are ready,' said Muneer Pasha. 'Go with dignity. There is no need for disguise any more. Go like princes and bring back my princess. Her mother longs to see her. She is growing old. She will live longer, with her daughter by her side.'

'Esteemed Sir,' said Idrees, 'shall we set out tomorrow?'

'Tomorrow, if it suits you and Anwar. There is one more thing, which you can do, after your return. I want two marriages to be solemnised together – yours and Anwar's. He is now of marriageable age. Find out a suitable girl for him, if he is not already in love with some pretty girl of Chahalgam.'

'There is no need to search for a girl. Anwar is self-reliant. He is in love with your fellow trader, Shaukat Husain's daughter, Roohi, a beautiful girl of fifteen. The girl passes all scrutiny of face, body, build, height and character.'

'You have taken a heavy load off my shoulders, Idrees,' said Muneer Pasha. 'I will send my wife to visit Roohi's mother tomorrow evening. They know each other very well. I feel that, considering our social and economic level, Shaukat Husain will be only too willing to give Roohi's hand in Anwar's hand.'

VII

'Anar,' said Salim, 'I am much disturbed today.'

'I know, Shahzada. Princess Maan Bai, your wife, has passed away.'

Salim was sitting on a carpet, soft round pillows supporting his back. He put down his empty cup and said, 'Anar, fill it again.'

Anarkali poured the red wine into the cup and brought it to Salim's lips. Salim took the cup in his hand and said, 'Anar, I am not in the mood today.'

'You will soon be,' Anarkali said, massaging Salim's thighs, the calves of the legs and feet with her long and pretty fingers. She did so, a few times and as the alcohol began to circulate in his blood, Salim seemed to become cheerful.

'Anar,' he said, 'Khwaja Jahan told me to drown my sorrow in the wine cup. I feel much better now.'

'Lie down, Shahzada and let me massage your head and hands.

It will make you further relaxed.'

'Do it,' said Salim, 'but fill this cup again.'

'This will be your last drink for today,' said Anarkali, picking the goblet and pouring wine into it. 'Drink slowly. After this, you will not have any more, because you will start snoring and I will have to let you sleep here, instead of in your bed.'

'You speak to me as if I were a child.'

'Yes, Shahzada, you are my master, but when you can't manage yourself, I have to play the role.'

'Anar, when you go away to your home in Kashmir, who will look after me as tenderly as you?'

'Gul Afshan will replace me. She is a good girl and she loves you. But let us not talk about it. The thought of my leaving you makes you sad.'

'Anar,' said Salim, gulping down the contents of the cup. 'One more.'

'No, Shahzada, not too much. You have already begun to feel sleepy. It is quite late now. Get up, put your arm on my shoulder and I will conduct you to your bedroom.'

Salim got up. His gait was unsteady. He had drunk a little more than was his wont. Anarkali led him to his room and made him lie down in bed. As soon as Salim was in bed, he felt the soft velvet touch of young female flesh, from which a faint perfume emanated.

'Whom have you put into my bed?'

'It is Gul Afshan,' said Anarkali. 'Now have a good rest for the night. I will see you in the morning.'

The Return of the Prodigal

I

Gul Afshan was disappointed. It was at Salim's request that Anarkali had bought this peerless pearl from a pearl trader, who had come from a distant land. Gul Afshan, in her late teens, was a Caucasian girl, at the fullness of her beauty. She had been bought and sold twice before. Her parents having died, she was brought up by a greedy maternal aunt in Samarqand. Salim had admired her sexuality. While her real name was Firdaus Khanum she had been named Gul Afshan by a fur trader in Kabul. Her second master, according to her own admission, the heir to a tiny tribal principality, had taught her some love pranks. She was a good swimmer. She could swim in the sea, as well as in bed. Salim complained she was ignorant of courtly manners. Anarkali had taken pains to raise her up to the mark.

Gul Afshan found no opportunity of displaying her erotic devices, or her newly acquired polite and pleasant manners. She lay beside Salim, who was fast asleep under the influence of alcohol. For him his sleep was good but for Gul Afshan it was otherwise. She had expected something exciting and new, but she gave or got nothing. At about daybreak, she heard Salim muttering in his sleep, something about painting and a married woman, whom he would like to make his Queen when he became King. Gul Afshan could not understand what all this meant.

When Salim opened his eyes, he did not recognise the girl who sat beside him. The hangover had not gone off completely.

'Who are you and what are you doing in my bed?' he queried.

'I am Gul Afshan', said the girl. 'Anarkali had sent me here.'

'Yes, I remember now', said Salim. 'Did you have a good rest at night?'

'I was wide-awake the whole night. My body was on fire.

There was none to put it out.'

'How do you feel now?'

'I would like to have a swim. But there is no sea here.'

'We have rivers – the Ganga and the Jamna – and a place where they flow together. But I would not like you to swim there. It does not suit a lady of my harem.'

'What should I do here?' Gul Afshan inquired. 'I was brought up in Samarqand. Perhaps I could go there. Perhaps my aunt is still alive.'

'I cannot arrange an entourage for you to such a far-off place. It may also be that your aunt has shifted to some other town or died. If she is still alive there, the possibility is, she will sell you again. Your next master may not be as good as the first three. Would you like to go to Kashmir? It is beautiful and cool.'

'I will be a total stranger there.'

'Anarkali is leaving the harem for good. Her brother is coming to take her away. Her family has settled at a scenic place called Chahalgam. I will speak to Anarkali. You may live with her family. She will also find a proper match for you. Get married and have a family of your own. I am preparing for a big war. When a man goes to the field of action, he cannot say whether he will be killed, or wounded, or captured, or return in one piece.'

'You have paid an enormous sum for me,' said the girl. 'I am yours.'

'It was my whim,' said Salim. 'I will give you enough, so that you can settle down, live in a good house, have a nice husband and pretty children.'

'Shahzada,' said Gul Afshan, 'I love you and want to marry you. If you can't marry me, let me remain as your maid.'

'You seem to have romantic ideas. You cannot marry a Mughal Prince. Your antecedents are little known. The Emperor will never allow it. I want to save you from possible trouble.'

Meanwhile, Anarkali walked in. She saw Salim and Gul Afshan discussing something. There was a look of frustration on Gul Afshan's face and of anxiety on Salim's. The Shahzada told Anarkali about the Caucasian girl's romantic aspirations. He asked Anarkali to persuade her to go to Kashmir. He unfolded the plan he had outlined for Gul Afshan's future.

'I understand,' said Anarkali. Turning to the girl, she said, 'Come, Gul Afshan. The Shahzada wishes you nothing but good.'

Gul Afshan's eyes were moist. She seemed to have developed an infatuation for the Prince. She, however, expected to be consoled by Anarkali, who would give her good reasons for the Shahzada's decision. She took Salim's hand gently in hers and put her sensual lips on two of his forefingers. Casting a long, lingering look at Salim, she reluctantly accompanied Anarkali into the ladies' quarters of the Allahabad palace.

II

When he had something important to communicate, Salim invariably called his chief advisor Khwaja Jahan, in whom he had full faith.

'Khwaja,' said Salim, 'an emissary has brought us a letter from our father, the Emperor. We have read it very carefully. Our dear adoptive mother, Sultan Salima Begum, is visiting us. We have to make the atmosphere in our palace more sober and more affable, to suit the nature of our most important guest.'

'Let us read the letter first,' the Khwaja said.

Salim, handing over the letter to his confidant said, 'Read it aloud. We may have missed something.'

Khwaja Jahan opened the scroll and read loudly and distinctly:

Our son Shaikhoo Baba, dear to our heart,

We would like you to come to Agra and live in love and peace, in the twilight years of our life. Having crossed the sixty-second year of our life span, we are aging fast. Your remaining far away from us and the untimely passing away of our dear daughter-in-law, has further shattered our failing health.

You want the throne, which will be assuredly yours, in the proximate future. It is therefore useless to proclaim yourself King, when you are going to be Emperor. It is also unnecessary to raise an army of mercenaries, when the entire imperial army will be at your command.

Let it be clear to you that we do not support the idea of our grandson succeeding us. We also discourage those who want to act as crutches, for Khusrau.

Unfortunately, it has come to our knowledge that a group of self-seekers have gathered around you and give you advice which, instead of promoting your best interest, is detrimental to it. We, as your father and well-wisher, understand better what is in your interest and what is not. We foresee a bright and peaceful future for you, if you come here and live before our loving eyes, which are longing to see you.

What we have written is also what your loving mother has in mind. She wants you to live as a loving son, with loving parents, in a family united together with bonds of love. Love unites, hate divides. The fruit of love is sweet; the outcome of armed hostilities is uncertain.

Your foster mother, Sultan Salima Begum, who loves you as much as your own parents love you, is coming to Allahabad on a mission of love and we wholeheartedly wish her success, in this noble errand.

Written by order and bearing the
seal of
Akbar Badshah

'Now analyse its contents and tell us what you make out of it,' said Salim.

Khwaja Jahan pondered for a moment and then said, 'Your Majesty, the letter conveys a spirit of sincerity. It makes an appeal to your sense of pity for the Emperor's old age. It assures you of succession to the throne, on his death. It appeals to your sense of filial love. Your foster mother represents the palace ladies and her visit to Allahabad means they want you and the Emperor to get reconciled.'

'These are all positive conclusions. Is there any negative one?'

'Yes, Your Majesty. 'The letter asks you to dismiss your ministers, disband your army and integrate your kingdom with the Empire.'

'How can we do all this?' said Salim. 'Can we give our ministers, officers and men of the armed forces indefinite leave, on full pay?'

'Your Majesty, I would not advise you to yield under pressure.

The reminder of filial love, parental ties, family bond and so on is nothing but pressure building.'

'We will have to think over it,' said Salim. 'At present, I am dying to see my foster mother. She often fondled me in her arms. I learnt to walk, by holding her finger.'

'Your Majesty, this is not the time for sentimentalism, but for sagacity. Resist Salima Begum's pressure. I must also tell Raja Gopal Das and Raja Bir Singh not to move freely in the open, as long as the Begum stays here. If word leaks out that you have given asylum to Abul Fazl's killers, all this drama of mutual love will come to an end.'

'You seem to be right, Khwaja,' said Salim. 'We have to be very cautious. Meanwhile, let us receive Sultan Salima Begum with all honour and courtesy.'

III

Anarkali had her expected guests. They were her brother Anwar and her prospective husband, Idrees. They had been allotted a separate room in a corner of the palace. Anarkali was given leave, to be with them. Gul Afshan was also asked to join them and cultivate familiarity with them.

As soon as Anarkali introduced Gul Afshan to her brother and her would-be husband, they were bewitched with the bloom of her beauty. Anwar was quite dazed. He forgot Roohi. If Roohi was a little twinkling star, Gul Afshan was the resplendent moon.

Anwar said to his sister, 'I have fallen in love with Gul Afshan. I went to marry her, when we return home.'

Gul Afshan looked at Anwar with surprise. She had not yet left the palace. A handsome youngster was talking of marrying her.

Anarkali said, 'Idrees told me mother has settled your marriage with Shaukat Husain's daughter, Roohi.'

'Marriage has not yet taken place,' said Anwar. 'A promise of marriage is different from marriage.'

'Promises are made to be kept, not to be broken,' his sister said.

'We are a family of traders,' retorted Anwar. 'Our accent is on beauty and quality.'

'I knew you will say so. Gul Afshan is irresistible. But she is a year older than you. She is a little over eighteen. You are about seventeen.'

'Difference in age does not matter,' Anwar said. 'Men marry girls below their own age and girls marry men, above their own age.'

'Will Gul Afshan agree?' Anarkali said.

'She is going with us and she will live with us. We shall get much time to be closer to each other.'

'What about father and mother?'

'They will accede to my wishes.'

Anarkali paused to think. Anwar was a little impatient. He asked her, 'When are we leaving?'

'I will introduce you to the Sultan. Seek his permission.'

'How is your Khwaja Sara?' said Idrees. 'Does the eunuch recognise us?'

'No', said Anarkali, 'You look different now. He has orders from the Sultan to spare no pains, in making his guests comfortable.'

IV

The two guests from Kashmir rested for three days, during which Anarkali spent most of her time with them, making inquiries about her parents and relatives and life at Chahalgam and relating how unexciting and monotonous life was in the seraglio. On the morning of the fourth day she led Anwar and Idrees to the Sultan's private chamber and introduced them to Salim, saying, 'Your Majesty, this is my younger brother Anwar and this is my betrothed, Idrees Pasha.'

Anwar came to the Sultan with a tray containing four of the best shawls. He lifted the velvet cover. The Sultan was delighted to examine their thinness and fineness and the exquisiteness of the delicate hand embroidery. Idrees then stepped forward to the Sultan with a rather heavy tray and uncovering it, displayed four little wall carpets. The scenery of Kashmir within the frame of ornamental borders pleased the Sultan.

Anarkali was dressed in her best clothes. She said, 'Your

Majesty, Anwar wants to say something.'

'Say it, young man,' said the Sultan.

'Your Majesty, we would like to beg your leave,' said Anwar. 'Our parents must be waiting for us.'

'You can leave after your midday meal. We have arranged a team of fresh horses for you. Ten armed soldiers will accompany you to Chahalgam.'

The Sultan clapped his hands and in response to it an attendant appeared. 'Bring Gul Afshan here.'

Gul Afshan was also dressed in smart clothes. Salim asked her, 'Are you willing to go with Anarkali?'

'She persuaded me. I am willing.'

'Good,' Salim said. Then he ordered an attendant to call Khwaja Sara. The eunuch came, saluted the Sultan and awaited his orders.

'Bring the gifts. The Khwaja went in and soon reappeared with another eunuch, who bore a tray, on which there were several little bags of different colours, perhaps as indicators of the amount of money. The Khwaja picked a bag and handing it over to Anarkali announced ceremoniously, 'Here are two hundred asharfis from His Majesty to you.' Anarkali bowed low in gratitude.

The Khwaja picked up another bag and said in the same ceremonious tone, 'Gul Afshan, here are one hundred and fifty asharfis for you.' Gul Afshan took the bag, looked lovingly at Salim and then curtsied.

'Anwar Pasha,' said the Khwaja, 'here are fifty asharfis from His Majesty to you.' Anwar accepted the gift and curtsied in the right, courtly manner.

'Idrees Pasha,' the Khwaja proclaimed, 'here are fifty asharfis from His Majesty to you.' Idrees also followed Anwar's example, in court etiquette.

'Anarkali,' said Salim, 'we bid you goodbye with a heavy heart. We shall miss you. Be happy. Some day, when we visit Kashmir, we will try to see you.'

Anarkali said, 'Your Majesty, I shall always remember your kindness and munificence.'

'Gul Afshan,' said the Sultan, 'we bid you farewell. We wish you a happy journey and a new life with Anarkali's family, at Chahalgam.'

'Your Majesty,' said Anarkali, 'Anwar seems to be drawn towards Gul Afshan.'

'Congratulations,' said the Sultan to Anwar. 'Go on wooing Gul Afshan, until she agrees to marry you.'

At these words, both the girl and the boy blushed.

'Idrees Pasha,' said Salim, 'marry our Anarkali and look after her well. She has been of immense help to us.'

The Sultan rose, saying, 'You may go now.' Turning to Khwaja Sara, he said, 'Provide them the ten soldiers and the four fresh and strong horses, which Prime Minister Khwaja Jahan has selected for them and supply them with enough provisions to last them during their long and arduous journey.'

V

Salim did not take his ministers and other officials with him and went alone, half a stage, to meet Sultan Salima Begum. His aide Khwaja Jahan, unknown to Salim, had taken the precaution of hiding some soldiers on both sides of the road, but so far away as to be invisible. Six bearers set down Salima Begum's palanquin. The escort commander recognised Salim. He came to the Begum's palanquin, turned his face the other way and said, 'Your Highness, Prince Salim has come to welcome you.'

The Begum got down from the palanquin as Salim brought his horse near. He dismounted and ran to embrace the Begum. Both were locked in each other's embrace for a few moments. Salim felt as if a lost treasure had been restored to him. The Begum gently disengaged herself and patted Salim fondly on his back, saying, 'Salim, my son, I am so happy to see you after such a long time. My God, you appear to have grown older than I thought! But no matter how old you become, you will always remain for me, the innocent child who played in my arms.'

Salim was overwhelmed. Recollection of his past floated across his memory.

'Your Highness,' he said, 'consider me your innocent child still. I feel I have been bereft of maternal care, since years and years. Welcome to Allahabad. Welcome to your son's humble dwelling.'

The Begum resumed her seat in the palanquin and with Prince Salim leading the way they entered the city gate of Allahabad. The public rejoiced to see the Prince leading the royal lady to his palace. Only a few people were upset – Khwaja Jahan and the other Ministers.

One of the best rooms in the palace had been readorned for the Begum, who looked handicapped by age and indifferent health. In the evening, Salim lay resting his head on her lap, like a child and inquired of the Begum how his father, his mother and his son were at Fatehpur-Sikri. The Begum related what she knew and Salim felt guilty of having kept himself away from his near and dear ones.

He said, 'Your Highness...'

'Don't address me as Your Highness,' the Begum snubbed him. 'Call me what you used to call me as a child.'

'Yes, Bari Ammi,' said Salim. 'There is no protocol between us. Your love is all I want.'

'I have always loved you. Your mother loves you much more than I and your father loves you much more than she. You are our son and you will always remain our darling son.'

'I have been disobedient to all of you, Bari Ammi,' said Salim with remorse.

'Forget Salim, my son, forget the past. There is basic goodness in the human heart and a human heart pulsates in your breast. The path of obedience is a bed of roses. The path of disobedience is a bed of thorns. In obedience, there is peace; in disobedience is turbulence and tension. God is Supreme and we feel peace when we obey him. In the same way, there is peace when we obey those who are elder to us. As God takes care of all, the elders take care of their children even if they are fully groswn-up like you.'

'How true!' said Salim with a sigh.

'My son, you must have received your father's letter. Without you, he feels like a fish out of water. You are the apple of his eye, the comfort of his heart, the peace of his mind. He wants you to be the future Emperor. He is angry with Maan Singh whenever he talks of Khusrau, your son. If you are in the palace, you will reclaim Khusrau as your only child. The poor boy has been bereft of his father's love and so he turns to the avuncular love of Maan Singh. Salim, my son, there is no comparison between a father's love and an uncle's love. They are widely apart from each other, as heaven is from earth.'

'How true!' Salim exclaimed again. 'Khwaja Jahan never talks like this.'

'Khwaja Jahan and others are opportunists. Pay no attention to what they say. They flatter you, but do not love you. Your near and dear ones may not flatter you, but they love you. There is no greater happiness on earth than love between a father and son and love between a mother and son. Come with me to Agra. Have no fear. They are waiting for you. Do not disappoint those who have fathered you and mothered you.'

'Yes, Bari Ammi, I will go with you. What there is, in family life, is not to be found in any other relationship.'

'Salim, my son, I have always known how sensible you were.'

'Bari Ammi,' said Salim, 'allow me a few days, to collect presents for my father, befitting his dignity and status.'

'Take your own time, my son; but do not keep them waiting for too long.'

'Only a week or so,' said Salim.

'That's a nice boy!' the Begum exclaimed. 'Despatch by special messenger the probable date and time of your arrival at Agra. It will fill all hearts with gladness.'

'I will do so, Bari Ammi,' said Salim, rising from the Begum's lap. 'Allow me to go and write the letter.'

VI

Salim went straight to his chamber. He made several drafts of the proposed letter, but no draft was to his liking. After several attempts, he hit upon the final draft. He made a fair copy and ordered a special messenger to deliver it posthaste, to the Emperor.

This done, Salim summoned Khwaja Jahan and said, 'My family wishes to see me. I must go to meet my aging father. I will come back, when the time is opportune. During my absence, you will look after the affairs of the State. Don't take any important policy decision. There are three beautiful girls in the harem – Zaitoon, who comes from somewhere near the Khyber Pass, Mahnaz from somewhere in Azerbaijan and Nilofar, from Tehran. The young commander of Sultan Salima Begum's escort party lives in single blessedness. Show these girls to him in your own way. If he chooses any of them, call the Qazi and marry them, at your residence. The ceremony should be simple and quiet. Give the bride a dowry of one hundred and fifty asharfis, in cash. Invite the commander this evening and take your wife into confidence. Create a suitable socialising climate and let the young commander see the girls in a casual way. He should not feel we are forcing a girl on him.'

'Your Majesty, this is all so sudden. I had never anticipated such lightning decisions.'

'Khwaja,' said Salim, 'you yourself enumerated the plus points of the Emperor's letter. You mentioned only one negative point – the dismissal of Ministers and the disbanding of the army. I am not going to do this. That is why I appoint you caretaker. I have told you, I will return when I have assessed the political climate of Agra.'

'So be it. There is meaning in what you say,' said Khwaja Jahan. 'As for the three girls you mentioned, they must be rare beauties – rare in Allahabad. I have a son and a nephew, Your Majesty. Both are officers in Your Majesty's armed forces. I will also invite them and the commander, this evening. If all the three girls are married simultaneously on some day before your departure, I would be doing my duty towards my King. Your Majesty, I suppose you are winding up your seraglio.'

'I am diminishing its strength. This will add to my public image. Had I done this before, my wife would have felt happy,' said Salim. 'By the way, how many elephants do we have, in the elephant house?'

'About a thousand, Your Majesty.'

'How much do we have in our Treasury?'

'I can't say exactly. There must be more than half a million gold mohars.'

'Good,' said Salim. 'I don't need a separate escort. Sultan

Salima Begum's escort is enough. Moreover, I will take some elephants. Their mahouts will add to the number of the escort squadron.'

VII

The Emperor called Jodha Bai and his mother, Hamida Bano. 'Read Salim's letter, mother,' said Akbar. Hamida Bano read aloud:

Esteemed father,

I am overjoyed to meet Bari Ammi. She is no less loving and worthy of love than Your Majesty, my father and the Queen, my mother. Bari Ammi and I shall be reaching Agra in about a fortnight, from today.

Your unworthy but loving son,
Shaikhoo

The letter filled Hamida Bano with excitement. She said, 'I will travel two stages, to welcome my eldest grandson and bring him to the palace.'

'No, mother, you are too old to travel,' Akbar protested. 'We will send somebody.'

Hamida Bano said, 'I am Salim's grandmother; I must go. What do you say, Jodha? I must make one thing clear. When Salim is here, nobody will ask questions and nobody will give explanations. Everything must be cordial. My Salim has suffered a lot. We must assuage his feelings. We must apply the healing touch.'

There was happiness on the Emperor and the Queen's faces.

VIII

News spread all over Agra that the Heir Apparent was coming, not to attack Agra and kill the Emperor, but to beg his forgiveness and live under his protective eye. The people were jubilant. They lined up the road leading from the city gate to the palace. There were also crowds in balconies, on roofs and on treetops, to have a glimpse of the prodigal's return.

Soon Salim's procession was sighted at a distance. The Governor of Agra spotted Salim and ordered the city gate to be opened wide. The procession entered. The first to enter was the young commander of Salima Begum's entourage. He had gone a bachelor, but returned a married man. He had chosen Nilofar, the Iranian beauty and was richer by one hundred and fifty asharfis. He was also a guest at the wedding of Khwaja Jahan's nephew and Mahnaz, as well as another of the Khwaja's nephews and Zaitoon. He was in a hurry to present his wife to his parents and win their approval, but he had to complete the protocol formalities first.

Behind the commander was Salim, Salima Begum and Hamida Bano, seated in the howdahs of their elephants. They were followed by the escort party, with the commander's wife Nilofer, in a palanquin in-between. Well-decorated elephants, their number running into several hundred, driven by uniformed mahouts, formed the rear.

When the procession moved on, there were showers of flower petals from the crowds, positioned on roofs, balconies, treetops, as well as people standing on both sides of the road. Wending its way to the palace gate, the procession came to a partial end. The two royal ladies conducted Salim to a chamber, where his parents were waiting for him. Salim embraced his father and then his mother. The warmth of feeling on both sides was unaffected and unostentatious. Salim said, 'Your Majesty, allow me to present some humble gifts.'

The Emperor smiled and Salim went outside the palace and beckoned twenty-four tray-bearers to follow him. The bearers entered one by one, saluted the Emperor and placed a tray of two bags – each bag having five hundred gold mohars – at his feet. The twenty-four trays contained twelve thousand asharfis. As soon as Akbar put his hand on each tray, it was lowered before him and an attendant took it away, to hand it to the Treasurer of the Palace.

'Your Majesty,' said Salim, 'Deign to step outside. I wish to present you, seven hundred and seventy elephants.' Akbar accompanied his son and saw the adorned elephants. Each mahout, standing beside the elephant, bowed to the Emperor and gave a command, at which the elephants raised their trunks to salute the Emperor.

Akbar was pleased at this spectacle. He took off his turban and placed it on his son's head. This was a symbolic declaration that Salim would be the Emperor, after his death.

'Shaikhoo, my son, you must be tired. Relax in your own chamber.'

'Sire,' said Salim, 'I beg a favour from you. Do not deny it.'

'Take whatever you want,' said Akbar. 'All is yours.'

'I would like Your Majesty to bestow upon me your favourite war elephant, Maula Rakkha.'

'All is yours, Shaikhoo,' said Akbar. 'Before your love and loyalty, all is valueless. At my age, gold mohars, horses and elephants have less worth than the love and fidelity of my Shaikhoo.'

IX

For the first few weeks, Salim was happy. His time passed with his mothers Jodha Bai and Salima Begum. He tried to be friendly with his son Khusrau, but the youngster remained morose. The idea fostered by his lobby that he would succeed his grandfather, had gone to his head. It led to an invisible hostility between him and his father. Being motherless and with the prominent ladies of the palace favouring Salim, Prince Khusrau passed most of his time with Maan Singh and his Rajput relatives. His father's return was not palatable to him. Salim now felt that his own, unruly conduct towards his own father, had boomeranged on him, in the form of an imperceptible rift, between him and his son. He felt sad when he realised that in the struggle for power, there was no room for father-and-son relationships.

Salim remembered the day when he was told by Princess Maan Bai that he was going to be a father. He had felt very happy. He had played a role in creating a new life. He wanted to know what fatherhood was. He learnt it soon. Fatherhood meant, being a child with a child and also satisfying the child's curiosity, by replying to his questions, in a language he could easily understand. When the child became an adult, fatherhood meant the cropping up of differences in the ways of thinking, between the senior and the junior. Under the existing circumstances, fatherhood meant that father and son were poles asunder, both aiming at a common object – the Mughal throne – in the establishment of which, they had no hand.

At these thoughts, Salim's spirits were at a low ebb. He began to dislike life at the palace. He felt as if unseen eyes were watching him from everywhere. He felt as if an invisible ghost was shadowing him, wherever he went. The most important figure in the palace was the Emperor. As compared to him, his own position was much inferior. His sense of self-importance, began to gain a hold on him. He saw the glaring contrast between Fatehpur-Sikri and Allahabad. In his little kingdom, he enjoyed the same supremacy that Akbar enjoyed, in his Empire. At Allahabad, his word was law; at Fatehpur-Sikri, Akbar's diktat was law.

At Allahabad, Salim had a harem of lovely ladies. He could pick and choose any girl, to warm his bed. At Fatehpur-Sikri, there was no harem of his own. There were maids to serve him, but they did not arouse him. He had no trust in these unfamiliar girls. Any of them could loosen her tongue and spread damaging reports about him.

At Allahabad, Salim had his own Council of Ministers, who fawned on him; at Fatehpur-Sikri, there was none to energise his ambition. At Allahabad, he had his own army and his own generals. At Fatehpur-Sikri, he was devoid of these symbols of power. With his own army, he could demonstrate his strength anywhere. Leading a life of contented passivity at Fatehpur-Sikri irked him. He longed for a life of struggle and activity, which only Allahabad could provide. Even an occasional ride on the elephant Maula Rakkha, now became a stale affair with him. He decided to take the famous elephant to Allahabad and one day, confront his father on the latter's own elephant, in the final war which would decide his fate.

Sometimes, Salim realised he was setting a bad example, to the sons of future Mughal Emperors. The sons would rise in revolt against their own fathers to capture the throne. Anyone who stood in the way, would be put to the sword, even if he were a brother, with the blood of the same parents flowing in his veins.

Compassion and sympathy would be rooted out of the heart and fear and suspicion would torment the head. No future Mughal Emperor would ever trust his son. The sisters of hostile brothers would take sides. The mother would be a helpless spectator to the break up, of a dwindling family.

The more Salim thought, the more gloomy he became. He took to painting again, to seek diversion. He would decide to paint a landscape but a beautiful woman seemed inevitably to find a place, somewhere in the landscape. The woman resembled Mehr-un-Nisa, wife of Ali Quli Istalju, who was on Salim's staff in the expedition against Mewar. The name Mehr-un-Nisa means 'the moon among ladies.' Her husband, Ali Quli Istalju, once killed a tiger single-handed and Salim gave him the title Sher Afgan (the conqueror of the tiger).

One day, when Akbar was alone, Salim approached him and said, 'Your Majesty, allow me to leave for Allahabad, to wind up my affairs.'

'I had a different plan for you, my son,' said the Emperor. 'I was going to suggest that you should prove your mettle and lead a strong military expedition to Rajputana. Amar Singh has the effrontery to make encroachments on our territories.'

'Your Majesty,' said Salim. 'The Rana and his Bhils fight a guerrilla war. I do not know guerrilla tactics.'

'It is not necessary for you to know them. We have raised separate divisions of guerrillas. Your presence will lend them moral support. You represent us.'

'Your Majesty,' Salim pleaded, 'give me some other assignment. I do not want to fight the Rajputs.'

The Emperor was incensed, 'We are not used to rebuffs. How will you bring Amar Singh to his knees, when *you* become Emperor? Will you gift away the whole of Rajputana to him? If he asks for more, will you, as Emperor of Hindustan, always go on saying *yes*?'

Salim was speechless. He had no answer to the Emperor's question.

X

All the friends of the Emperor had breathed their last. He was growing old and lonely. The nine jewels of the court were no more. Only a solitary jewel remained. He was Raja Maan Singh. Although Akbar was sometimes inflamed, whenever the Raja tried to put in a good word for Khusrau, as the likely successor to the throne, yet it made no difference to the Raja. He was unflinching in his loyalty to his Emperor.

Salim's obduracy distressed Akbar. If Salim, as the Emperor's representative, did not wage war against Amar Singh, who else would? If oral orders failed to have any effect, written orders would. He therefore issued a *farman*. Non-compliance of a royal decree was a penal offence. It could be stretched as far as treason, for which the punishment could be death.

The *farman* sent shivers in Jodha Bai, Salima Sultan and Hamida Bano. They knew that Salim would not take the *farman* seriously. He was prepared to fight for his own rights, but not for the Emperor's. He was a bundle of contradictory impulses. The three ladies begged the Emperor, severally and sometimes jointly, not to press the matter, but to take Salim out of the quagmire, into which he had recklessly dragged himself. They argued that, even if Salim made a show of compliance, he would ensconce himself at Ajmer. The argument seemed to convince Akbar and he withdrew the *farman*. The three prominent ladies of the palace breathed a sigh of relief.

Maan Singh said, 'The cancellation of the *farman* is an unfortunate decision, Your Majesty. It means that the resumption of hostilities against Amar Singh is shelved, almost indefinitely.'

'We are fed up of Shaikhoo,' Akbar said. 'He will think we are powerless. We feel he will be encouraged in future to defy our orders with impunity, because his mothers are there to plead for him.'

'Your Majesty, the withdrawal of the royal decree may send the wrong signal to the Shahzada and his timeservers. They may misconstrue it, as a sign of weakness. The Shahzada is nursing unworthy ambitions of which Your Majesty is aware of,' said Maan Singh.

Akbar said, 'Shaikhoo wants to return to Allahabad. We will now grant his request. Between the two evils – his lukewarm compliance of our orders to engage Amar Singh in war and his return to Allahabad – packing him off to Allahabad would be the lesser evil. We know Allahabad is his stronghold. We also know he will foment trouble for us. Let him do his worst. No matter how large an army he may raise against us, he and his officers know, he lacks consistency and courage. He is used more to wine and women, than to the sword. With a man without leadership qualities at the helm of affairs, his flatterers and mercenaries will take to their heels, rather than face the wrath of the imperial troops, in a bloody battle. They do not have a cause to back them up; while our forces have one – to defend the Empire and the Emperor.'

'Your Majesty, the policy of appeasement does not yield lasting advantages. It is not like giving Salim enough rope to hang himself. It is like inviting more trouble for ourselves. But I must submit to what Your Majesty has decided and remain prepared to meet the worst, when it comes.'

'Maan Singh,' said Akbar, 'we understand what you mean. We have made ourselves a victim of conflicting loyalties. We owe a duty to our son and a duty to the Empire. Sometimes, our duty to our son gets the upper hand and sometimes, our duty to the Empire prevails.'

Maan Singh said humbly, 'Humayun and Babar, of revered memory and Your Majesty, have built this Empire, bit by bit. Your Majesty's duty to your Empire should prevail over all other considerations. There is hardly any duty, to an undutiful son,'

'Maan Singh,' said Akbar in anguish, 'your words are daggers to our heart.'

'Pardon me, Your Majesty, if I have transgressed in my duty to you. You are free to order me to lay down my life, for the preservation of the Empire.'

Promises and Propaganda

I

Sohani and Nannoo were intelligent young men. Sohani was picking up applied accountancy, under the guidance of his munim. Nannoo was doing the same, in a different way. He gave cash receipts to customers, noting down the name of each item purchased and its prices and then, totalled the sum. He gave a copy of these vouchers to the munim, when the shop closed for the day, to be entered in the sales register. His employer appreciated this innovation.

Nannoo asked the munim, with his employer's permission, to prepare bills of dues outstanding against each customer. Taking time off during the lean period of the day, he went on foot to each creditor and succeeded in recovering the whole, or part of the sum, due to him. The recovery rate increased and more rolling money was now available to his employer. The elder Sohani now asked him to contact the Head Accountants of those of the Sultan's commanders, who ordered grocery from him. During his frequent visits, Nannoo developed contacts with the Head Accountant of Raja Jai Kishan, one of the six Generals of Salim's army. The Head Accountant was pleased with Nannoo's proficiency and polite manners. A Junior Accountant having retired on superannuation, the Head, offered Nannoo the job. The elder Sohani was reluctant to relieve Nannoo, but was finally persuaded to do so, the debt which Nannoo's stepmother owed to him having been repaid, with compound interest, in a little less than a year.

When Nannoo got his first salary, he rented a small house, in a decent locality and shifted his stepmother there, asking her to devote her time in keeping the house. His stepmother found herself rehabilitated and looked after herself, her stepson and her house. She had been rescued from the Sultan's fun-loving soldiers. In a few months, she regained her lost respectability and her health also improved.

The elder Sohani wanted his son to take charge of his establishment, so that he could take rest and attend the shop for only a few hours, but Sohani kept putting him off. The young Sohani would leave the shop after five in the evening, go to the river for a bath, put on fresh clothes and wait for Bibbo, at the market corner. He accosted her one day and said, 'Bibbo, here is your rupee. I have been giving you a rupee every day for the last one year or so, besides the occasional little sums for your vegetables. What have I got in return, from you?'

'One rupee a day is my fee for the pleasure you get in talking to me. As for the random little sums for vegetables, they are my fee for the pleasure you get, in walking with me, to your favourite greengrocer's.'

'Do you meet Nannoo?'

'Now and then. He is a Junior Accountant in Raja Jai Kishan's office. His performance in his official capacity is being appreciated by his colleagues and his employer.'

'Does he appreciate your performance with him?'

'I never perform with anybody.'

'Not even in secret – without my knowledge?'

'There is no secret between Nannoo and me. He is devoted to his work and to his stepmother.'

'And to you?'

'He is as devoted to me as you.'

'Bibbo,' said Sohani, 'my father wants to hand over charge of his establishment to me. Do you like it?'

'If you start running your father's business, I won't marry you. You will come home tired, thinking of rising market and falling market, profit and loss. You cannot leave your parents and live in a separate house.'

'Bibbo, if I persuade my parents, we will get married. Surely you can adjust yourself in a joint family.'

'I can't,' said Bibbo frankly.

'Then I will ask my father to give me a decent monthly wage and we will set up a separate home. But you must marry me.'

'Look here, Sohani. You know my terms – enough money,

separate home, no outside interference.'

'All right, Bibboo,' Sohani said. 'Enough money, separate home, no outside interference. Agreed.'

'No. There should also be fixed hours of work, as Nannoo has. I can't wait for my husband's return, at late hours.'

'All right, Bibbo,' said Sohani. 'Fixed hours of work. Right?'

'Let us wait and see. I understand the Raja of Sironj has taken a liking for Nannoo. He wants to employ him at Sironj on a higher salary and a rent-free house. I would like to go with him.'

'But will not his stepmother interfere with your doings?'

'She dare not. I will keep Nannoo and his stepmother under my thumb.'

'Who is the other boy I saw you with yesterday?'

'He is Tari Ram, my new friend. His father died only last month, leaving him his land and his money.'

'Do you meet him often?'

'Yes.'

'Where?'

'In the forest.'

"What do you do there?'

'Whisper sweet nothings in each other's ears.'

'Will you marry him?'

'If he sticks to my terms.'

'Does Nannoo know?'

'Yes, he does.'

'Bibbo, you are always on the lookout for a good bargain. First, you wanted competition between Nannoo and me. Now, there are three competitors in the field.'

'Competition among lovers is good for a girl. She can choose the best. But I don't want that you should fight among yourselves.'

'We are not dogs – at least, not I.'

'I am a girl with my own self-respect. I want the good things of life. I would not like to be treated like chattel, as women are often treated. I am nobody's personal property. I am no dumb-driven animal. I have my own, free will. I will live my own life. I don't suppose I will be born again. This life is most enjoyable, if one has the means to enjoy it.'

Both Nannoo and Sohani worked hard, to earn Bibbo's favour. Both were amazed to learn that Bibbo had eloped with her new find, Tari Ram, who had taken a lot of cash with him. Where they had gone and where they would settle, was anybody's guess. Nanno did not take Bibbo's elopement to heart as much as Sohani. He was disconsolate for several months. It is said that love is good, but the fulfilment of the loved one's aspirations is better.

Nannoo went to Sironj, taking his mother with him. The heat being off now, Gopal Das and Bir Singh returned to their respective States. The elder Sohani introduced his son to Bir Singh, who took him into his service as Controller of Accounts, at Orchha. To their surprise, Nannoo and Sohani discovered that each of the two States had a Treasurer, but their account keeping was defective, there being no auditing and no way of knowing misappropriation of funds.

II

Salim was happy to be at Allahabad again. There, he was the reigning monarch. His first task was to summon Khwaja Jahan. On entering Salim's chamber, the Khwaja greeted the Sultan and said, 'Your Majesty, it is a pleasure to see you again. You stayed too long, at Agra.'

'I told you I would be back. I was waiting for an excuse. It came, when the Emperor asked me to wage war against Rana Amar Singh. When I declined, he issued a *farman.* But my mothers succeeded in getting it cancelled.'

'Your Majesty, it is good you have returned to your Kingdom. I suspect there was some foul play, in sending you to Rajputana. Amar Singh's Bhils could have killed you with their poisoned arrows.'

'Rubbish!' said Salim. 'Don't try to frighten me.'

'I am not trying to frighten Your Majesty,' said Khwaja Jahan. 'Suppose Your Majesty could not accomplish the task. The failure would have brought Your Majesty a bad name.'

'Certainly,' said Salim.

'Suppose, God forbid, Your Majesty were captured. The Emperor might not have ransomed you. Those whose ransom is not paid, are killed. The Emperor could have thought it a good riddance.'

'Nonsense!' said Salim. 'I know my father better than you. He loves me.'

'But the relations between Your Majesty and the Emperor seems to me, a love-hate relationship.'

'Whatever it is, let us not talk about it,' said Salim. 'Tell me what happened in our Kingdom, during my absence.'

'Nothing important happened, Your Majesty,' the Khwaja said. 'Your Ministers sent proposals, which involved the sanction of more funds. I asked them to wait, until your return.'

'What else?'

'Gopal Das and Bir Singh came to me. The search of the Emperor's men for the two Rajas proved a wild goose chase. The Rajas wanted to return to their own States. On Your Majesty's behalf, I allowed them to depart in peace.'

'What else?'

'Many soldiers of Sironj and Orchha wanted to enlist themselves in our army. They were screened. Those who passed the tough test were sent to be retrained, in the orientation course.'

'How many were taken?'

'About seven hundred and fifty, Your Majesty.'

'What else?'

'Your Majesty, I recognised Maula Rakkha. How could the Emperor part with him? He was his favourite. The Emperor has won many a battle on this elephant.'

'The Emperor was in a very generous mood,' said Salim. 'He said, everything was mine.'

'Everything will be yours only when you are the Emperor.'

'That day is not far off. The Emperor is aging and lonely. I seem to be his chief source of comfort.'

'Why did you leave him then?'

'Life at Fatehpur-Sikri was boring. I felt as if I was under ceaseless surveillance.'

'You were, Your Majesty. Here you are a monarch.'

'I also felt starved in the other way. I would not trust the maids, who were placed to serve me.'

'It was wise of Your Majesty. Call Khwaja Sara and he will see you are not starved.'

'Where is Mehr-un-Nisa?'

'Does Your Majesty mean Sher Afgan's wife?'

'The same.'

'Your Majesty, she must be where her husband is. If you wish, I will find out, where Sher Afgan is posted.'

'Do soon. I seem to be drawing her picture unconsciously, in my paintings.'

'Does Your Majesty want me to eliminate Sher Afgan?'

'Not now. We have a lot to do.'

'What, Your Majesty?'

'Prepare for a conclusive confrontation with the Emperor. I am impatient. No other Mughal Emperor before my father, has lived as long as he.'

'Hush, Your Majesty,' said Khwaja Jahan. 'We must not speak like this. Even the walls have ears.'

'Your ears are walls, Khwaja,' said Salim.

'Your Majesty, what I have heard has entered one ear and gone out of the other. I know nothing.'

'Very good,' said Salim. 'This is what I call, loyalty.'

'I am Your Majesty's most humble subject.'

'You are my most honoured and trustworthy dignitary, Khwaja. I am proud of you,' Salim said. 'I feel hot. I must call Khwaja Sara.'

III

Well, Khwaja, Sara, what is the news of the harem?' Salim inquired of the eunuch.

'Bad, Your Majesty,' said Khwaja Sara. 'The harem is not quiet. The girls feel frustrated. They give vent to their frustration by quarrelling with one another, over trivial matters. The petty squabbles among them, have grown out of all proportions.'

'Why? Earlier, it was not so.'

'Your Majesty understands. Anarkali was an expert in keeping the girls. She had charisma. How long can a girl, who knows why she is in the harem, wait? Sending away some girls to their families or getting them married, has spread dissatisfaction. They all grumble. They say they have been discriminated against. They all expect you to find their parents and, if parents are not found, their near relatives and restore them to their families or near relatives.'

'Khwaja Sara, use your influence and restore peace, somehow. Assure the girls that all possible attempts will be made, to locate their parents or near relatives. Tell them it will take time, a lot of time. They cannot be sent away in the twinkle of an eye, but by and by. I have their good in mind. I don't want them to get married to fortune-hunters. They will marry them for the one hundred asharfis I will give, as dowry to each girl. Having pocketed the money, the dowry-hunters will ditch them soon. In that case, the girls will find themselves in the streets.'

'True, Your Majesty,' said the eunuch. 'I have come to like the girls. I have never spoken a harsh word to any one of them. I feel as if I am their father and mother. They have also great regard for me.'

'Khwaja Sara, you say Anarkali was a magnetic personality. She charmed everyone who came into contact with her. You are right. Is there any girl who, in your opinion, has qualities of leadership, a pleasing personality and a real concern for the girls – one who can love the girls and be loved by them?'

'Your Majesty, there is one. She is Nastaran from Lahore. She cannot duplicate Anarkali. Anarkali was one in a million. But Nastaran has the will and the capability, to reach a higher level.'

'Send her to me. Dress her yourself. You know my taste. There were no girls at Agra. You can guess how impatient I feel.'

'Your Majesty, Nastaran will cool you down. She has never come to you before. She may feel nervous. Approach her tenderly. Make her feel relaxed and she will make you feel relaxed.'

'Don't worry,' said Salim. 'Let me see her.'

Khwaja Sara went in and in a few minutes a girl entered and stood respectfully before Salim, awaiting his orders. What Salim saw before him, was a feast for his eyes. The girl had no make-up. She was tall. She had sparkling eyes and long eyelashes, a Grecian nose, rosy lips, smooth cheeks and, when she smiled, she showed pearl-like teeth. Her neck was long and her shoulders bare.

'Sit down,' said Salim.

The girl obeyed her master and took her seat, in a dignified posture. She did not lower her eyes but seemed to scan the man before her, from limb to limb, until she added the parts together, into a proportionate whole.

'What is your name?' Salim asked.

'Nastaran.'

'What does it mean?'

'It is the name of a flower.'

'Do you remain cheerful as a flower?'

'Not always, but I try to bear a smiling face.'

'Where do you come from?'

'Lahore.'

'How did you come here?'

'I was a victim of riot.'

'Who is your father?'

'He was an officer in the army.'

'Which army?'

'The Emperor's army.'

'How did the riot occur?'

'A soldier misbehaved with a woman. The people resented it. Some hooligans infiltrated and started a riot. There was panic, loot and arson. I was trying to run away, when I was caught.'

'By whom?'

'By a hooligan.'

'Did he mishandle you?'

'He was dragging me somewhere.'

'Where did he take you?'

'Some good people rescued me from his clutches. They searched my parents. Everyone was trying to run away from the fury of the mob. We all ran away, in different directions. The army men put down the riot. My rescuers wanted to restore me to my parents. They couldn't find them. Khwaja Sara happened to be at Lahore. They handed me, to him.'

'Did they demand any money?'

'No, as far as I know. They treated me well. They thought I would be safe here. They believed you could find my parents and send me, to them.'

'Why did you not tell me this before?'

'I never got an opportunity. You were away at Agra. I was waiting for your return.'

'How long have you been here?'

'About two or three months.'

'Girls in the harem are for the pleasure of the master. Did you know this?'

Nastaran replied, 'I came to know it here.'

'Did your rescuers know it?'

'No. They said the girls in the harem are well treated and well protected. Khwaja Sara has been very kind to me.'

'Have you ever been wooed by a man?'

'Yes. A boy was in love with me.'

'Where is he?'

'I don't know. His name is Ghulam Ali.'

'Did he ever touch you?'

'No. He was too shy.'

'Did you want him to touch you?'

'I wanted him to take me in his arms and caress me.'

'Nothing beyond that?'

'Nothing.'

'How do you like harem life?'

'Some of the girls are very naughty. They have taught me things I never knew before.'

'Such as...'

'Self-excitation.'

'Do you like it?'

'I do.'

'Why?'

'It is natural.'

'Is there no shame in it?'

'There is no shame in what is natural.'

'Do you do it alone?'

'Alone.'

'Why not before others?'

'It is shameful.'

'You just said there is no shame in what is natural?'

'I mean there is no sense of shame when one does it alone; but it is shameful when it is done before others.'

'Will you do it before me?'

'Not willingly.'

'Why?'

'I will do it unwillingly because if I don't, you may turn me out and I have no place to go to.'

'You are a good girl. I won't ask you to do anything which you think is shameful. But I would like you to do one thing for me.'

'What?'

'To work as the Chief Lady of the Harem – the place Anarkali held. Your duty would be confidence building, among the girls. I will try to locate your parents, as well as Ghulam Ali. I will also try to get information about the families of other girls and send them back to their homes. Do you know how to read and write?'

'I do.'

'Then take down the name of each girl, the names of her parents or near relatives, their last-known address and give the list to Khwaja Sara.'

'Very well.'

'You may go now. I had called you for some other purpose. I was feeling hot. Now I feel anxious – about you, about you all.'

Nastaran bowed in a dignified manner and went to report to Khwaja Sara.

IV

Salim called a meeting of the Council of Ministers. All the thirteen Ministers were present. The differences in apparel, the various forms of turbans, the style of wearing them and the refurbished darbar hall, added grace and grandeur to the court. Salim said, 'We have to make an important announcement. Khwaja Jahan holds two portfolios. He is Prime Minister as well as *Sipah Salar*, or Chief Commander. We wish to lessen the burden of his responsibilities. He is a very capable man. His tenure as Prime Minister has been above reproach. He believes in team work. That is why there is hardly any dissension among our Ministers. He does not believe in the iron hand. He believes in persuasion, consensus and co-operation.

'You all know we are preparing for an all-out attack on Agra, in defence of our rights against the evil designs of certain sections at our father's court. This section wishes the Emperor to derecognise our rights and put his stamp on the so-called right of our misguided son Khusrau, who is too young to understand the ins and outs of politics and statesmanship. The defence of our rights includes the defence of your rights.

'We therefore propose to handle ourselves, the important office of Chief Commander of our armed forces with immediate effect, while retaining the title of Supreme Commander. Our gallant Generals – Raja Jai Kishan, Raja Chandra Bhan, Raja Mohan Das, Mirza Aslam Khan, Saiyyid Bashir Ahmad and Turkman Khan – will report to us and discuss all military matters with us.'

Everyone in the darbar applauded. The six Generals were elated at the opportunity of coming closer to the Sultan. Even Khwaja Jahan seemed to be satisfied. Perhaps it was his own suggestion to Salim to disburden him of this responsibility so that he could devote more time to supervising the administration.

'Raja Nirmal Singh,' said Salim, 'we understand you have come with some proposals. Let the other Ministers hear what you have to propose.'

Raja Nirmal Singh stood up. He held a paper in his hand, on which he had made some notes. 'Your Majesty,' he said, 'the prosecution of war, in defence of your rights needs funds, enormous funds. Your Majesty was gracious enough to realise that your rights include our rights. No one can say how long this war will last. Our army must be well trained and well equipped. We had put certain proposals before the honourable Prime Minister, but he asked us to wait for Your Majesty's return. Now that Your Majesty has sent a wave of joy among the people, with your return to your God-gifted kingdom, we assure you we are solidly behind you. We will wage a war, but we will do so with the conviction, that we will be victorious. We would like Your Majesty to assume the reins of the Government of Hindustan as Emperor.

'War, as Your Majesty and everyone present here knows, has to be adequately funded. We do not want usurers to lend us money. We do not want to go from one *mahajan* to another with a begging bowl in our hand. It does not behove us. We want to be self-supporting and self-reliant. This war will also be the people's war, not that of Your Majesty and ours alone. For this reason, the people – the well-to-do – will have to contribute their mite.

'Before I proceed further, allow me to recount briefly why, among other reasons, the State finds itself faced with a shortage of funds. The State has borne Your Majesty's travel expenses to Agra. The State has lost seven hundred and seventy elephants and no less than twelve thousand asharfis. A rough estimate of the total loss of the State exchequer, would be to the tune of twenty thousand asharfis. The State considers this expenditure necessary and does not regret it.

'In order to make up this loss and to mobilise more funds, certain fund-raising measures are both necessary and urgent.'

Raja Nirmal Singh paused to examine the reaction of the Sultan and the other Ministers. There was no sign of disapproval on anyone's face.

'Go on, Raja,' said Salim in an encouraging tone. 'Announce your proposals and let the Ministers discuss them.'

'Your Majesty, I propose to impose certain taxes.'

The Raja consulted his notes and said, 'I propose to impose a tax of five per cent on salt. Everybody consumes salt. The effect of this tax on the poor will be negligible. The rock salt, which people buy for the cows to lick, will be tax-free. The State does not manufacture salt. Sea salt comes from Gujarat and rock salt from the hills of the Himalayas. The wholesalers of rock salt run their establishments at Lahore. Salt enters our State through different routes, in cartloads, donkeyloads and boatloads. The tax will be collected at entry points, for which honest tax-collectors will have to be appointed. They will assess the wholesale value of the salt and calculate the tax. The tax will be totally abolished at the end of the war. Do Your Majesty and the Ministers agree?'

'We agree,' said some Ministers. A few remained silent, raising no objection.

The Raja continued, 'I propose to withdraw all incentives currently in force, on non-agricultural products. The producers earn huge profits. I propose to impose a tax of five per cent on all production and value added goods. There will be a negligible burden on the citizens. But purchases of products necessary and useful to the army, will be tax-free. This means that military purchases of non-agricultural products will cost us as before. This tax will also be withdrawn at the conclusion of the war. Do I have the assent of Your Majesty and the ministers?'

The Ministers nodded assent. The Raja consulted his notes again and said, 'Three-fourths of our people are farmers and landless agricultural labourers. Not all among them pay land revenue. The land revenue is assessed on the quality of soil, the extent of land one has, the average of three years' produce of the total land in one's name. I propose to raise the existing land revenue by five per cent. This will raise the price of agricultural produce nominally, but I hope the people will not grudge it, because of the exigencies of war. The purchase by the military, of agricultural items like cereals, pulses and fodder will be tax-free. This tax will also be done away with after the termination of the war. Do I have Your Majesty and the ministers' consent?'

The Ministers said nothing. As no one raised a voice of dissent, the proposal seemed to have been carried through.

Raja Nirmal Singh paused again, to consult his notes and then resumed, 'Your Majesty, I have shown only one side of the coin. Let me show you the other side. Existing laws, provide for a nominal sum as family pension to the next of kin, of those army personnel who die in service. The soldiers and their families are largely illiterate and ignorant. The family pension seldom reaches the beneficiaries. We can guess where it goes. I therefore propose that the amount of family pension be raised to equal the total cash emoluments last drawn by the deceased, in cases where there is no able-bodied son to replace his father in the army, or is unwilling to join the armed forces. This will improve the condition of young widows, who sometimes fall upon immoral means, to sustain themselves and their dependants. This welfare scheme will remain in force as long as the army remains and cannot be withdrawn. Do I take it that this ameliorative step has been approved?'

'It is approved,' said General Turkman Khan. 'This is an incentive for the men to join the army. A soldier will know that when he is no more, the State will provide for his family. The details of how this benefit reaches the bereaved family, have to be worked out carefully.'

Having finished his speech, Raja Nirmal Singh took his seat.

Salim said, 'The tax proposals seem to be a necessary evil. They have only our tentative approval. If they spread dissatisfaction among the common people, or if prices rise disproportionate to the amount of tax, the proposals will have to be reviewed.'

'Yes, Your Majesty,' said Raja Nirmal Singh. 'They are open to review, modification, even cancellation, depending upon their impact on the people.'

Salim said, 'There are many big and prosperous jagirdars and zamindars in almost all parts of the State. They have also to contribute to the war effort.'

Khwaja Jahan stood up and said, 'Your Majesty, I have contacted about five hundred most prosperous jagirdars and zamindars. According to their approximate annual income, as furnished by the revenue records, I have persuaded them to agree to a levy of a certain number of soldiers, to be armed and paid by these big landlords. Their training expenses will be borne by the State. The levy ranges between ten and fifty soldiers, depending on the known sources of income of the big landowners. I have given a promise that the expenses incurred by the jagirdars and zamindars will be reimbursed to them, if the proposed war comes to a successful conclusion.'

'These landowners will pray for our success,' said General Chandra Bhan.

'I share the feelings of General Chandra Bhan,' said Thakur Tomar Singh, Superintendent of the Artillery.

'The meeting is over,' said Salim. 'It will be convened again, when Raja Nirmal Singh has had sufficient time to study its full force on the common people.'

V

About six months later, the Council of Ministers met again. Raja Nirmal Singh, addressing the throne, said, 'Your majesty, the people have not responded well to the new taxes. Most of them are dissatisfied. The traders have become profiteers. They have raised prices much above the taxes imposed. The people's goodwill is necessary for the war to come. I have some alternatives.'

'Let us and the Ministers hear your new suggestions,' said Salim.

'Your Majesty,' I have certain fresh proposals. I propose to reduce the salt tax, the production tax and the recently enhanced land revenue, from five per cent to two per cent. This will please the people. Our officials will lay down clear-cut guidelines and see that increase in prices is in proportion to the tax. As a deterrent, I proposed a penalty of one hundred rupees on those who do not comply with the guidelines.

'To make good the loss of State revenue, I propose to levy a tax of six per cent, depending on the value of all goods entering or leaving our State. For this purpose, *nakas* or check posts have to be set up on all entry and exit points, by land and river. The daily collections at each check post will be deposited in the local treasury, throughout the State. I ask Your Majesty and your Ministers if they have any objection or amendment.'

'None,' said Khwaja Jahan and the six Generals.

Janbaz Khan, Superintendent of Intelligence and Posts said, 'Your Majesty, I would suggest the launching of a mass awareness campaign in each town and village of our State, through the prevailing public address system, highlighting the need for defending our people against possible aggression by the Emperor. I will work out the publicity details.'

'A good idea.' said the Sultan. 'You have our permission to carry it out.'

General Sayyid Ali Haider said, 'We have to build an ideal or near-ideal image, of our Sultan. A successful propaganda is the repetition of lies, again and again. I would like the honourable Minister of Intelligence and Posts to keep this in mind.'

Amin Sarhadi, Mir Bakhshi or Incharge of Military Establishment said, 'Your Majesty, we have to rouse the passions of the people against the Emperor, bearing in mind that everything is fair, in love and war. We have to build a war hysteria.

We have to arouse a sense of patriotism among the people by instilling in them the fear of the Emperor's aggression and present a horrid picture of the devastation of people's lives and property that is bound to follow, if people are unprepared for defence.

'I stress again that we have to infuse a sense of fear among the masses. Patriotism thrives on fear of aggression. Before leading our army to Agra, we will have to proclaim that the Emperor is the aggressor and we are the aggressed. We have to play the role of injured innocence. The most vulnerable among the masses are the women. They fear the death, or the incapacitation of the breadwinners of the family. They fear being rendered homeless. Most of them will donate their ornaments for the war effort. We can melt the ornaments and turn them into gold and silver coins.'

Janbaz Khan said, 'I agree.'

VI

A man beat the two-headed drum – hanging from his neck – with a stick, in each of his hands. This was the public address system. The loud sound of the double-headed drum was a signal for people to collect and listen to an important official announcement. When a sufficient number of men had gathered, an official proclaimed at the highest pitch of his voice:

'The land is of God; the order is of Sultan Salim. Akbar Badshah has evil designs on this God-gifted Kingdom, which gives us bread. Akbar Badshah wants to snatch our bread from our mouths. He is coming with a huge army to do this. There may be a holocaust. Akbar Badshah has become an unjust man. He does not want us to live in peace. He wants to slaughter us. We have to defend our hearths and homes. Sultan Salim will protect our lives, the honour of our women and the innocence of our children. This announcement is made in the public interest.'

Having made the announcement, the drummer and the official went to their next stop.

A man in the audience said, 'We had heard many good things about Akbar Badshah. Why does he want to snatch our bread? We have done him no wrong.'

Another commented, 'Satan must have tempted him.'

A third man said, 'Akbar Badshah has become greedy. A greedy man is like a glutton. Give him enough to eat: he still wants more.'

A fourth man remarked, 'It is our good luck that we have Sultan Salim as our ruler. We trust him. If anyone can save us, it is Sultan Salim.'

A fifth man observed. 'Let us convey this ill news to others. It is good if we put them on the alert.'

VII

The next week, the publicity took a new form. The drum-man beat his drum, calling the audience to assemble and listen to the latest:

'The land is of God; the order is of Sultan Salim. Akbar Badshah has gone senile. He is more than eighty years old. He is unfit to remain a Badshah any longer. He likes the shine of our gold, silver and copper coins. He has ordered Maan Singh to invade our Kingdom and carry away all our gold, silver and copper coins. His soldiers will break into every home and kill those who will not willingly give them the gold, silver and copper coins. Sultan Salim is the defender of our lives, the honour of our women and the innocence of our children. This announcement is made in the public interest.'

The comments of some among the audience were varied. One man said, 'I was told Akbar Badshah was in his early sixties. The announcement says he is over eighty. May be the announcer is right. My memory seems to be failing.'

Another man observed, 'If Akbar Badshah is more than eighty, he must really have gone senile. Old men are often greedy. I know of an old man whose soul refused to leave his body for days together. Then someone told his son to put gold, silver and copper coins in a pot, cover it with his hand and shake the pot. It was only when the gasping old man heard the jingling sound of the coins that he could breathe his last.'

Another person commented, 'I had heard Maan Singh was a good man. Why did he agree to Akbar Badshah's order?'

Another man said, 'There are a number of families who have

only a few copper coins. It is a pity that Maan Singh's soldiers should kill an entire family for a couple of copper coins.'

The fifth man said, 'Wealth, however little, is a curse. It takes a lifetime to earn it, but minutes to snatch it away. What then is the difference between robbers and Maan Singh and his men?'

'The whole thing is terrible,' said another man. 'Let us warn others and ask them to bury their cash beneath their fireplace, or the tulsi plant. These are the most unsuspicious of places.'

VIII

Seven or eight days later, the sound of the drum was heard again. This time the announcer had a fresh version:

'The land is of God; the order is of Sultan Salim. Akbar Badshah is ill and out of mind. The Hakims are attending on him. Maan Singh has taken the administration of Hindustan in his hands. Sultan Salim and Maan Singh are old enemies. Maan Singh is planning to attack this God-gifted Kingdom which gives us bread. Sultan Salim has always led a pure and noble life. Maan Singh tried to draw him to the wrong path. He sent casks of wine and a number of women for his harem. Sultan Salim has ordered all wine to be thrown away. He is sending the harem women to their families. Sultan Salim is prepared to meet Maan Singh in a one-to-one combat at any place Maan Singh would like to choose. Sultan Salim will cut off Maan Singh's head and have it hung under the big *bargad* tree in Gole Market, for everybody to see how the enemies of the people of this God-gifted Kingdom must be treated. Sultan Salim protects our lives, the honour of our women and the innocence of our children. This announcement is made in the public interest.'

A man in the crowd remarked, 'I pray the Hakims succeed in restoring Akbar Badshah's balance of mind. He is a man among men.'

Another said, 'Whether Akbar Badshah's balance of mind is restored or not, is not our problem. That Maan Singh and Sultan Salim are enemies is also not our problem. That our bread is snatched away by Maan Singh is our problem. We should stand united with our Sultan against Maan Singh.'

Another man observed, 'Our Sultan had the wine thrown away into the gutter. He is sending the harem women back to their parents. Nothing can be nobler than this.'

Another man tried to show he could also make comments. He said, 'I would love to see Maan Singh's body hanging from the bargad tree. Those who try to dishonour us and our Sultan, deserve such punishment.'

IX

The people were waiting for more news. About ten days later, the news came. The drummer beat his drum furiously, suggesting the importance of the news as well as the need for a large gathering. The official accompanying him, announced at the top of his voice:

'The land is of God; the order is of Sultan Salim. Akbar Badshah has left his palace. He passes his evenings in wine sheds and gambling dens, and his nights in the arms of public women. Maan Singh is behind all this. Sultan Salim cannot tolerate this indignity on the part of his father, to his dynasty. Sultan Salim trusts that all his people will stand by him, in foiling the nefarious designs of Maan Singh. Our Sultan is the protector of our lives, the honour of our women and the innocence of our children. This announcement is made in the public interest.'

The big crowd felt the earth slipping beneath its feet. A man remarked, 'Akbar Badshah has gone mad. He seems to be beyond cure. It is all Maan Singh's doing. A mad man does not know where he is. How can he go to wine sheds and gambling dens and women of ill repute? It is unbelievable.'

Another man interposed. 'Some man may be taking him by the arm and leading him there.'

'Nonsense,' exclaimed the first man. 'Gambling needs money. A mad man has no money. He does not know how to cheat or how he is being cheated.'

A third man opined, 'Whatever may happen to Akbar Badshah is not our concern. The danger that threatens us and our Sultan is all-important, at the moment.'

A fourth man said, 'I am sure the evil intentions of Maan Singh can never succeed, so long as our Sultan is there to protect us, our women and children.'

X

The multitude of Salim's territories was utterly confused. Rumour and gossip were the order of the day. For about a fortnight, no public announcement was made. The army was being organised. The elephants in the Sultan's stables were being sold. Only Maula Rakkha would be retained. The war would be fought with cavalry and cannons. Elephants were not as good as horses. Then one day, the sound of the drum was heard once again. The announcer was also there. He proclaimed aloud:

'The land is of God; the order is of Sultan Salim. Maan Singh has arrested Akbar Badshah. The Badshah is now more than ninety years old. Sultan Salim wants his subjects to show their loyalty to him, by condemning Maan Singh's treachery. Sultan Salim himself will lead his mighty army to Agra, arrest Maan Singh and put Akbar Badshah under medical care. Our Sultan is the protector of our lives, the honour of our women and the innocence of our children. This announcement is made in the public interest.'

'What has happened to Maan Singh?' a man inquired of the person standing next to him. 'Does he want to be Emperor?'

'What is the arithmetic behind Akbar Badshah's age? Fifteen days ago, he was over eighty. Now it is announced he is over ninety. Either the earlier figure was wrong, or the present figure is wrong.'

'Don't bother about figures,' the second man answered angrily. 'Let us hold meetings and condemn Maan Singh's treachery.'

'We wish every success to our Sultan and his army,' said a third man.

'The arrest of Maan Singh will be justified,' a fourth man remarked.

'After all, a father is a father,' said a fourth man. 'How noble of our Sultan to think of putting his old father under medical care.'

XI

Propaganda was having its pernicious effect among the masses. Many believed in what was dinned into their ears, time and again. A few were too perplexed to separate the chaff from the grain. Months passed and no further announcement came. At last, one day, the sound of the drum was heard again and the drummer and the official made their presence felt again. The official announced:

'The land is of God; the order is of Sultan Salim. Maan Singh has started preparations to attack our Kingdom from three sides. Maan Singh is a habitual drunkard. No woman's virtue is safe wherever he goes. He is the enemy of our people. Sultan Salim will lead his army in a day or two, to teach a lesson to the traitor. Sultan Salim is the protector of our lives, the honour of our women and the innocence of our children. This announcement is made in the public interest.'

Most people among the audience were indignant at Maan Singh. 'A three-pronged attack on our kingdom is something menacing,' said a frightened old man. 'The Sultan will have to divide his army into three parts.'

'Don't worry,' the second man comforted him. 'A habitual drunkard can never be a good General.'

'Maan Singh is certainly the enemy of the people. I should say, he is a villain, a downright villain.'

'I should be happy if our Sultan teaches the traitor the lesson of his life,' another man remarked.

'We will have to await the outcome of the armed conflict. All the time we will be edgy,' said another man, in despair.

Ambition Fulfilled at Last

I

Akbar was highly incensed at the hostile activities of his insubordinate son, particularly the lies spread against him and Raja Maan Singh. The Raja was his sole, surviving friend. The Emperor held private consultations with him. The Raja was an embodiment of reverence and loyalty. He said, 'Your Majesty, things have gone too far and, if action is deferred, they may go out of hand. Where persuasion fails, force succeeds. The Empire needs strength, stability and continuity. All fissiparous activities have to be curbed with a strong hand. Those who aim at the fragmentation of the Empire are our foes, not our blood relations. There is nothing which the imperial army at present cannot do. It has shown the excellence of its performance times without number. A word from you is enough to put me into immediate action. My purpose would be to bring the schemers into submission, not to take their lives.'

Akbar caught the hint. He said, 'Maan Singh, Shaikhoo has taxed our patience beyond endurance. We have now made the boldest decision of our life. We order you to make a strong force ready for action. We ourselves will lead it. We do not want to include you. Your presence could be misunderstood as a personal vendetta. We do not want any blame to fall on you. We also know we are old. We are sixty-two. Our mother, Hamida Bano is ill and weak. Yet we will go, because time is running out.'

'Your majesty, pardon me if I venture to say something that may not be very pleasing to your ears,' said Maan Singh. 'The Queen and the Oueen-Mother will plead with you, to shake your resolve. Once a decision is made, it must be carried out. There should be no question of going back.'

'Maan Singh,' said Akbar, 'we appreciate your foresight.'

'Your Majesty,' said Maan Singh, 'I would humbly request you that this time there should be no ladies in your entourage.'

'Maan Singh,' said the Emperor, 'there will be no ladies this time. They will be an unnecessary encumbrance. We want the matter to come to a speedy conclusion. Send the army by land. Despatch five hundred scouts to spread the news about the size and strength of the imperial forces. Let the news be blown out of all proportion. I know Shaikhoo. He will panic and seek submission. The use of force may not be necessary. We ourselves will take a shorter and easier route. We will go by river, in our little man-of-war, accompanied by the royal flotilla. The river Jamna has a lot of water and is navigable. We will join our forces near Allahabad.'

'As you wish, Your Majesty,' said the Raja. 'This will be done.'

The fleet of small ships was decorated with coloured banners and white sails and oars painted afresh. A huge crowd of nobles and common people came to see off the Emperor. No sooner did all take their seats in the vessels, than the Flotilla Commander blew a shrill whistle. The men on the river bank waved their hands in return. The nobles wished the Emperor a safe passage and success, in his mission.

II

The fleet had hardly moved a few miles from Agra when there was a vicious storm. Dark clouds overcast the sky. There was roaring thunder and serpent-like flashes of lightning and a heavy downpour of incessant rain. The small ships that had moved in an orderly manner from Agra, now tossed upon the splashing waves of the river. The Pilot of the Emperor's little warship tried to avoid the rushing waters of the midstream. He wanted the ship to move closer to the bank, where the turbulence of the waves was minimal. In trying to do so, a strong blast of wind pushed the ship, grounding it into the wet Jamna sand. Hundreds of boatmen were pressed into service to refloat the royal vessel, but the mighty gusts of wind and the lashing of ceaseless rain, hindered their efforts. The storm continued unabated for two days and two nights. When the tempest was almost subsiding, a special messenger came speeding from Agra. He was the bearer of bad tidings. The seventy-seven year old Hamida Bano's illness, had taken a turn for the worse. Ill health had already enfeebled her. She wanted to see Akbar, before she closed her eyes forever. Akbar was sceptical about the veracity of the message. He thought it was a womanly stratagem, to thwart his plan.

Soon a messenger arrived from Sullivan, a famous Goanese physician of his times. Sullivan's message was more disheartening. Her Majesty, Hamida Bano Begum, was engaged in a hopeless struggle between life and death. The Emperor had to abandon his plans to proceed further and rush back to Agra, to be at his mother's deathbed.

The lustreless eyes of the dying Hamida saw Akbar. A weak smile came on her lips. She said in a faint voice, 'You have come, my son. Lay down your head on my breast so that I may caress you.' There was moisture in Akbar's eyes. He did what his mother told him. Hamida Bano touched Akbar's head with her emaciated fingers. 'This is my last look at you, my son. You have the blessings of a dying mother. In my death, I see that the conflict between father and son seems to have been averted, perhaps forever.'

Akbar sat beside his mother's bedside for four days and four nights. Sullivan was on his toes administering life-saving drugs and frequently feeling her pulse, which became weaker and weaker. Hamida Bano's eyes lingered on her son. When the pulse stopped beating, Hamida's head tilted towards one side of her pillow. Akbar gently closed her eyes with his hand.

The death of his mother was a great emotional blow to the Emperor. One more comforter of his life had gone away, leaving him more desolate. Nine uneasy days had passed, between his stepping into his mini war vessel and the demise of his mother. He recalled his army and sent a tender message to Salim, informing him of his grandmother's death.

III

Salim read his father's letter. He was upset by the sad news. He thought his consistent disobedience had been the root cause of his grandmother's death. She had always counselled restraint and reconciliation.

Khwaja Jahan however, thought otherwise. He said, 'Your Majesty, this is no time to become sentimental. Fortune favours us. The tempest that grounded the Emperor's vessel has been a blessing to us. Had the vessel been set afloat, the imperial army led by the Emperor himself, would have engaged us, on our own ground. The death of Her Majesty the Queen-mother, also augurs good. The Emperor is depressed and desolate. Our cavalry and cannons are ready. We have more than eighty thousand men. Let us march to Agra and stage a coup. Your dream of being an Emperor will come true.'

'The time does seem to be ripe.' said Salim. 'Let us give the orders to march.'

Khwaja Jahan said, 'Diplomacy demands Your Majesty must have two faces. I would like Your Majesty to send word to the Emperor that you are deeply touched at the passing away of your beloved grandmother and that you are coming to Agra, as a dutiful son, to offer condolence to the Emperor and the bereaved family.'

Salim agreed.

IV

Salim came to the banks of the Jamna and encamped some ten miles away from Agra. He had eighty thousand armed men, including fifty thousand cavalry. Yet he did not dare to attack Agra. In spite of Khwaja Jahan's constant prodding, he refused to budge even an inch. He told the Khwaja he and his troops needed rest. The Emperor was not deceived by his son's ostensible, condolatory role. Salim had not come to offer sympathy in sorrow, but to fight. Evidently, a mourner does not come with infantry, cavalry and artillery. The Emperor, sent him a message couched in mild words.

Our beloved Shaikhoo Baba,

We are happy to learn you have arrived near Agra, safely. Perhaps the way from Allahabad to Agra has become so dangerous as to need such heavily armed escort. Your security is also our concern and, had you asked us, we could have provided you with a suitable one. However, this is your own affair and it is not for us to make any comment.

Ever since we received your letter, your mother and I, had been waiting for you anxiously. We would be glad to receive you in the Diwan-i-Aam, the public audience hall, so that the nobles and other invitees pay the respect due to you and be eye-witnesses to how our beloved son acquits himself. You enjoy our and your mother's love – we want you to gain the love of the nobility and the other invitees, too.

You are most welcome to your future court. We would advise you to enter Agra in a manner that befits our Heir Apparent, accompanied by no more than a few hundred of your followers. If you bring all your army with you, clashes may occur between your men and the common soldiers of our army, over trivial matters, which both of us should take care to avoid.

Written by order of and given under the seal of
Shahinshah Akbar

Salim read the letter over and over again. He showed it to Khwaja Jahan, who commented, 'Your Majesty, the Emperor is a shrewd man. His Intelligence officials have conveyed to him the size and strength of our army. However, go and offer condolences. The Emperor will ask you to stay for some days in his palace. Obey him, but keep in touch with us. Send us a word and we will make a surprise attack, at midnight.'

Salim presented himself at the public audience hall, in mourning robes. The Emperor received him with all ceremony. Salim presented his father ten thousand asharfis and the elephants that had remained unsold, at his Allahabad stable. The whole court watched Salim right from his entry in the Diwan-i-Aam to the gift-presentation formalities. Each person present there, looked at Akbar's unpredictable son, from his own viewpoint.

Akbar rose from his throne and led Salim by the arm, into his own private chamber in the palace. 'Be seated,' he said, 'and relax.'

Salim took his seat. The aging Emperor still struck awe among those who beheld him. Salim's courage failed him. His father was right. Salim could never face his father in a clash of arms, on the battlefield. The Emperor said, 'Shaikhoo, it is not a wise step to leave your mercenaries ten miles away from Agra. They cannot come to your rescue, in case you need their assistance.'

'They are not mercenaries, Your Majesty,' said Salim tactlessly. 'They form my army. They are well trained and well equipped.'

'Why should you raise such a huge army when we are there to help you?'

'I thought that, if you do not abdicate or die, I would have to fight and declare myself Emperor.'

'Do you want me to abdicate?' Akbar roared. 'Do you want me to die?'

'Your Majesty,' said Salim shamelessly, 'you have lived longer than your father and grandfather.'

'You came here to offer condolences on your grandmother's death. Condolences are expressions of sorrow. If I die, will you rejoice, or console your mother?'

Salim was speechless.

'Why did you send drum beaters all over the towns and villages in the neighbourhood of Allahabad, vilifying me and Maan Singh?'

'It was an exercise in the formation of public opinion, Your Majesty,' said Salim. 'It was validated by my Council of Ministers.'

'Your Council of Ministers!' Akbar sneered. 'Ungrateful man! You bite the hand that fed you.'

Salim had never expected what was coming. The Emperor rose from his seat and gave a slap on his son's cheek with such force that Salim fell down from his seat. The five fingers of Akbar's hand left their imprint, on Salim's cheek.

Akbar called out, 'Is anyone there?'

Four armed guards appeared immediately. The Emperor ordered, 'Arrest this man. Confine him in one of the *ghuslkhanas* (bathing chambers) in our palace. See that no alcohol or opium is served to him.'

Salim found himself in a *ghuslkhana*, which was a multi-room complex. It had all the amenities for relaxation and pleasure. Guards were posted outside. They had searched Salim from top to bottom, before they put him in. 'Take it easy, Your Highness,' one of them said. 'Just tap the door if you need anything. We are all your servants.'

For one whole day and night, there was neither wine nor opium to make Salim oblivious of his degradation. He had become a chronic addict. He preferred wine, to opium. Without either of them, he was in agony. He raved like a mad man. He begged the guards to seek the Emperor's permission, for only a cup of his favourite wine.

The Emperor called his personal physician Hakim Ali and deputed him to examine Salim every morning and evening and report to him. 'You must rehabilitate the Prince,' he said, 'You can prescribe only such quantity of wine, as you think fit.' Akbar could never imagine that Hakim Ali could be bought and that, later, Salim would make advantageous use of the Hakim's services.

The rehabilitation of Salim proved no easy task. Rani Jodha Bai and Sultan Salima Begum exerted all the pressure they could, to get him released from the ghuslkhana and shifted to his own palace. They vowed to stand guarantee for his good behaviour.

The Emperor relented. He allowed Salim to move into his own palace. He had remained in confinement for ten days, during which he had made friends with Hakim Ali. The Emperor sent men of his army, under a diplomat, to disarm Salim's men and persuade them to return to their hometowns or villages. The surrendered arms were stored in the Emperor's armoury, the cannons sent to the imperial artillery and the horses and elephants to the royal stables. Salim realised his foolhardiness. A self-proclaimed Sultan was not an independent sovereign, but a rebel, in Akbar's vast Empire. A new Governor of Allahabad was appointed, with express orders to do the clean-up and dismantle the so-called God-gifted Kingdom of the Ganga and the Jamna of the self-styled, His Majesty Sultan Muhammad Salim.

V

Early that year, astrologer Parmanand sought an audience with the Emperor. As he was sent by Raja Maan Singh, the Emperor had him admitted.

The learned Brahmin said, 'I have studied the movement of the planets in regard to what they presage, for Your Majesty. The present position of the planets is identical with what it was in Emperor Harshavardhan's reign. This foretells danger. Emperor Harshavardhan was advised to perform a grand *yagya* to avert the impending peril. He did so and was saved. It will be in Your Majesty's interest to perform the mahayagya.'

'Thanks for forewarning us,' said Akbar. 'We are busy in other affairs. Take your fee and wait for further orders. We will call you, when we are free.'

'Your Majesty,' said Parmanand, 'I cannot perform the mahayagya alone. It needs a hundred Brahmins to do it.'

'You will arrange for the hundred Brahmins and the *samagri* (material) for this complicated ritual,' said Akbar. 'We will meet again.'

Parmanand took the hint, collected his fee from an attendant, bowed and went away. Akbar was too engrossed in cleaning the mess Salim had created, to take seriously, what the astrologer had said. The forecast, however, continued to disturb him occasionally. Salim seemed to be settling down to the life of an obedient Prince, partly because of the ten days' chastisement he had undergone and partly because his mothers had stood surety, for his orderly conduct. Akbar also seemed to be satisfied and soon forgot all about the Brahmin's warning and the performance of the mahayagya.

VI

Akbar had three handsome sons – Salim, born of Rani Jodha Bai, Murad, born of Salima Begum and Daniyal, born of a concubine at Ajmer, in the house of a Jesuit missionary from Goa. All the three were alcohol addicts. Salim took to drink at the age of eighteen. During the next nine years, he gradually increased the quantity to twenty cups. He drank fourteen cups during the day and six at night, with the result that wine failed to intoxicate him. He was on the look-out for some drug that would give him the thrills.

All the three Princes made a bid for the throne. Murad was camping at Burhanpur, when he was stricken with epilepsy. As his condition deteriorated, the hopes of the physicians attending him, began to recede. His premature death left only two brothers as contestants to the throne – Salim and Daniyal. The thirty-three year old Daniyal, was in the South. Contrary to the advice of his well-wishers, he did not give up drinking to excess. This affected his brain and stomach. He suffered from acute, abdominal pain. He lay in bed for forty days and occasionally opened his eyes, only to beg for a cup of wine. His physicians failed to save his life. His wife, Jahan Begum, was the daughter of the powerful Abdur Rahim titled Khan-i-Khaanaan. She was so grief-stricken that she wanted to be buried alive with him. The rest of her life was one of mental morbidity. Those who looked at her, felt as if she was in a state of trance.

One after another, the Emperor's near and dear ones were dying. He sent for the astrologer Parmanand. He asked him if the crucial years had passed, with Daniyal's death. The Brahmin did his readings again. He did not give a well-reasoned reply. He talked about the inevitability of fate. The Emperor sent him away, with a handsome gift of one hundred gold mohars.

With the death of his two brothers, Salim was the sole, surviving son of the Emperor. With no rival to compete for the throne, Salim reverted to his old habits. He began to assume airs. He behaved as if he was already Emperor. He became haughty and arrogant. Akbar desisted from taking any action against him. He continued to take a lenient view. Old age and successive bereavements mellowed him. He came to believe that clemency would have a salutary effect on his son. To lose two sons was more than he could bear. He was weary and forlorn. He often called aloud to Shaikh Salim Chishti. He was convinced that the Shaikh's prayers had given him the gift of three sons.

The Emperor was also concerned with the continuance of his

dynasty. He feared alcoholism might drive Salim to an early grave, like his two brothers. He had three grandsons – Khusrau, Parvez and Khurram. They were in their green years, too young to understand the intricacies of statecraft and take high-level decisions, on their own. Men with unsettled principles were waiting in the wings. There was no man like Bairam Khan, to save the seams of the Empire. The warning of Parmanand haunted him. He felt a sense of guilt. Had he performed the mahayagya, he thought, the misfortune might have been averted.

VII

Out of the nine jewels of Akbar's court, six had shed their lustre, because of the dark hands of death. Only three remained – Abdur Rahim, Raja Maan Singh and Mirza Aziz Kotaltash. The trio were loyal to Akbar but divided on the question of the Emperor's successor. To resolve their differences, they met at Raja Maan Singh's residence.

The Raja said, 'The future of the Empire is at stake. Let us discuss the issue of succession, in a dispassionate and objective manner.'

'Raja Maan Singh,' said Abdur Rahim, 'you are an old guard. Let us hear your views first.'

The Raja said, 'I am not an old guard alone. Both of you share that honour with me. The issue before us is: who should succeed the throne – Prince Salim, or his son Prince Khusrau. You will agree with me that only a person with a liberal outlook, a broad vision and an unblemished life, can prevent the Empire from bursting at the seams. I therefore propose that we should debate impartially the eligibility of Prince Khusrau, as the most suitable successor to the Empire.'

'Raja Maan Singh,' said Abdur Rahim, 'Humayun Badshah succeeded his father Babar Badshah and Akbar Badshah succeeded his father Humayun Badshah. On this principle, Prince Salim should succeed his father, the Emperor. There seems to be no plausible reason why the father-son chain, should be broken. What is your opinion, Mirza Kokaltash?'

The Mirza replied, 'As the Raja said, we should discuss the

matter of succession dispassionately and without bias. I have been watching Prince Salim's career carefully. I have nothing against Prince Salim personally. He has three unpardonable vices, which rule him out of our consideration. One: he is a thorough drunkard. Two: he has repeatedly revolted and openly defied the Emperor's authority. Three: his lately assumed arrogance, disqualifies him for Emperorship. In his eyes there are visions of a hundred colours of sovereignty. His father is still alive, yet he thinks he is at the top of the world. A man who drowns his senses in liquor, a man who sets an example of disobedience to others, a man who heaves his head in haughtiness, in my opinion, cannot prove a just and successful ruler.'

'Presuming that Raja Maan Singh and you have the correct perception, how will you overcome the hurdles in your way?'

Raja Maan Singh said, 'The biggest hurdle are the two most prominent ladies of the palace, who wield great influence on the Emperor. They are my close relatives – Rani Jodha Bai and the late Prince Murad's mother, Salima Begum. They are all set on Salim.'

'I asked you, how you will overcome the hurdles,' said Abdul Rahim.

'It is not an easy task,' Maan Singh replied. 'I rely on the Emperor's clarity of thought and soundness of judgement. We will move carefully, taking one cautious step after another. We will step up our lobbying and show that compared to Prince Salim his son Prince Khusrau is a better candidate.'

'What, in your opinion, are the plus points of Prince Khusrau, Mirza Kokaltash?' inquired Abdur Rahim.

The Mirza answered, 'Prince Khusrau has not one, but many plus points. I will enumerate only a few. One: Khusrau is now eighteen and amenable to reason. Two: he is a liberal intellectual. Three: he has charming manners. Four: he is not interested in women. He has only one wife and he is devoted to her.'

Abdul Rahim said, 'Where there is some relationship on account of matrimonial alliances, we cannot say, we have been dispassionate and unbiased.'

'What are you driving at, Khan-i-Khaanaan?' asked Mirza Kokaltash.

'What I mean is that you are the father-in-law of Khusrau. Your daughter is Khusrau's wife. Khusrau being your son-in-law, your bias is natural,' replied Abdul Rahim. 'Similarly, on his mother's side, Khusrau is the adoptive son-in-law of Raja Maan Singh. It is an open secret that Khusrau prefers the Raja, to his father. The Raja's championing of Khusrau's cause therefore, cannot be free from bias.'

'Who is your candidate?' Mirza Kokaltash queried.

'I have no candidate. I agree that Khusrau has many superb qualities of head and heart. I believe in the father-son succession. I do not want that a son should supersede his father. Supersession creates bad blood. I am not in favour of making the rift between father and son wider.'

Since no consensus was arrived at, the meeting ended in a fiasco. But one good thing emerged. Each of the trio showed his cards. The Raja and the Mirza were one, in their support for Khusrau, while Abdul Rahim believed in hereditary succession.

VIII

An aggressive campaign was launched by the Maan Singh-Mirza Kokaltash combine. Others who opposed the combine were Shaikh Rukn-ud-din Rohilla, a powerful nobleman, Zia-ul-Mulk, a warrior of no mean rank and Sayeed Khan Chughtai, a polite, persuasive and soft-spoken orator. Akbar was perplexed. Belief in omens bedimmed his perspicacity. Somebody suggested a fight between two equally powerful elephants – one belonging to Salim and the other to Khusrau – under the vigilant eye of an unbiased umpire. The owner of the winning elephant should succeed to the throne. The elephant fight was a pure gamble, as much depended on chance. It was not a rational way of deciding the issue.

The Emperor consulted Salim and Khusrau and both agreed. The elephant combat, they thought, would humour the Emperor and also provide excitement to the supporters of both the warring camps. The fight was open to the public and would entertain all, even the ladies of the palace.

An open space, outside the Fatehpur-Sikri palace, was chosen and tents were pitched around the vast arena, for the royal and other distinguished visitors. On the eastern side of the arena was a red pavilion for the Emperor. On the western side was the blue pavilion for the senior ladies of the palace. On the northern side was Salim's green pavilion and on the southern, Khusrau's yellow pavilion.

On the day of the fight, all were clad in colourful costumes. Akbar sat with his grandson, Khurram. The latter was Salim's son by Rani Balmati, daughter of Raja Udai Singh. Balmati was a famous Rajput Princess and Khurram was Akbar's favourite grandson. Khusrau was seated with the Raja-Mirza combine and Salim with Shaikh Rukn-ud-Din Rohilla, Zia-ul-Mulk and Sayeed Khan Chughtai. Salim's celebrated elephant bore the name Giranbar, while Khusrau's famous elephant was called Abrup. The two animals had been fed on honey and herbs, to vitalise them for the occasion.

At a signal from the umpire, the two animals entered the arena – Giranbar from the north and Abrup from the south. These elephants were a sight worth seeing. They looked like huge chunks of a mountain and like their mahouts, smart and warlike. As they eyed each other, both elephants rushed forward, with the full ferocity of an offensive. Giranbar rushed upon his opponent and with one mighty thrust of his massive head, knocked Abrup down. There were loud cheers from the blue and the green camps – the ladies' and Salim's. Giranbar severely mauled the fallen elephant. The umpire sent another elephant to bear the brunt of Giranbar's ferocious attack and to save Abrup, who was by now on his feet again.

Salim's supporters began to shout, 'This is unfair. The fight is between Giranbar and Abrup and not between Giranbar and Ranthaman. Stop it.'

When the umpire paid no attention to the shouts of Salim's supporters, they began to pelt stones, wounding both Ranthaman and his mahout.

Akbar was distressed at this turn of events. He sent word to Salim, to restrain his followers from violating the rules of the elephant fight. If one elephant is knocked down and injured, a substitute elephant is sent to prolong the fight.

Salim sent the answer that he disapproved of the stone missiles and that he would order that the elephants be separated. For this purpose, fireworks were sparked off to scare the elephants. The three huge animals ran away, in sheer fright. They ran as far as the Jamna and threw themselves into its waters, not only to cool but also to save themselves from stone pelting and the uproar of the fireworks.

The Emperor was dressed in plain, cotton clothes. He called both Salim and Khusrau. He congratulated his son on Giranbar's victory. He sympathised with his grandson, for the shabby performance of Abrup. He distributed gifts of great value both to the winner and the runner-up. Giranbar's mahout was rewarded with one hundred gold mohars and a family pension, after the mahout's demise.

Khurram was fourteen, neither a boy nor a man, but an adolescent. He was excited over the elephant fight. He liked Zinhar, the biggest elephant in Akbar's stable. He wanted to get him trained, for an elephant fight he hoped to stage, some day. He told his grandfather he would like to own that mountain-like elephant. The Emperor ordered Zinhar to be shifted to the stable of Prince Khurram, the future Emperor Shah Jahan.

IX

Next day, the Emperor happened to fall ill. He complained of an upset stomach. Spasms of abdominal pain increased his agony. His personal physician, Hakim Ali, attended him. He was fully conversant with Akbar's anatomy. He knew which herbal medicines agreed or disagreed with the Emperor's physical constitution. Akbar had complete faith in him. Salim also trusted him, for another reason. The ladies of the palace and the nobles were alarmed, when the illness continued for nine days, with no sign of relief.

Rani Jodha Bai summoned Ali to her presence and severely reprimanded him. 'Ali,' she said, 'you have been in the Emperor's service for years. Earlier, the Shahinshah would recover from a stomach upset in two or three days. Today is the tenth day. You do not seem to be anxious about his health, as we are. Why are you so negligent? Why don't you consult other physicians? If you can't diagnose the disease, others might. Do you want to be dismissed?'

'Your Majesty,' said Ali humbly, 'the Emperor has a strong constitution. I am not administering high-potency medicines for fear of side effects. I want to relieve him of the spasms, hoping that with the Emperor's powerful body, nature would do the rest.'

Rani Jodha Bai was incensed. She said, 'Are you poisoning him? Has someone hired you? Why don't you take the advice of other Unani or Ayurvedic practitioners and arrive at a correct diagnosis? Without a precise diagnosis, any medicine, unrelated with the disease, will have no effect. Will it? Answer me.'

'Your Majesty,' said Ali, 'my life is in your hands. I cannot poison the Emperor when I have cured him several times. I cannot be hired, when the Emperor gives me enough to live in comfort. I shall obey your orders and consult other Hakims and Vaids.'

'Go and do it just now,' Rani Jodha Bai commanded.

Ali retraced his steps, with a sullen face. He examined Akbar again. He diagnosed the disease as a form of chronic diarrhoea. As the Emperor grew weaker, day by day, there was panic in the palace, in the mansions of the nobles and in the humble dwellings of the commoners. There was no end to rumours.

The pro-Salim and pro-Khusrau factions revived their activities, with renewed fervour. The first move was made by the Raja-Mirza combine. They had planned a meeting of the more important noblemen and with inflammatory speeches, hoped to secure approval for Khusrau's succession to the throne. The warrior Zia-ul-Mulk, an ardent Salim-supporter, got scent of the plot. He advised Salim to go out of Agra, as quickly as he could. If Khusrau was proclaimed heir, his supporters would be thirsty for his father's blood. Salim also realised what would happen to him if he was caught by the Maan Singh-Mirza Kokaltash clique: his death would clear the way for Khusrau. Zia-ul-Mulk took Salim, in the darkness of the night, to the Jamna and made him board a boat for Allahabad. He told him that he would launch a counter offensive and as soon as the scenario improved, he would send him word, to return to Agra.

X

Raja Maan Singh and Mirza Kokaltash held a crucial meeting of the prominent noblemen, interested in a solution to the succession issue. Zia-ul-Mulk, Shaikh Rukn-ud-din Rohilla and Sayeed Khan Chughtai had raised their counter-offensive against the pro-Khusrau elements, to a high pitch. When enough pressure had been built up and hopes of support mobilisation soared high, Zia-ul-Mulk quietly brought Salim back to Agra.

The debate in the meeting, excelled in eloquence. Mirza Kokaltash and Raja Maan Singh delivered great orations. But Sayeed Khan Chughtai questioned their motives. 'It is clear,' Chughtai said, 'that the Raja and the Mirza will derive great advantage for themselves and their families, if Khusrau succeeds the Emperor. They are Khusrau's relatives by matrimonial ties. Can they deny this? They cannot. They dare not. If they do, their self-interest is evident. Their hearts are their best mirrors. Let them see their face in a mirror. It will tell them that their faces are covered with a deceptive mask. They want us to believe that if there is a sinner in the world, it is Salim; and if there is a saint in the world, it is Khusrau.

'We respect the Mughal tradition. Till now, it has been of father-son succession. It would be the most unfortunate day for all of us, if a bad precedence is set up. To uphold the questionable claim of a son arbitrarily, bypassing his father, is a bad precedence – bad in intention, bad in principle, bad in law, bad in history and bad in example. It amounts to revenge. It is like as if, when our eldest son does not listen to us, we disinherit and disown him and make our grandson our sole legal heir. Those who agree with me should stand up. Those who disagree with me, should remain in their seats.'

A majority of the dignitaries stood up. The game of the Raja and Mirza was up. Both were quick to realise it. The Raja apprehended that his presence at Agra would be an open invitation to trouble-brewers. He therefore hurried for Bengal, taking Khusrau with him. Mirza Kokaltash, on the other hand, did not panic. He stayed on at Agra, in the belief that, once the dust had settled down, all would be well.

XI

With the majority of noblemen on his side, Salim felt reinvigorated. He decided to pay homage to his bedridden father. Hakim Ali had come to him the previous night, under cover of darkness, to intimate to him that he would soon hear news that would sound like music to his ears. Salim had caught the hint.

The guards at the eastern door of the Emperor's bedchamber admitted the Heir Apparent. The Shahinshah lay on a thickly cushioned bed. His breathing was irregular. He gasped for breath. His eyes were closed. He had also lost his speech. Ali, the Emperor's personal Hakim, stood in a corner, along with several practitioners of other systems of medicine, studying the changing expressions on his face. Ali had been administering an astringent, a medicine that contracts organic tissues. This led to strangury, on account of which the Emperor's urethra contracted and he felt pain in passing even a few drops of urine. Ali turned his eyes for a passing second, with a meaningful glance. This signified some secret understanding between the two. At a little distance away stood some nobles, among them being such celebrities as Abdur Rahim, Mirza Kokaltash, Zia-ul-Mulk and Meer Murtaza Khan. The only other person of distinction, who was conspicuous by his absence was Raja Maan Singh.

Salim went straight to the Emperor's bed and stood at its foot, with the utmost reverence. He waited for the Emperor to open his eyes. He wanted to convey his absolute and unconditional submission, to his dying father. A few moments of suspense seemed to last for centuries. Gradually, the Emperor's tired eyes half opened. Akbar recognised his son. Salim bent down on his knees and laid his head on the Emperor's feet. He then rose, showing inimitable reverence for his father. He hoped that the Emperor would say something. Akbar's lips began to move. He tried to speak. Everyone went near the Emperor and bent their ears to his lips but they could not make out what he was trying to say.

Unable to communicate his wishes, the Emperor made a gesture towards his turban and Salim's head and then to his ancestral sword, hanging on the wall behind his bed and to

Salim's waist. Mirza Kokaltash got the meaning. He placed the royal turban on Salim's head and girt him with the sword of Taimur, the ancestor of the Mughal dynasty in India.

Seeing his son decked in the royal turban and the Taimurid sword, an integral part of the Mughal insignia, the Emperor was so happy that his eyes filled with tears. He tried, with his feeble hands, to prevent them from rolling down his cheeks. Akbar tried to speak again, but without success. Salim realised that his father was breathing his last. Hakim Ali came to Salim and requested him to step back and let the patient rest. As soon as Salim did so, the Emperor's eyes shut again.

XII

People of all castes and communities had gathered outside the Fatehpur-Sikri palace. They numbered thousands. The vast assemblage of such a multitude was an indicator of the immensity of Akbar's popularity. They were anxious to hear the latest news. A pensive attendant came out of the palace and informed a couple of men that the Emperor's condition was deteriorating fast that there was a recurrence of dysentery, which pointed to the utter failure of medical treatment. He also informed the gathering that the dying Emperor had chosen Shahzada Salim to succeed him. If there was any happiness among those who were inclined towards Salim, they suppressed it. Their hearts were filled with grief, at the agony of the Emperor's numbered hours. A few of them turned inwardly hostile to Hakim Ali who, in spite of the skill for which he was known, could not rescue the ailing Emperor from the gaping jaws of death.

The palaces of the Begums wore a grim look. There were shadows of gloom over the senior ladies of the family. Rani Jodha Bai sat in despair, trying to resign herself to what was to come. Salima Begum thought of her second widowhood, the first being when Bairam Khan died. Rani Balmati, Khurram's mother, feared the loss of a loving father-in-law. The other ladies were uncertain of the treatment they would receive, when a new Emperor ascended the throne.

The mansions of the noblemen wore a ghastly appearance.

There was no certainty who would retain and who would lose his position, with a new Emperor in power. Those who had propped up Salim, knew how mercurial he was. Those who had opposed him could not say for sure, whether he would forgive and forget. The fortunes of the nobles are so interwoven with those of the reigning monarch, as to be put in peril with the advent of a new sovereign.

As the shades of the night spread, the vast concourse of increasing numbers of people, grew more uneasy. Some whispered fresh rumours. Some feared that the Emperor's journey, from the cradle to the grave, was coming to an end. Sikandra, a place six miles away from Agra, was designed and partly completed by Akbar himself. Some prayed for the restoration of his health and hoped he would be hale and hearty again.

No news came till midnight; but the people still waited. A little past midnight, cries of lamentation rose from the palace. The suspense had come to an end. The Emperor was no more. An attendant rushed out of the palace and sobbed, 'I had served Akbar Badshah all my life. Now he belongs to history.'

XIII

A Mughal Emperor's bier was never *taken out* of any of the palace gates. The custom was, to make a breach in the walls of the fort and carry the bier to its resting place. Akbar had built a mausoleum for himself at Sikandra. The pallbearers had to journey for six miles, to lay the deceased to rest. According to tradition, every person accompanying the funeral lends his shoulder to the bier, for a few steps. This practice is regarded as a virtue in itself. It is also aimed at relieving the pallbearers of their burden. In doing so, one also expects that at one's own death, others will reciprocate similarly.

Salim, Parvez and Khurram, were the first to lift and carry Akbar's bier. Khusrau was in Bengal with Maan Singh. He was deprived of having a last look at his grandfather. Almost all dignitaries accompanied the bier, making a long funeral procession. They walked slowly and silently, as a mark of respect for the departed soul. The partly built mausoleum at Sikandra was later completed by Salim, as a mark of his submission and repentance, after he mounted the throne, as Emperor Jahangir.

Akbar was the first Mughal sovereign who was born, brought up and buried in Hindustan. He loved the land of his birth, his childhood, his boyhood, his youth, his manhood and his old age and returned to its soil.

XIV

Hakim Ali was richly rewarded by Salim. He rose high in his favour. He was most helpful in translating Salim's ambition into reality, before the Prince was too old to enjoy the power and privilege of an undisputed monarch. He brought Akbar's life to a premature end. He was, however, removed from the post of court physician. Another man replaced him.

When Salim and Ali found themselves alone, Salim said, 'Ali, we gave you twenty-five thousand gold mohars to make the Emperor ill. We paid you another twenty-five thousand asharfis when his condition worsened. In this bag, there are fifty thousand gold coins in full and final settlement, of what was agreed between us. How did you accomplish your work?'

'Slow poisoning, Your Majesty. Mixed with medicine.'

'What poison?'

'Arsenic, Your Majesty.'

Glossary

Abhinay: Acting

Akbarnama: The Book of Akbar. It contains Akbar's life and the important historical events, till its writer's (Abul Fazl) death

Allama: A man of learning and scholarship

asharfis: Gold coins

Badshah: King

bairagi: An ascetic

Bargad: A wounderful Indian tree: some of its stems hang down like ropes and, on touching the ground, take root, prolonging the tree's life

bazar: Marketplace

Bhils: Name of a primitive tribe

Brahmachari: One who refrains from carnal desire in the belief that it disturbs meditation, for spiritual attainment

darbar: Court

darwesh: A man of God; a hermit

Diwan: Prime Minister

farman: Royal decree

faqir: A holy and other-worldly man

hamaam: Turkish bath, with a set of several rooms

harem: Seraglio

jagir: Ownership of large tracts of land, including villages

Kathak: A form of dance, popular in the courts of Princes, in Mughal times

madarsa: School for secular and religious education

mahajan:	Moneylender
Maharaj:	Great king
Mahayagya:	Purification fire on a grand scale, to propitiate the gods, to avert evil
mahout:	Elephant trainer and driver
mohars:	Asharfis; sovereigns; gold coins
muezzin:	A person in a mosque who calls the faithful to prayer five times a day
nakaa:	Check point
munim:	Accountant
rubai:	A poem of four lines
rani:	Queen
sanyasi:	Ascetic, one who abnegates the world
Shahinshah:	Emperor
Shahzada:	Prince
sufi:	A Muslim mystic
Sultan:	King
tulsi:	A plant with medicinal properties, often found in the courtyard of pious Hindus, watered and worshipped by women
Ustad:	Teacher
zamindar:	Big landowner